# THE LADY OF LYONESSE

# THE LADY OF LYONESSE

Dea Hicks Langmead

The Book Guild Ltd
Sussex, England

First published in Great Britain in 2003 by
The Book Guild Ltd
25 High Street
Lewes, East Sussex
BN7 2LU

Typesetting in Baskerville by
IML Typographers, Birkenhead, Merseyside

Printed in Great Britain by
Antony Rowe Ltd, Chippenham, Wiltshire


A catalogue record for this book is available from
The British Library.


ISBN 1 85776 777 2

*To all who have helped bring this book into being,*
*but especially my daughter, Anne Carol.*

# CONTENTS

*The Lady of Lyonesse* began as a musical entertainment called *Lyonesse* and was performed at local venues, the short story being told by the author, accompanied by music written, played and sung by Cornwall's Sally Brown.

# THE LEGEND AND KNOWN FACTS THAT FORM THE BASIS FOR THE STORY OF *THE LADY OF LYONESSE*

Lyonesse was an island believed to have once flourished between Cornwall and the Isles of Scilly. Its inhabitants were reputed to have been remarkable for their piety and industry and there were many churches. It was recorded in the *Anglo-Saxon Chronicles*, a form of Church diary comprising a continuous register of events, 'that the Lioness [sic] was destroyed on Saint Martin's Mass Day, the eleventh of November at the end of the eleventh century, in a single night of a new moon when a very high tide occurred.'

\* \* \*

The Seven Stones Reef, which lies close to the Isles of Scilly, is still referred to as 'The Town' by the islanders, and the Wolf Rock, which now supports a lighthouse, is the top of a pinnacle of greenstone slate that I have called Carrag Uthek, the Awesome Rock.

\* \* \*

Legend informs us that one landowner, Richard Trevelyan, managed to escape the destruction of Lyonesse solely by the strength of a white horse and was borne to safety at

Perranuthnoe. The one other person said to have reached the mainland was a Lord of Goonhilly, a proprietor of Lyonesse, who came ashore at Sennen Cove, where he founded Chapel Idne, the Narrow Chapel, as thanks to God for his deliverance. Recently, and sadly, the remains of the ancient oratory were removed to accommodate a new car park.

I venture to make the suggestion that the title 'Lord of Goonhilly' came about later when, in 1426, a John Vyvyan, whose earliest recorded ancestor was a Vivian of St Buryan, married into the family who owned Trelowarren, an estate which lies on Goonhilly Downs in the west of Cornwall. It should be noted that the figure of a white horse is incorporated into the iron gates on the property, and for many years a similar animal was always kept ready saddled in the stables.

\* \* \*

Before Saint Michael appeared to some fishermen on St Michael's Mount, it was known in Cornish as *Carreg cowse in clowse*, which means 'the hoar rock in the wood', indicating that it was once surrounded by trees. Even today in times of very low tides stumps can still be seen, and in A.D. 1824 it was written that under the sand could be found black vegetable mould, full of tree branches, leaves and nuts, pointing to the fact that an irruption must have occurred in the autumn.

\* \* \*

The story of Olaf Tryggvason, a Viking pirate-king, is part of Scandinavian history. In A.D. 980 Snorri Sturlsuson recorded in the *Heimskringla* that Olaf had heard of a hermit and seer, thought to be Saint Elidius, and visited him in his cell on Scilly. He was so impressed with the power and sanctity of the seer that he and his followers were baptised. The place where the hermit had his cell was named after him, becoming St Lide's or St Elid's Isle, which subsequently, with usage, became St Helen's.

*   *   *

Martin's prayer in Chapter 14 consists of relevant phrases taken from the *Stowe Missal*, the earliest known book of prayers, which was written by monks about A.D. 1,000, and is now held in the Royal Irish Academy, Dublin, Eire.

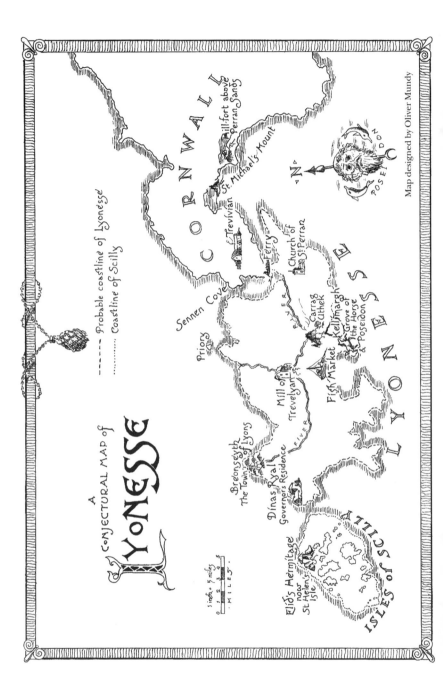

A CONJECTURAL MAP of

# LYONESSE

3 inches = 5 miles

MILES.
0  1  2  3  4  5

------ Probable coastline of Lyonesse
············ Coastline of Scilly

CORNWALL

Hill-fort above Perran Sands

St Michael's Mount

Trevivian

Sennen Cove

Ferry

Church of St Perran

Priory

Carrag Cothek

Kellmargh

Grove of the Horse & Poseidon

Fish Market

Mill of Trevelyan

River

River

Breanseyth The Town of Lyons

Dínas Pyal Governor's Residence

LYONESSE

Elíd's Hermitage near St Helen's Isle

ISLES of SCILLY

N

POSEIDON

Map designed by Oliver Mundy

# 1

---

*The Prophecy*

By midday a pervasive mist had veiled the August sun. It drifted in to envelop the carn, bringing an added chill to the fear already felt by the grim-faced men whose progress up the steep slope had slowed to a snail's pace. Their leader, his rugged, bearded face glistening with droplets of moisture from both the vapour and the sweat from his exertion, was some way ahead. He looked around and halted, leaning on his staff.

'Why hold back? What d'ye fear? The shades of those who can hold neither bow nor spear to harm you? You shiver and shake like maidens stolen away by pirates from the sea! Keep abreast of Old Jowan – he limps along with a good grace despite his old bones – not a-creeping like you ghost-ridden dolts! Tread in my steps and let not the dead make cowards of you all!' With renewed determination he strode on, a powerful, stocky figure, impatiently brushing back untamed, dark hair already tinged with grey, his woven cloak catching on brambles and scrub.

Many of the men remained unconvinced, acutely conscious that former dead heroes had been rowed across from the Cornish mainland for burial on Scilly, as departed spirits were known to be unable to travel over water and thus be powerless to return to trouble their successors. Also, the summits of the carns were high, enabling the dead to be placed nearest their gods, and undoubtedly most of this

1

visiting party felt they could be climbing up into the arms of numerous trapped, spectral wraiths lying in wait, eager to take their revenge upon the living.

Stunted trees and brushwood amid the rocks aided the mist to restrict their vision, until with sudden, surprised horror, they found their way barred by a row of black, shapeless, hooded and faceless forms. They pulled up sharply, some with a shriek and making as if to turn and run, but there also came a swish of swords drawn from scabbards and arrows pulled from quivers.

'Hold,' ordered their leader, lifting a restraining hand as he let his staff fall to the ground. 'You have naught to fear – this is the Hermitage – a holy place.'

He went towards the unbroken line, palms held open before him. 'I'truth – we are your neighbours from Lyonesse come here in peace, and bear arms only to guard against the pirates from the north who plague our shores. See, we bring gifts, wine and cloth, meat and fresh fruits.' The men bearing the offerings reluctantly shuffled nearer, dropping the packs from their backs before fast retreating to what they hoped would be a safer distance.

'Whom do you seek?' came a muffled voice.

'I seek Elid the hermit, the saintly man of God called the Seer. You must be the Brothers who care for him.'

A figure stepped forward, hands tucked in the sleeves of the habit, face hidden by the cowl. 'Who are you and what is your purpose?'

'I am Richard of Trevelyan, owner of the mill which grinds corn for our island. These men also farm my land and work tin from a lode running through, and my purpose is to seek an answer to certain strange, unexplained happenings that I believe only Elid can reveal.'

'Ay, you were expected long since. Come,' said the monk. Then, as an old man moved to Richard's side, he added abruptly. 'You alone may follow.'

Richard glanced at his companion. 'There is no danger to me, Jowan. 'Bide with the others 'til I return.'

The line parted to let them pass to where several stone huts could be seen through the haze, and the monk guided Richard to one set aside and bade him enter. He stepped inside onto straw scattered over the earth floor while trying to accustom his eyes to the dim light – a small opening in one wall served as the only window. He became aware of an altar table and tall, tallow candles burning in sconces on either side of a finely carved cross, then smoke from a turf fire smouldering in a crude hearth obliged him to cough.

'I hear you – come near that I might see.'

Richard, following the direction of the voice, found himself before a raised pallet on which an aged man was supported half sitting, covered by thick-furred animal skins. He appeared to be so frail that it seemed the merest amount of skin and flesh held the bones in place, the puckered mouth incapable of having spoken the words. A mass of white hair was spread over the head and face and, as Richard's gaze lingered there, two eyes pierced into his own, having an intensity that seemed to convey all of man's joy and suffering in their profound depths.

Elid broke the silence. 'My son, bend your knee to God and tell me what troubles you.'

'O holy man,' said Richard, falling to his knees. 'I have seen of late the waters of the sea encroach upon Lyonesse and the rivers make inroads to devour the pasture. At each full tide they recede less and less and foam with fury around our shores, making much white water. This very day we had to take oar to reach here, though ever before at low tide we could ride across with ease. Ay, and the animals show anxiety, too; they yield less milk and bring forth fewer of their kind. I have concern for my family and dependants – and my countrymen.'

'Listen, and heed well my words,' said Elid, after

deliberation. 'Can you hear the bells ringing on Lyonesse, calling your people to prayer? They might be doomed to toll forever when moved by storm, though their tongues be muted. Wickedness is abroad and rife on your island, which has not escaped the all-seeing eye of God and which he finds intolerable. Havoc threatens the land unless you, Richard of Trevelyan, seek out this evil and destroy it. You must forewarn the people of their danger and persuade them to aid you in the search – as the wickedness is well hid.'

Startled, Richard leapt to his feet, but Elid, disregarding him, continued: 'If, as I fear, they will shut both ears and eyes and ignore the warning, t'will be their choice and you will be constrained to leave them to their fate – should you be unable to succeed by your own efforts. You would then need to act speedily to move those beholden to you, and your livestock, to the safety of the mainland by Saint Martin's Mass Day ere the new moon rises after the setting of the sun.'

Richard lifted his chin, which had sunk lower and lower on his breast as he tried to grasp the full import of this very grave news, having been unprepared for the extent of its severity despite his misgivings. 'But – so soon? 'Twill be early November, as I recall – just three more rebirths of the moon away...' He paused. 'My eldest son is named for the saint. He is a devoted priest, ordained in the church of Saint Perran, and would never be persuaded to leave should that be demanded of him. How, then, could he be saved?'

Elid regarded him with a look of compassion. 'With God all things are possible. Were he to be pure in heart he would be lifted up out of chaos by the hands of Jesus himself. As for you – you would lose two things that mean much to you – one to right and one to wrong – and also have to carry the burden of painful memories concerning those who refused to aid you in your search.'

Richard tried to push away a sense of dread and foreboding to allow reason to unravel the meaning of this enigma, but

4

without success. 'How can this be? Why have I been chosen to find some unknown evil that I might not even recognise? You cause me great distress,' he protested. 'What power have I to persuade men to aid me in the search? And for those that do, and we meet with no success, to order them to leave homes and land and follow me? Whither could I take them? And how could I bring myself to abandon the last resting-place of my beloved wife, Ysella?'

'Take comfort that nought can harm her bones,' Elid murmured, 'you must look to the living. The answers you seek lie in the trust you have in God – but beware of Satan tempting you from your path!'

'We are a pious people who keep no slaves in thrall.' Richard spoke in a bewildered way. 'Once there was evil in the land but that was stamped out long ago, like a dying fire. Now, I cannot conceive of a secret wickedness anywhere in our midst, and my skull is empty of a notion as to where to begin to look for it!'

'Nevertheless, it does exist and you were brought here by God, with whom you commune daily, to be entrusted with the task of attempting to remove the threat that hangs over you all.' The light began to fade in Elid's eyes. 'Keep faith,' he whispered, 'and do not defer to worldly neediness. Now, return home and spread the message throughout Lyonesse. You have my blessing…'tis over…'

Richard was loath to leave with question upon unanswered question filling his head, but his guide had entered to grasp his elbow and escort him outside.

'He may be the chosen prophet of God but is an ancient man and quickly tires,' came the rebuke from the folds of the cowl. 'You have received that for which you came, now gather your men and depart in peace.'

Richard, bemused, moved toward the group waiting uneasily, Old Jowan coming anxiously to meet him. He brushed aside their curious enquiries and they fell silent, catching his sombre mood as they observed his cheerless face.

He was recalling the time when he first noticed that ordinarily predictable events had begun to behave in an irrational manner. Small things, insignificant in themselves, were causing him such concern that he had resolved to seek advice from someone he considered a reliable source, the safety of his family being the prime reason for undertaking this journey. Since the death of his adored wife he had done all he could to protect his children, a family well-disciplined and close-knit, secure in its own little world. Living, loving and growing older, they busied themselves with daily tasks, time meaning nothing more than day and night, spring, summer, autumn or winter, working days, rest days, celebration days and Church days. In any event, there was always work to be done.

He gave a deep sigh as he regarded the faces of his men, eager to be gone. 'Let us make haste homeward', he said, 'to the cooking fires and full bellies that you crave. Once there, of a truth, you will find me to be the bearer of the dire tidings I have been bidden to share with you and all our countrymen.'

Upon their return, Richard immediately set about alerting the people to the Seer's prophecy. He spoke to the crowds in the marketplace of the Town of Lyons and the smaller fish market on the quay of the wide, sheltered bay to the south, but to no avail – no one heeded his plea for information or to help him search. In time, having visited every small community and finding the same negative response, he had become dismayed. Whatever reactions he had expected, those had not emerged. He had thought disbelief perhaps, but indifference? Amusement? Ridicule?

He pressed the men of the Church to urge the congregations of the churches spread over the island to aid him, but was firmly put off with: 'Would it be wise? This is only hearsay and there may be no truth in it. Panic might arise if we appear to confirm these tidings, and where would everyone repair to, pray? Some strange land over the sea holding unknown dangers, and with nowhere to lay their heads? Why, they could even be enslaved by any landowner finding them gathered there! No, better remain where God can continue to watch over them as usual. We must not beget alarm without good reason!'

'But, for sure, that is exactly what I do want to do – alarm the people for their own good and for the reason that it is what God wants!' Richard was exasperated. 'Has no one else noted the agitation of the waters – amongst other things? And there would be no need for panic to take hold, just an orderly withdrawal to the mainland. But that circumstance could be avoided altogether should you aid me in finding the devilry that lies hidden somewhere in our midst!'

However hard he tried, he was unable to convince them. The small church dedicated to Saint Ana, which served the locality of Trevelyan, was also unresponsive to his appeal, the clergy complacent and lacking concern, and, excluded from their support, Richard felt helpless. As the days advanced he had to accept the fact that he was looked upon as an agitator or, at best, a credulous person influenced by soothsaying. Even friends were unwilling to admit their lives were threatened.

'You are a dullard in accepting the utterances of an aged man on Scilly,' they muttered, smiling smugly. Others displayed annoyance: 'You possess the only mill on the island. Who will grind our grain if you heed this nonsense and leave?'

Richard exercised his patience. 'If I am wrong and the allotted time passes without incident I will speedily return with my millers to Trevelyan, but if I am proved right – you will have no further use for your grain!'

The only ones who did believe, trusting him implicitly,

were his own family and retainers, but although they searched, looking for they knew not what, they failed to find any trace of concealed corruption.

Watching the weeks pass as September crept away, Richard began to despair. He would have to start thinking of himself and his own, and of what he could do to safeguard their future. If the source of the evil were not found he would be compelled to move to the mainland, but where to? The only lands he possessed were here, so where could he transfer to safety all those who looked to him for protection? Greatly troubled he resolved to pursue each problem in turn, and for the present he would have one last try to stress the urgency of the situation, determining to visit some locations again. If then he failed to find what he sought and the people yet ignored the warning, he would address himself solely to his own domestic removal.

After a sleepless night, tormented by demons in dreams, he arose at dawn and rode away for as long as the day should last for one final search, unaware that before his return a distraction would re-enter his life that would cause the tenuous, diverse threads interlacing the lives of the people on Lyonesse to become twisted, and none remain the same. All would be affected by the arrival of the catalyst.

# 2

---

## *The Catalyst*

Lyonesse was an island said to have once flourished between Scilly and Cornwall, separated from the county by a narrow, surging strait fermented by waters pounding down from the Irish Sea and Bristol Channel, a promontory thrusting out like a tongue into Mount's Bay. It was a fertile land with many churches, the major sources of interest and entertainment, where congregations met and upheld those who preached the Gospel, thus being provided with a sense of belonging to a body greater and more dignified than themselves. Some said the churches had been built to impress with sanctity, but others declared it was to bring together all the singing and praying voices at regular times so that God could arrange to hear them.

Near the centre of the island stretched Nansvelyn, a valley formed by the convergence of two rivers flowing out to the north coast and the sea. The source of one was from an area known as Breonseyth, the seven hills surrounding the Town of Lyons, the place of government, commerce and barter. The other was fed by a spring gushing from the side of Carrag Uthek, the Awesome Rock, the site of pagan sacrifices long ago. A high, sinister, craggy pinnacle of greenstone slate, its base a quarter of a mile in diameter, it yet retained the power to inspire awe by dominating the lower southeastern region.

At the confluence of the two rivers lay Trevelyan, the mill

house, with a high wall encircling it. The mill itself was built into the wall, forming a part of it, so that a stream flowing past on the outside could provide the millrace necessary for grinding the grain. The only entrance was through a wide gateway, the gates usually left open unless lookouts at points around the coast signalled, by the ringing of the church bells, the possibility of an imminent attack by the fierce men from the Northlands sighted in their longships, pirates who pillaged and killed, but when shut and barred the place could be well defended. Inside, two levels had been constructed, one above the other, the higher level comprising the rooms used by Richard and his family, their doors opening onto a gallery, a wooden platform boxed in to waist height. This platform extended right round above a spacious courtyard and could be reached by both outer steps and inner stairs. The lower level contained everything pertaining to the small community, safe within the wall, the mill, granary, stores, the smithy and stabling, shelter for livestock and the dwelling places of the retainers.

A lofty, spreading tree grew in the courtyard by a well. Beneath it had been placed a long table, benches and a carved chair with arms – clearly the social hub of the residents. It was the peaceful setting for the scene about to unfold in the afternoon sun, on what had begun as an ordinary day when Richard had ridden out with the firm intention of making a last, desperate search. His retainers had rallied from the initial shock brought about by the news from Scilly and, having been unable to find, as yet, any evil to sustain the anxiety of the threat, had decided to trust both master and God to save them from harm before lapsing back into their everyday routine.

Just after noon, Martin, the eldest son, having heard that the churches had united against his father's plea for them to support his warning, arrived to discuss the matter with him. The young priest's time was normally restricted as, being an adept scribe, he helped to produce small missals for priests to carry to enable them to provide services for worship at any time, anywhere, so having stabled his horse he went in search of company, coming upon his youngest sister in the largest kitchen as she prepared fruit and berries for supper.

'How fares Tressa, my third and smallest sister?' he asked cheerfully.

'Not so small – 'most full grown!' she snapped, tossing her long, russet curls over her shoulders as she snatched a bowl from out of his reach, annoyed that he should choose to ignore the fact that she was fast coming to an age when wedlock might be considered.

'And just as plump – but not as ripe as this plum,' he quipped, stretching over and plucking one from under her nose.

Hastily escaping from the possibility of retaliation, Martin found his little brother polishing metal pots in the armoury. 'Where is Father busying himself this day, Hicca?'

'Abroad somewhere.' Hicca was engrossed in completing his chore. 'Hopefully to return by sundown he said.'

Martin walked to the door and stood looking outside. The mill was idle, the millers taking a rest in the heat of the day, as were all the other inhabitants, everyone staying in the cool of the interior. It was very quiet, with only the faint splashing of the waters and the clucking of hens to break the silence – even the dogs had taken refuge from the sun. He moved into the courtyard, the heat beating down on the tonsure crowning his blonde head, and went across to the shade of the tree. Sitting on a bench he put his back against the trunk, his black habit merging into the shadows. From an inner pocket he drew out an assembly of small reed pipes and began to play, the sweet notes filling the heavy air. With eyelids closed in his finely moulded face Martin gave himself up to the music, and so was unaware when his brother came out to drink at the well.

11

Hicca was eight years old, a mischievous, brown nut of a boy, dark-haired and stocky like his father, resembling him also in that he was ever alert and querying. He wore a knee-length tunic, held in at the waist by a belt, which overhung cloth breeches. He was joined a moment later by Tressa, two years older and anxious to leave childhood behind. She was wearing a loose smock-frock the colour of bright marigolds, pert features softened by a pair of wide, light grey eyes that her doting father said always reminded him of a pigeon's breast, licking fingers stained red by the berries she had been preparing.

The children's fingers were always stained in the fruit-picking season since one of their tasks was to keep the baskets filled. They also helped the community's children to gather kindling for the fires, but of late Tressa had begun to consider herself too old for such a childish pursuit, planning to refuse to concern herself with it any more. Hicca, knowing her thoughts, teased her mercilessly. She usually took his jesting in good part unless feeling fractious – as she was today. When she came to the well, walking in a studied, dignified way as befitted one on the verge of maturity, or so she chose to regard herself, she wanted a drink of water – quickly! Hicca was already drinking from the ladle and held it away from her, increasing her vexation.

'Give it me,' she said crossly. 'I have a great thirst!'

Hicca moved out of reach. 'You will wish for the heat when the cold comes and there are no fires for warmth 'cos you would not fetch kindling!' His cheeky face grinned annoyingly.

'Stop your chiding, you witless babe!' she fumed.

He was stung by being referred to as a 'babe' and pranced away even further, making impudent noises at her.

'Martin, make him give it to me!' she demanded, appealing for him to intervene in this aggravating game. Martin, however, was lost in a realm where music reigned and

12

failed to hear. She was left with no other choice but to discard her assumed dignity and run after her tormentor – having longer legs, she invariably caught up with him.

'Bide still 'til I catch you!' she called. 'Then you will surely be put down the well – and good riddance!'

By this time they were racing round the courtyard, bare feet thudding in the white dust from the mill. Hens and geese scattered with a beating of wings and indignant clucking and honking. The children were yelling, laughing and gasping for breath, Tressa's ill temper forgotten, and she all but had her brother in her grasp as they reached the big gates when he was suddenly swung away above her head. Unable to check her headlong rush she struck something soft but unyielding, at once becoming aware that her face was buried in what she knew must be someone's stomach, while hearing Hicca squeal from somewhere on high.

'Oh! For shame!' she gasped, pushing herself away while peering up to see who had brought about this hindrance. Shyness enveloped her when she realised that it was not a familiar face smiling down at her but one belonging to a total stranger.

'I am contrite,' said the man, in a disarming manner, as he lowered Hicca to his feet. 'Allow me to shoulder the blame for our sudden – and forceful – meeting.'

Hicca straightened his tunic, still recovering from his surprising flight into the air and, at present uncertain as to how to deal with this event, quickly edged behind his sister. She, standing her ground, noted that the newcomer was wearing fine garments and was of a distinguished appearance. As he threw back his cape she saw a glittering, ornate badge on his breast indicating a person of some importance, although she had no idea that he was Vivian, Governor and Lord of Lyonesse, born and raised there, but absent from the island for some years past.

When Vivian was barely out of his teens, his father, the

governor then, had been crippled in a hunting accident and soon chose to transfer to his only son his authority, which included Dinas Ryal, the official residence, sited near the Town of Lyons. Afterwards, he moved to property he owned on the Cornish mainland, and when he died a few years later Vivian went over there to claim his inheritance of the estates that covered an area stretching to what was called the 'end of the land' and stayed on. His wife, Kweras, had much preferred to live there, and for his part he had reason to feel a certain reluctance to return to Lyonesse. His absence had not seemed to be of concern to anyone other than his friends, as activity there continued to be uneventful and did not present a need for governing, though some elders spoke darkly of disloyalty and default. But, now in his early thirties, changing circumstances had persuaded him to resume his duties, and only later would he reproach himself for having neglected both birthright and obligations for so long.

As Tressa regarded him now, momentarily robbed of speech, she noted that his hair was of a chestnut colour untouched by rime and, though his smile was a mite askew, thought he was by far the most handsome man she had ever seen – apart from her father, of course! Hicca was seldom at a loss for words though and, showing bravado, emerged from behind her back and stood gazing upwards.

'You are well come,' he greeted the tall man cheerfully, hardly pausing to breathe. 'How are you called? I am Hicca and my sister here is Tressa and this is our home – d'ye wish to speak with anyone or mayhap find yourself in need of guidance?'

The man waved a restraining hand, a twinkle evident in his kindly brown eyes. 'Whoa there, boy – you rob me of my breath! One question at a time, if you please! Now, the answer to the first is that my name is Vivian, and I am honoured to meet with you both. Secondly, I am intent upon finding Richard, who owns this mill, and am well acquainted with my whereabouts.'

'Oh, you want Father,' said Hicca. 'He rode out early for his busyness of the day but should be back by sundown. Can you stay? You can sup with us – there is always plenty to share.'

'If that is your wish then 'tis my command and I will gladly await him. But my mount needs care – she has been hard ridden.'

'She seems spent and needing mash.' Hicca eyed the mare critically, seeing that it was furnished with an elaborate harness. 'I am skilled with horses – let me look to her.' He handed the water ladle to Tressa and led the mare towards the stable.

His sister was still feeling uncomfortable about her inelegant introduction to this person who, she was sure, held some high rank, and also cross that Hicca had left her to entertain him. Another thought intruded – what if Father should be displeased to find him waiting? They might be old enemies, although – she glanced quickly at the stranger's smiling eyes – she very much doubted it. She decided to shift the responsibility.

'May I offer you drink to quench your thirst?' she asked, waving the ladle in the direction of the well. 'You can rest in the shade there,' she added, leading the way across the courtyard to where Martin, eyelids fast closed, was lost in his music.

Vivian followed her to the tree, loosened his sword-belt and cast it on the table. The thump of the scabbard brought Martin rudely from his daydreaming and the tune ceased abruptly. Startled, he scrambled to his feet.

'I beg pardon for causing you alarm – 'twas not by design but clumsiness,' Vivian apologised. 'You are a gifted player on the pipes,' he continued, while studying the face of the discomfited young priest. 'Pray continue.'

'No matter.' Martin was hastily trying to assess the situation as he failed to recognise this eminent person. 'Please to be seated. What seek you at Trevelyan?'

Vivian was regarding him also with uncertainty as he lowered himself on to a bench. 'Unless I err mightily, you must be Richard's son, Martin.'

'Ay, 'tis true.' A frown creased the brow above his boyish features. 'But how…?' The frown cleared as he realised that this was no stranger. 'We have met before – a long time since. I well know your face but fail to put a name to it.'

' 'Twould indeed be strange if you should remember the governor who has been away for far too many long years. You were but a young colt when I left.'

'Of a certainty – you are m'Lord Vivian! You spent much time here with us before travelling to the mainland. Mother – and 'specially Father – were grieved by your absence. 'Twas plain to see that you were sadly missed.'

Vivian nodded. 'Ay, and I longed for their company, too, having thought to be gone but a short while when my father died, but I was held protecting the property and people who had passed into my care. Moreover,' he dropped his gaze, 'my Lady was loath to leave Trevivian, our home there.' He lifted his eyes again. 'My steward managed my lands here well enough, rarely needing advice, but situations change and so I am returned to resume my role at Dinas Ryal – and friendship with you all.' He felt a touch on his arm. 'I am obliged to you, Tressa,' he went on, finding her proffering a ladle of water dripping on the white dust as she lifted it from the bucket.

Martin realised that he was failing in his duty as host by not providing hospitality for this honoured guest. His father's tongue would flay him should he hear of this lack of manners! 'Forgive me – my head is in the clouds,' he confessed. 'Tressa – leave that be and tell the women to bring food and wine – and hurry!' He returned his attention to Vivian. 'Father should be back by sundown.'

The governor rested his arms on the table, smiling after Tressa as she scampered away forgetful of her recently assumed decorum. 'So your brother said. Now, tell me all your news. There has been little enough reaching me, though I did hear of your mother's death. I sent word of my regret.'

Martin nodded. 'Ay...she died when Hicca was born.'

'I can imagine your grief – I felt it cruelly myself. Ysella...On my word, if your father, who is a mite older than myself, had not wooed and won her in far off Cornouaille before he brought her to Lyonesse, I would have begged for her hand in my own right, but I was yet a callow youth while she had attained womanhood – gentle and lovely – the more so than any I have set eyes upon,' he ended absently.

'Our sister, Meralda, favours her, as alike as any two people could be. She, and Lowenna, who is younger, now have control over the household.'

Vivian appeared surprised. 'What? Has your father not wed again? I would have expected it, though not having heard tell...but then, I have received no word of your own progress and am taken aback by the sight of you in the cloth. I would have avowed that you were aiding Richard here and been wedded long since.'

'None of us seem desirous of becoming espoused to another – except Tressa!' Martin grinned in amusement as he watched her walking back sedately in the wake of two women carrying food and wine, her eyes on Vivian. 'And she is most impatient to find her own true love! As for me – well, I am content.'

'But your father had such plans for you, as I recall. Whatever chanced to turn you from that path?'

Martin hesitated, reluctant to expose his feelings. ''Tis hard for me to say,' he conceded. 'I once fell in love, deeply on my part, but she was yet a child and made sport of me.' He sighed. 'I was unhappy for a while, but one night I had a

17

dream and knew what I must do.' He warmed to his story. 'It was as if the idea had been in bud in my head all my life, then blossomed so I could grasp and pluck it out. I could not deny the yearning for the cloth, so Father, being persuaded, set me in the church of Saint Perran. He felt I had more to offer than would be required by our own small church of Saint Ana, although I had preferred the nearness to my mother who lies buried there.'

He poured a goblet of wine, passing it to Vivian just as Hicca came running from the stable with his usual vigour. 'Your mare has been fed and watered and rubbed down,' the boy announced, breathing hard. 'She rests in comfort in a stall.'

'Ho! Such service! I cannot remember the like when I was here before!'

Hicca registered disbelief. 'And I cannot 'member you being here before. See, Tressa has surprise on her face, too.'

'Nor should either of you recall me – your mother had not borne you then, lad, and Tressa was too small to know – a tiny child forever sitting in her beautiful mother's lap. I can see the two of you even now, Tressa, your arms about her neck...' Vivian pulled his wandering thoughts back to the present. 'I assure you that I have long been your father's friend...' he broke off, hearing a shout from the gateway.

'My horse is lame – fetch another with all speed! By my troth, I am conspired upon by the Devil! Can there be such a curse upon my quest that I have to be thwarted at every turn? And why do I find, when I return earlier than expected...'

'Father's here!' cried Tressa, starting to run towards him to be first with the news, but Hicca forestalled her by calling out: 'Father! Your friend Vivian is come to sup with us!'

At the first sound of the voice of the master of the house the whole place had been startled into feverish activity. Women appeared carrying baskets, men heaped logs into piles and moved barrels. Dogs barked and stablemen came running, the miller and his underlings appearing as if by magic to lift sacks of grain and flour, and the noise made by the millstones put into motion began to dominate the whole. This sudden industry could have been due to the cooling of the day coinciding with the master's return, but whatever the reason, none of it was lost on Richard as he strode in, beating his whip against any inanimate object that he passed.

'...you seek to befool me into thinking you have not been idle!' He finished the sentence with a roar. 'Get you all to...' he paused as he made sense of Hicca's words. 'Vivian?' his voice was querying.

Then, as his eyes confirmed what his ears had conveyed, he bounded forward. 'My dear friend – I can hardly believe I am not suffering a disorder of the mind! Is it really you – or a delusion? Have you been brought here in answer to my prayers? Then I thank God for opening His ear to me! Each day when I speak with Him I have begged – merciful God, I pray You send aid to help me find the place which conceals the evil that offends You, and...'

He stopped again in mid-sentence. 'But I digress – am in error – you may have no knowledge of my dilemma. We must talk of it at length when I have ceased to marvel at your coming – I cannot heed aught else for now!'

Vivian had risen and moved to meet him. They clasped one another in a tight bear hug for some long moments before loosing their arms, though continuing to hold elbows as if afraid that in parting they might lose this joyous instant, to vanish as vapour under the rays of the sun.

Richard cleared his throat of the lump that was threatening to choke him. 'It has been so long...We go about the daily tasks and the years fly by without us heeding their passing. How did we allow this parting to happen, doing nought to hinder it? Making no effort to beat a pathway one to the other in order to enjoy our friendship to the full? Let me regard you.' He held him at arm's length, beaming with delight. 'Veritably the same – time has dealt kindly with you. I have aged the most, with many more lines etched upon my face.'

'Well, I am younger than you – remember how we used to jest?'

'You have brought it to my mind again! We will talk of that anon. Tell me what happy chance returns you to us? Many have censured you for neglecting your duties, but not I, though I cannot understand what has kept you away.'

He did not await an answer, the exhilaration having sent his senses bubbling as water in a boiling kettle. He picked up a goblet. 'Bring more wine! Martin, have you met our guest's needs?'

With Vivian the same euphoria applied. Gone were the years of separation – it was enough that they were together once more. The children had been standing by, mouths slightly agape at the unusual sight of two grown men behaving, in their eyes, like tender young maids. Besides, this was a new experience – their loving father had never before ignored them for so long.

Hicca tweaked his sleeve. 'We abide here, too, Father.'

Richard turned and hugged them. 'Halloa to you, my dears. I have been so taken by surprise that my wits are scattered! Vivian, have you met with my children?'

'These three have occupied me agreeably enow, but I have yet to glimpse the others.'

'What? That is very remiss and must be put to rights. Tressa, find your sisters. Order them to cease whatever tasks concern them and attend us here. Vivian, please be seated while we wait.' He sat himself in the heavy wooden chair obviously reserved for the head of the household and contentedly stretched out his legs. 'Now, what of you and your family? We saw too little of your wife, Kweras, before you left. There was talk here that you had begat an heir. Are there others – and all with you?'

Vivian smiled ruefully. 'You delve into the sadness of my heart. There were no others, and my son and Kweras are gone – both taken by the pox these twelvemonths. 'Tis a lonely life without kin, but as for Kweras...' he paused. 'No matter. I know that Ysella is gone too, and that you remain without a consort. Will you not wed again?'

'Not I!' answered Richard, giving a saucy wink. 'I do very well as I am!' He gave a passing serving wench a slap on the rump. 'Besides, where would I find another such wife? I have luck enow to be blest with a loving family to give me company, my daughters seeming loath to leave my hearth. But for you, my friend, I feel disquiet. Have you no one?' As Vivian shook his head he went on: 'I know you love me like a brother, but that cannot take the place of passion and you are a young man. You must recall how much you are missing when, in the dark of the night, you find yourself lying next to no one?'

'Only the admitted chance of being unable to fall out of favour with a person other than myself – which is a circumstance for which I am truly grateful!' Vivian's tone was sharp.

At that moment Tressa intervened. 'I have done as you asked, Father, and they are coming.'

''Tis well.' Richard cast a puzzled look at his friend, obviously disconcerted by his response, but decided to dismiss it. 'My maidens, Vivian, are known as the three swans because they have such grace and beauty. Tressa here is the cygnet.'

'What about me?' demanded Hicca, impertinently 'Am I not beautiful?'

'You are nothing but a saucy young gosling!' Richard ruffled the dark head. 'My other swans are Meralda and Lowenna – surely you remember them? Here is Lowenna now. Come and meet my old friend – do you not find his face familiar?'

21

She had come into the courtyard, a basket of fruit on her arm. Long, shining black hair, framing a lovely, heart-shaped face, hung below her waist. She wore a loose, purple garment, a colour she favoured, which accentuated the violet of her eyes, the draping tending to obscure her already sensual, rounded figure. She was of a practical and kindly nature, her discernment belying her sixteen years, and enjoyed domesticity and cooking though Gweniver, a widowed matron once their wet nurse, ruled over the kitchens.

Putting down the basket, her breath coming quickly and a high colour suffusing her cheeks, Lowenna eyed Vivian with a shy, sidelong glance before curtsying low. 'I remember well,' she answered. 'I never forgot. I had a certainty you would return to us one day, m'Lord. Do you recall this ring?' She held out her hand to display a large, black stone set in silver. 'You lost it once when you were here with your Lady. When I found it you let me keep it and so it has stayed on my hand ever since, going from finger to finger as I grew older.' She looked around her. 'Does your Lady visit with you?'

'My Lady will nevermore be with me but that must occasion you no distress.' Vivian smiled gently, taking the hand and kissing it. 'I well remember this ring and how could I fail to hold you in my mind?' He remained with her hand in his for longer than was necessary, gazing into those welcoming, violet eyes.

It was then that Meralda made her entrance. She had been in an upper room and was making her way down nearby steps, lifting the edge of her green-blue gown, so like the colours of the waters of the sea, just above her ankles. It matched her large, luminous eyes that you would swear were blue on sun-lit days and yet became green, and even grey, when clouds covered the skies. Her pale, fair hair was looped up and pinned around her shapely head, as befitted a maid who had almost attained eighteen years. She was coolly beautiful, moving like a queen with a natural grace, yet unaware, giving the impression that her eyes were turned inwards and focused upon something unseen. Many youths had tried to court this desirable creature, only to find she was disinterested in boys of a marriageable age. Men had wooed her but said she was without warmth, as if she dwelt in the dark depths of the ocean, soon to discover that she preferred to be alone on the seashore gazing over the waves into the far distance, aloof, but poised as if waiting for something unknown. All eyes were upon her now as she reached the courtyard.

'And here is my other swan, Meralda,' said Richard proudly. Then to her: 'Join with us in gladness that our Lord of Lyonesse pleasures us with his presence.'

Vivian was still clasping Lowenna's hand but looked past her and let it fall. The instant he glanced at Meralda he thought his heart would stop its beating, and he ceased to see anything else. She filled his entire horizon – dazzling him. The sight of her swept him joyfully back to his younger days when he was madly in love with...Was it her yet? No, impossible. He swiftly chased that thought from his mind, temporarily sending it scuttling out of harm's way as Meralda bent to kiss her father then turned to him.

'My Lord,' she said, giving a deep curtsy.

He took her hands, drawing her to her feet, enraptured. 'Meralda – there has been such a change in you from the small maid I used to see at her mother's knee – though it seems but yesterday. I beg you...sit by me here.'

He had not meant to be cruel and, indeed, was unknowing that Lowenna had been left standing by herself feeling hurt and rejected as she drooped her head and went to sit by Martin. Her brother, noticing her abrupt lapse from radiance to despondency put an arm around her, pulling her close, while suddenly being assailed by a deep, unexpected disquiet.

Richard watched with interest how the meeting with Meralda was affecting Vivian, noting his evident attraction to her, and was seized with an idea as to how to advance this desirable possibility.

He rose to his feet. 'What say we celebrate when we sup this even? Let us eat, drink and make merry! Can you tarry here, Vivian? And Martin?'

When they both nodded he called to the servants: 'Prepare a feast – M'Lord graces us with his presence! Let us offer the best we have – and with no tardiness – you have but a short space to set a good board.'

His eyes alighted on Gweniver, the buxom, motherly figure who once cared solely for his children and who now shared that task, since they were fair grown, with presiding over the food. 'You hear, Gweniver? Make a feast to surpass all – let the boards creak and groan with good provender!'

With a broad grin she nodded as he turned to his offspring. 'All of you make yourselves of use while I converse with my old friend, happily returned. We have much to review.'

Martin held back, hesitating. 'There is a matter I would discuss with you, Father, which is why I am here. The Church buzzes with rumour and hearsay.'

'There will be time enow when we have supped, my son. For the present, aid the others in preparing all to my satisfaction.' Richard moved away, dismissing him.

'Then, shall I go fetch the priest and brothers of Saint Ana? 'Tis usual for them to join us in celebration as they form a part of our community,' Martin persisted.

Richard showed impatience. 'Let them be!' he said sharply. 'We no longer share such courtesies for reasons which will be made obvious to you. I bitterly regret that your dear mother lies at rest there since I have fallen foul of them with their complacency and intolerant manners! They incline to scorn my beliefs and those of the Seer, saying he has prophesied a false vision. They smite him with their tongues, calling him a mere soothsayer who should be disregarded – as did the merchants, the fishers and most others! They all deny that our Maker has spoken through the mouth of this holy man because, as I fancy, they find it incommoding!'

Spluttering with annoyance he swung around, inadvertently pushing against a man well advanced in years displaying sparse, white hair and a full set of whiskers. He quickly calmed his sudden temper. 'Oh, Jowan – I ask pardon.' He rested a hand on the bowed back. 'Vivian – you must remember Old Jowan here – my father's steward. He taught us to hunt and divert ourselves when we were young.' He paused, conscious of Vivian's eyes turned elsewhere. 'You show no recognition, friend. Has it faded from your mind?'

Having been lost in contemplation of Meralda, Vivian was at last able to tear his gaze away as she disappeared through a doorway. He forced his attention back, although he would have much preferred to let his imagination follow her inside.

'Why…indeed, ay…I mean…nowise!' He squeezed the old man's arm. 'You saved us many a beating by covering our foolishness, Jowan,' he admitted hurriedly. 'We must take up those past tales anon, for our diversion.'

'Whenever it may please you, m'Lord.' Jowan bobbed his head before turning away. 'Master, you lately called for a fresh horse – it awaits you at the gate.'

Richard smote his forehead with the heel of his hand. 'I swear, my brains are as addled as an egg with the whirling of my senses at your glad arrival! I cannot centre my thoughts on trivia – there are better things to occupy me. Stable it.'

'I have no desire to tempt you from a prior plan,' said Vivian.

Richard waved aside the very idea. 'Forbear to mention it! It is simply that ere the day was ended I had planned to question yet again the fishers in the bay, before riding eastward 'til I reached a certain area – by chance upon your land. You know it, the region around Carrag Uthek and Kellimargh, the Forbidden Place where no one ventures, hoping against hope that I might at last find what I seek but lacking any true expectation. I have already ridden out there, it seeming to be an obvious place to search for evil, as it was once the centre of pagan activity and is now the supposed haunt of ghosts, but found it utterly forsaken as always. Howbeit, I had determined to traverse every portion of Lyonesse twice over, being held back now only because my horse became lame – but I am remiss – you may be ignorant of my quest. Have you heard aught of the events I have proclaimed these many days, giving tongue all over the land?'

Vivian shook his head. 'Not one word, just having set foot back on Lyonesse soil, but I sense a mystery unfolding. 'Tis many years since I went near the dark side of Carrag Uthek myself – I know my steward shuns it yet. He says that with its dire history 'tis only wise to avoid it, however brave you be, but haply we both were raised to discount the existence of ghosts...'

His thoughts went to the Forbidden Place, seeing it in his mind's eye. A stream, fed by a spring, gushed out from about halfway down the south side of Carrag Uthek, diverging just above the base to form two sides of a triangle containing Kellimargh, the Grove of the Horse. The streams marked its boundaries, forests on either side keeping it secluded, to hold safe within the lurking, unquiet spirits of the victims of pagan sacrifice as was believed by the fearful, superstitious population who kept safely away.

He returned his attention to his host. 'But, since 'tis on my land and should you so desire, I will willingly ride out there with you now.'

Richard shrugged his shoulders. 'As all my efforts have so far come to nought, I doubt 'twill matter overmuch should I abandon my mission for this day. I can search it later with you, mayhap on the morrow, trusting that another pair of eyes may reveal what has lain hidden from mine. Instead, let us go inside to converse and I will acquaint you with all that is affecting me.'

That decision made, they climbed the steps to Richard's chamber.

# 3

## *The Forbidden Place*

When Richard first rode out to the Forbidden Place he had seen no need for caution, believing it to be deserted, unaware of silent watchers hidden in the trees at all times with orders to lure away, frighten or kill anyone foolhardy enough to venture into this place of spectral ill-repute.

In the ancient past, the pagan worship of the sun had predominated and, as fire gave the appearance of reproducing it on earth, rituals involving sacrifice by fire were practised. Carrag Uthek, known as the Fire Rock, had been the ceremonial site – approached from Kellimargh, the Grove of the Horse, by a lone pathway that led up the sheer north face to the summit, the nearest place to supplicate, and make sacrifice to, the sun god. Though that custom had long ago been abandoned, awareness had been kept alive by word of mouth and the brooding nature of the Fire Rock itself. Its stark south side, facing towards the sea, loomed over Kellimargh with the open glade at its centre, where it was almost obscured from sight by a shield of foliage formed by the trees.

A later cult had succeeded the worship of the sun, that of the worship of the sea. The fisher folk venerated the god Poseidon, whom they looked to for protection and to provide the means to support their livelihood. His deification had been suppressed by the advent of

Christianity, the monks who brought the Word to the island affirming that paganism was an abomination to be outlawed. There were many who were reluctant to relinquish their traditions, afraid to accept this new religion and abandon the gods who had earned their loyalty – it might be the wrong choice and they would suffer for it, and so they only pretended to be converted. Their sacred Grove of Kellimargh had then become the Forbidden Place, shunned by the Christian population, but the fisher folk over the years had gradually managed to ease it back into resuming its former role, re-establishing their gatherings while observing the utmost secrecy. They nurtured tales of hauntings by those who had been sacrificed at the top of Carrag Uthek, feeling safeguarded by the stream that flowed down from the rock, diverging on each side of the grove and so on to the sea. Within that watery triangle the devotees of the sea god felt immune from any harm essayed by ghosts and shades unable to cross water – the living presented a greater threat. All paths leading to the glade had been carefully blocked by what appeared to be naturally fallen tree trunks to deter mounted intruders from riding along them; sentries accounted for unwary interlopers.

So, the hidden glade continued to be undisturbed by outside influences on that peaceful afternoon when Vivian arrived at Trevelyan, the day when Richard had intended to make his second search of the area. The sunlight radiated through the leaves, picking out the scene like spotlights illuminating the setting where a modest temple stood amongst cypress trees, steps leading up to its pillared doorway. Near it, a post used for tethering was stood by a long, stone altar, and further along a large circular stone with a sizable hole in the centre above waist height, resembling a millstone, rested upright on its rim. Close by, two marble statues predominated, the larger being an impressive, naked male depicting the god Poseidon, flowing, curly hair surrounding a powerful, bearded face above a muscular neck and body. He clasped a trident in one hand, the shaft resting on the plinth with a dolphin at his feet. Next to him was Cleito, his consort, the only one of his many lovers to have been mortal, her voluptuous body draped in what was skilfully sculpted on the marble as a transparent garment, her sightless eyes staring up at him in ardent adoration.

It was before these images that white-robed figures were moving in a circular pattern forming a rhythmic progression. The low humming noise issuing from their closed lips sounded like the wind stirring up the waters of the deep to echo among empty caves as they began to fill with the tide. These were the fisher folk, the men acting as lesser priests, the women as priestesses to minister to Cleito.

Outlined against the dark interior of the temple stood an amorphous form of above-average height emanating authority, directing the proceedings by holding on high a silver trident with a long shaft. A white cloth covered the head, the folds concealing the features, which were hidden from the gaze of inferior mortals with the intention of distancing them from this deputy of a higher power, to shroud it further in an aura of mystery. Eyelet holes in the cloth permitted observation without being observed, the head being bared only during important ceremonies when an ornate silver head-dress was worn, but no person dared to glance directly at it.

Tardhamor, the high priest, was zealous in his service to his god. He lived alone in the temple served by acolytes, seeking companionship from no one. He subsisted on offerings brought to Poseidon – whatever he desired he had only to pretend to interpret the god's needs in the hearing of the assembly for a bountiful supply to appear. The fisher folk revered and feared him, never questioning his slightest command, regarding the aloof figure with awe. They might have believed that the visible covering concealed nothing more tangible than an inhabiting spectre, had it not been for a thin, greyish beard jutting from below the edge of the cloth and two lean hands projecting from the sleeves of the robe. These, when their owner was angered, would pluck at the material as if to tear it apart, then shake with rage when thwarted in the attempt.

The high priest was now calmly descending the steps, and when he waved the trident all movement and sound ceased for a few moments and even breathing was suspended. As he came to face the statue of Poseidon, breaths were expelled in a loud sigh, and the company prostrated themselves.

Tardhamor made a low obeisance, raising his arms in supplication. 'O great God,' he chanted. 'God of the seas, horses, storms, earthquakes – and god of Atlantis and Lyonesse – hear me! What has made you so angry? Why do you roar and beat upon our shores as if to swallow us up? What can we do to placate you?'

He stood, hand cupped to ear, listening. From the far-off coast, whether imagined or not, the sound of surf breaking on the shore became audible to all. He nodded, as if agreeing to a request. 'I hear your words, O great One. Your bidding will be obeyed without respite or regard for the progress of time or tide.'

He turned to the recumbent forms. 'Rise!' he ordered. His eyes scanned the various faces, passing over and discarding until they reached one that pleased him. 'Atlan!' he cried. 'Come forth and offer yourself. Your father Poseidon calls to you – his son!'

A tall youth, with broad shoulders and golden curls above a face bearing the fine outline of a Greek sculpture, pushed his way into the inner circle. His skin, too, was golden, and dreamy blue eyes gave the impression of pools of sea water surrounded by sun-warmed sands. He was never idle, and much more astute than the others as Tardhamor well knew, ever eager to serve his god in loyal, blind obedience.

Kneeling before the statue, the youthful fisherman thought he was about to be told to steal a bull-calf, his usual task, but this time he was mistaken.

'Atlan,' continued the high priest, 'you are entrusted to seek the fairest maiden in Lyonesse and to bring her here to become a bride for Poseidon. She must have the same calm beauty as a swan, whose soft, white breast glides over the waters, and 'tis paramount that she has known no man – she must be pure, a virgin – and preferably a Christian!' He spat, as if to cleanse his mouth of the word. 'She will be taught to abandon her foolish notions. Cleito has consented to her lord's wishes without spite and, after their union, the seas will be at peace. You are allowed but one more coming of a new moon to increase to the full, but be very sure you deliver the maiden before the rebirth of the second or the result may be dire! Your reward will be a favour granted by our god. Now, mount your horse and ride!'

Atlan rose to his feet and broke the circle, flinging off his robe as he ran to reveal a fisherman's short tunic, belted at the waist. Attached to the belt was a sheath holding the obligatory knife, carried by all men in whatever occupation they followed for attack and defence. A distinctive medallion, a cross-within-a-circle finely wrought in bright silver, hung around his neck. He did not question the mission, it had been made clear enough, and although he had no idea as to how to attempt this novel undertaking, he had faith that Poseidon would present him with both the opportunity for, and means of, success.

As he reached the edge of the glade he saw his horse moving towards him. There had never been a need for tethering, an intuitive understanding between the two being apparent from the beginning. No bridle constricted its head, neither bit nor rein, merely a finely woven halter about the neck and a surcingle to hold a cloth over its back. It was rare for a lowly fisherman to own a horse of such quality and strength, although Atlan would have denied that he owned it – the horse seemed to have become an extension of himself.

Sailing homeward in his boat with his catch some long time before, he had noticed, as he rounded the point into the bay, a movement far out in the sea. Watching, he saw what appeared to be a white horse swimming vigorously in his direction, the fine spray sent up on each side as it breasted the waves resembling great, white wings. Briefly, Atlan had thought this was so and the horse was skimming over the water, being reminded of an ancient tale of a winged horse called Pegasus, said to signify immortality, which had been fathered by his own god, Poseidon. It had sprung from the blood pouring from the neck of its mother, the winged monster Medusa, her head of writhing snakes severed by Perseus, the son of Zeus, king of the gods.

As it swam up alongside he was aware of lengthy, pale green ribbons of seaweed entwining its neck and floating out around it, and when they reached the shore the stallion trotted from the water and quietly stood by as the boy beached the boat. He had no idea from whence it had come, and since it showed no inclination to leave his side he named it Mordon – 'sea-wave'. It had soon ceased to have an indefinite gender, becoming Atlan's friend and brother, taking the place of the father and mother he had lost when too young to remember them. He knew only that he had been found and raised by a solicitous, but unresponsive, childless couple who remained distant toward this child who seemed to be different from others they knew – although they would have had difficulty in explaining that difference.

When unobserved, Atlan had a distant look in his eyes, as if transported afar to dwell in a place remote from the humble fisherman's hut that sheltered them, but it was more than that. From an early age he had been attracted to the temple in Kellimargh, and as he grew older spent much time there learning from the priests, while displaying an unusually high intelligence and proving an apt pupil. He also excelled as a fisherman, and soon left the hut to live and work in the stalwart boat he had built himself. But first and foremost came his utter loyalty to his god.

He gently stroked Mordon's muzzle. 'We have an irksome task ahead,' he said softly. 'I shall go wherever you take me – guided, without doubt, by Poseidon in his wisdom. Who knows whither this maiden will be found?' He mounted the white horse with an obvious lack of enthusiasm and they headed out towards the bay and the comfortable familiarity of his boat.

# 4

## Celebration

'What say you, friend? Am I acting like a man in his dotage to take on so? Addressing myself solely to this matter to the exclusion of all else? You are now aware of the reason for my fretting, my belief that calamity lies dormant at our gates. Having heard my case, would you consider there is just cause for alarm? I place much value upon your ruling.'

His fears disclosed, Richard rose from his seat and began pacing while awaiting answers to his questions. Passing the couch on which Vivian lay sprawled, he anxiously scanned his friend's face, fervently hoping for his support.

Vivian took his time before replying. His judgment would not be hasty as he was a man shrewd in his assessment of any dilemma. 'It seems I have returned at an opportune moment,' he said at last. 'I, too, have noted the increased activity of the seas and my steward has made known to me the unease affecting the animals. I have also heard of the surety of the Seer's prophecies – so, all in all, I am inclined to give credence to your alarm.'

Richard had been prepared to continue with his pleading and was taken by surprise. 'Wh-what? You are in accord with me? I was of the opinion that none outside of Trevelyan would ever be convinced of my prudence. God be praised! Then will you follow me to the mainland with your own people?'

'I will fain take a chance upon't!'

Richard felt heady in his relief. 'Let's drink a toast to it, then.' Having sipped the wine he wiped his lips. 'Perhaps you can aid me in a further problem. 'Tis your good fortune to have another abode on the mainland, and thus able to transfer your chattels to safety. My mind is set to find another domicile for my family and dependents, but where 'tis hard to surmise. Time flies on apace and we have but a few weeks left 'til Saint Martin's Feast. I am blest that harvesting is almost done.'

His thoughts busy, Vivian had shut his eyes. Opening them now, he said: 'I would have it that everyone from Trevelyan could stay with me on my estate at Trevivian, but with the influx of my people leaving from here...And the pasture would prove too scant for both all your stock and mine.'

Richard waved a deprecating hand. 'I swear, such an idea had not entered into my head. I have no wish to encumbrance you – 'twould afford me no pleasure...'

'Let me finish,' broke in Vivian. 'I am able to offer you a place to stay as brief or lasting as you choose. There is a hillfort upon a piece of my land over there, able to accommodate your dependents and with land enough to provide for the livestock. 'Tis on a cliff looking over what is known as Perran Sands at Perranuthnoe and was built to house a small troop of men, though of late it has not been fully manned, so I would welcome your people, 'specially those bearing arms. 'Twould be a base for shelter 'til you decide which way your future beckons, and it might also be possible to put your workers of tin to labour nearby as rich workings are already sited there and dwellings could be built for them.' He paused, smiling. 'Saint Perran watches over those who pursue the obtainment of tin – or so I have been told – and that must include you as their master. 'Twill not be so easy to restore your livelihood as a grinder of grain,' he went on, pondering, ' 'til you find a place to settle and build another mill, if 'tis your wish, so must be suffered to wait. But, for now, I must insist that you and your family stay at Trevivian with me 'til your future plans are fixed – I long for the hollowness of the house to be filled.' The image of Meralda's face came into his mind. 'The rooms are so empty that they resound with doleful echoes.'

Richard felt overwhelmed by gratitude, and with the lessening of the strain so apparent earlier, the two men relaxed in reactions of relief and anticipation, for differing reasons, until roused by a tentative knock on the half-open door.

Lowenna stood there, watching them uncertainly, unsure of her reception, but seeing their smiling faces she curtsied, with a glance at Vivian. 'It moves towards dusk,' she said. 'All is made ready. We await your coming.'

The two men became aware of the tantalising smells of cooking food invading their nostrils, and the hum of cheerful voices reached their ears. Before, they had been too absorbed in themselves to give consideration to anything else.

Richard went to his daughter and kissed her, lifting her up. 'I should have known that my good friend here would resolve my problems. He has taken the heavy load bearing upon our future domicile from my back! Why ever did I think that my prayers might not be answered?' He set her down. 'Come, Vivian, let us join with the others and begin the celebration in earnest!'

All was bustle and excitement in the courtyard below. The labourers had returned and herdsmen come in from the pastures, everyone doing his share, making himself part of the festivities. A great fire was roaring, its flames giving light to the scene in addition to the lanterns and torches. The family table had others placed before it, and what a goodly spread there was! Platters of cheese and baskets of bread, cakes and fruit, and flagons of wine, drinking horns and vessels covered the boards, with butts stood beside. Children ran about adding to the noise, and an air of merrymaking pervaded Trevelyan, in sharp contrast to the low-spirited atmosphere displayed since Richard had returned from Scilly full of gloom.

The two men descended the steps and began making their way to the top table, passing the cooking-fire where various roasts were spitted. Richard unsheathed his knife and carved a slice of beef, chewing it slowly while judging the quality. He offered a second piece to Vivian on the point of the knife.

'There cannot be a tastier meat anywhere,' he said with satisfaction, wiping the blade on a cloth. 'My oxen are renowned for their tenderness and flavour. It seems their repute has proved a temptation for several bull-calves have gone astray, according to the herdsmen, and no trace found. It is doubly strange because we deem it dishonour to steal amongst ourselves, and for what purpose, pray? If anyone should find himself in want he need only ask for it to be given him – as is well known.'

''Tis possible a pack of wolves has ventured from the forest.' Vivian knew it to be a half-hearted reason – wolves would have been detected, bones found – but he was finding it hard to concentrate on anything other than that for which his eyes anxiously searched, but without success as yet.

Richard resumed his way to the top table, finding his intake of wine was beginning to have an effect as both men were demonstrating an unsteady gait, though conducting themselves with seemliness. It seemed as if everyone wished to talk to the governor, welcoming him back, and by the time the two men gained their seats they were dry-mouthed – which they at once set about rectifying with zeal!

This was the signal for the master's family to take their places, Meralda and Lowenna, with Tressa changed into a long, creamy-yellow dress, appearing together to sit by their father's left hand, while Vivian, Martin and Hicca were

38

seated on his right. They faced the assembled company as a king and his family preside over their court, which, to a lesser degree, they were doing. To add to the illusion, the three maidens had woven colourful circlets of flowers in their hair, which resembled the precious jewels worn by true princesses. Vivian would have preferred Meralda at his side, but urged himself to be amiable and patient and bide his time. Happily, he found that whenever he turned to Richard, he was able to glance past him to catch a sight of the lovely profile that sent his heart racing.

Servants cut off ample portions of the roasts to be put on platters for serving maids to pass around, while the fat dripped steadily on the blazing logs making them sizzle and flare, the flames highlighting the hot faces near by. When all was ready the master rose to his feet and banged on the table, the hubbub dying down and passing into silence as he motioned to Martin. 'My son, we await God's grace.'

As all bowed their heads Martin gave thanks for the feast, then enthusiasm was unleashed and for a time all activity centred upon everyone eating and drinking their fill, after which a comfortable lassitude settled on the gathering, marked only by occasional belching and sighs of contentment.

Richard and Vivian had apparently drunk themselves back to sobriety, because they were quite sensibly discussing how the move to the mainland was to be accomplished and the right time for the people with allegiance to them to be told. Richard could see no reason to withhold the news so stood up, rapping on the table until every face was turned to him.

'My worthy people,' he began. 'Each of you depends upon Trevelyan for his livelihood. It has provided a good living, enabling you to enjoy the best of all things, and so it gives me grief to remind you of the Seer's prophecy. I had hoped with all my heart to be able to tell you that the danger had been averted but it seems I may have failed in my undertaking – though bestirring myself these several weeks.'

An immediate silence fell on the assembly. Mothers put their arms around children and pressed them to their bosoms, the men staring ahead with blank faces, and Richard began to realise what a drencher he had put upon the festive scene.

'Stay!' he cried, lifting a hand to dismiss this unwelcome mood. ''Twas not my intention to create misgiving and despond this night but quite the reverse. My purpose is to dispel it.' He waited for a lessening of the tension as expressions eased and a faint hum of conversation arose.

'We are gathered together this even to welcome m'Lord's return, but he, too, has deemed it wise to heed the warning and plans to retreat to his other home over the sea. My misgiving concerning our own possible departure was caused by the lack of a suitable place to which we could remove, but this has now been determined. M'Lord has offered us the use of a hillfort which lies upon his land, close by the mount once called "the Grey Rock in the Wood" ere Saint Michael appeared in a vision to some fishermen, and which can be seen from the east of this island rising above the forest surrounding it. There we can remain safe 'til the future is decided.'

The hum of voices grew louder as Richard paused to drink. Somewhere in the background a man gave voice to a matter of prime importance to them all. 'Master, at what shall we labour and be occupied with? Shall our skills go to waste?'

Richard shook his head. 'Your worry is groundless. The tinners, those who work the land and those who see to the stock are accounted for. The rest will be kept busy with tasks to suit them, never fear.'

Another voice. 'When must we make ready to leave?'

'That will be told you when m'Lord and I arrange how best to effect the move – you will be forewarned. There is much to be done in the short time left to us.'

'And what of those who resist the offer to leave the land where they – and their forefathers – were born?'

Richard's eyes sought out the questioner. He had found no trouble in recognising Jowan's guttural tones. 'Would you abandon me and mine after all these years, old man?' he queried. 'Would you, perforce, be content to stay? Leaving us to wonder about your condition and yet without the means to give you succour?' He returned his gaze to the others. 'Everyone must answer to his own conscience. I bring no duress to bear, but those who follow me must have flown Lyonesse before the rising of the new moon on the day of Saint Martin's Feast.'

He was aware of a movement to his right as Martin stood up as if in response to the name. 'And if any will not be turned from their intention to stay, they can join with me for prayers in my church when the rest have gone, thus replacing the anguish of separation with comfort and companionship,' the young priest said with gentle finality, making very clear his own resolve.

Richard was quick to reply. ''Tis a fool's way to flout danger! Join the prudent amongst us, if only for the support and help you can render, then should this prove to be a great ado without substance and no calamity occurs we can all return together – albeit with our tails between our legs!'

Icy fingers touched his spine as his eyes silently pleaded with his son, although in his heart he had always known that this would be the way of it and he appealed in vain. He recalled the Seer's words: 'But you – you would lose two things that mean much to you – one to right and one to wrong', and since his search had so far proved ineffective it seemed likely that the prophecy might well be fulfilled. But what was the meaning of the riddle? Could it be that he would lose Meralda to Vivian as he was secretly hoping? That would be right – but what could the wrong be? And whom or what would it take? Martin would insist upon staying here – but that was unthinkable! He banished the shivery feeling as he remembered the Seer had said that in the event Martin would be saved, lifted from chaos, so he decided the loss would likely be the destruction of Trevelyan, his dearly loved home. He forced his mind from further disquiet concerning his adored children, knowing he would protect each of them with his life if need be, and what harm could come upon them now they were repairing to a place of safety?

Yet there remained a subtle constraint upon the evening as if wickedness lurked leering in the darkness beyond the gates, eager to get in. Richard, on whom the burden of effacing it rested, felt the threat most keenly, so to keep it at bay he determined to silence the serious murmuring already filling the air. 'Let us commence the games,' he called. 'Clear a space before us and have the jugglers and wrestlers show their skills!'

At once the uncertain mood was lifted and all hands put to shifting tables and benches, throwing bones to dogs, removing platters and replacing empty wine butts with full, and the freely flowing wine brought a rosy glow of well-being to the company settling down to indulge itself with pleasant diversion. The jugglers elicited oohs and ahs from the mouths of those admiring of their dexterity, and then two sturdy wrestlers in coarse shirts, muscles rippling in flesh spare of fat, stepped forward. Wagers were laid on each before they began their bout.

After watching the strenuous grappling, throws and falls for a time and noting that his choice of contestant was gaining the most points, Richard turned to Vivian. 'D'ye recall when we used to wrestle in our youth? And once you broke my nose? You did it a'purpose, confess it now, because I looked to be the victor!'

'I swear, 'twas caused by you having me in a stranglehold and refusing to let go, you knave!' Vivian grinned. 'And, of a truth, for your part, you pushed me in the water whenever we went a-fishing!'

'Because you always caught the biggest fish! I should have done that as I was the older – you shamed me!' Richard warmed to his memories. 'And the time Old Jowan was teaching us the use of the bow when we were hunting game and you shot him in the backside! I had the blame for that as I recall.'

'You usually warranted a beating for something or other, so the error hardly came amiss!' laughed Vivian.

'And what of the day when Ysella and I were wed? We two scamps were so filled with wine we could scarcely find our feet and were frowned upon by priest and congregation alike!'

They both roared with intoxicated mirth. Recovering his breath, Richard continued more soberly: 'Ay, and I also 'member that Ysella was too tender a maid to give me the tongue-lashing I deserved when I failed to bed her that night! Howsoever, it occasioned but a petty delay in Martin's arrival...'

They fell silent, meditating, ears disregarding the rowdy crowd alternating between boos of disapproval and cheers of encouragement as each wrestler gained or lost ground.

Vivian, disturbed by the memories, sought to lead the talk away from them. He put his back to the priest, noting that he was engrossed with the contest, and quietly said: 'Richard, do you regret allowing Martin to enter the Church? You must find it irksome that his duties now lie elsewhere.'

'I cannot but agree I felt disappointed when he chose to leave Trevelyan, 'tis true.' He rested an elbow on the table, chin upon palm. 'I wondered, for a fleeting moment, if 'twere laziness or cowardice the motive for him renouncing the world. Then I recalled he had never once, to my knowing, been reluctant to perform wearisome tasks or ever to adopt the semblance of a snivelling churl, while showing true courage in adversity – albeit with a gentleness that matched his mother's! At last I accepted that my entreaties were to no avail – there was as much chance of my diverting him from his choice as of changing the courses of the rivers at my door.' He smiled. 'Nay, better to take what God had planned with a good grace. He said he had been determined by a dream, but did not suffer himself to make its content known.'

'He spoke of his dream to me,' Vivian agreed. 'I must avow we all dream, but most of us allow our dreams to fade in the harsh reality of day, and as we grow older wisdom overshadows desire and attainment.' He idly watched without pleasure the heaving bodies of the two wrestlers.

Richard regarded his friend with concern. 'Do I hear the voice of regret?' he enquired. He smote the table hard. 'Beyond all doubt, I am a witless fool! The loss of your family must give you grief. Kweras alone...'

'I do not heed her absence,' Vivian broke in, sharply. 'But my heir occasioned my many tears when he withdrew from life.' He gave Richard a quick glance. 'I realise I should offer some unfolding of the happenings. The wine has loosed my tongue or I would have forborne ever to show my true and honest face regarding my marriage.'

He hunched himself over the table, and Richard, sensing the intimacy, brought his head closer. Those nearest, seeing their gravity, drew away. Vivian continued. 'Now, you were wed a few years before me, and despite my wealth and advantages I missed our togetherness immeasurably – you had been the brother I lacked. I longed, above all else, to follow in your steps and establish my own household, filled with laughter and happiness as was yours whenever I entered it. I searched without success for a maid as warm and lovely as Ysella – I adored her from afar, you know.' He flashed an apologetic look at Richard.

'I was aware,' Richard said, nodding. 'As was Ysella.'

'Well, in time I conceded that no one comparable to her trod this earth and found none other acceptable, though many laid siege to my affections in order to become the Lady of Lyonesse. Then my father chose to move over the water, and seeing that I was reluctant to succeed him here thought I needed the inducement of a wife. He sought for a damsel he deemed fit to bear our name and his heirs and selected Kweras, her suitability being judged by the lands that adjoined his own on the mainland of Cornwall where she had been bred and which she would inherit.'

He seized a clay pitcher to replenish his goblet, the handle snapping with the force of his grip. 'Forgive me. If I show bitterness to you, my trusted confidant, 'tis because I tasted a cup of gall for so many years that it flows out of me yet.' He had forced himself to look directly at Richard as he made this confession, passing a hand across his eyes before resuming. 'My father persisted in his persuasion for me to wed and I finally yielded since I had no preferment with which to counter him and because, being sickly, he was anxious to depart. You knew nought of this, my friend. I feared your disesteem in allowing myself to be prevailed upon.'

Richard laid an arm about his shoulders. 'There would have been no disesteem. I wish, with all my heart, you had made me aware that yours was not a love match, although Ysella had a notion of it. I did not favour the lady myself, finding her cold.'

'Cold and forever dissatisfied, there was no pleasing her. She had no contentment in living here – she missed her companions on the mainland too much – and when we made what was meant to be a brief stay there when my father died, she had no desire to return here – even to visit. Deep in my heart, I believe it could have been jealousy of Ysella and yourself. We three fitted into the same mould, making her feel excluded and somehow belittled. There, you have it.'

Richard took time to reply. 'I am saddened by your tale. I

was aware that Kweras seldom visited and that we met only in church or when hunting, but gave it no further thought. I fear I was delighting too much in my own family to heed the lessening of our time together, and after…' he paused. 'What do you plan for your life now? Have you considered being joined in wedlock again?'

'Considered? Ay, long enow to become a fugitive from the very thought – to beware of falling into a similar trap! To consider returning to a misery from which chance has released me…? I could not a'bear it! Kweras had a tart mouth and an eye for other men – she cared not an empty husk for me. I can live without that ever again and could never be induced to put myself at the mercy of another wife – have no doubts upon it!'

Richard was saved from having to express his surprise at these revelations by a sudden roar from the throng, indicating the end of the bout. One wrestler had a hold on his opponent who begged for mercy, releasing him only when his arm was raised as the winner. The spectators began to move, stretching their legs and easing discomfort, while those who had wagered successfully went to collect their reward.

Taking advantage of the activity, Hicca escaped from the constraint of his seat by diving beneath the table to the other side. He was now helping himself to wine, pouring it down his throat so fast that it dribbled down his chin onto his chest, staining his garments. His father was transferring his attention from Vivian, at a loss to know how to bring comfort to one so disturbed in spirit, when his eyes alighted on his youngest son. He delivered a sharp slap to Hicca's person.

'Ow!' wailed the boy. 'I meant no harm!'

'Maybe not,' returned Richard, 'but I did! I will not have you lying at my feet overcome with liquor! Get you back behind the board this instant!'

Hicca ducked under the table again, this time coming up

beside Tressa. He pulled her hair in his annoyance, the wine already making him reckless.

'Oh, you little toad!' she gasped, giving chase.

'Ha! Try to catch me...' he mocked, poking out his tongue, and for the second time that day was swept off his feet and held aloft. He yelled in fear lest it was Richard. 'Mercy – I saw nought in my path!' he panted, breath scared out of him.

Vivian released the squirming boy. ''Tis not to be wondered at if you run backwards whilst tormenting your prey!'

Hicca retreated in confusion, trying to evade his captor's gaze by hiding behind Gweniver's ample girth, but Vivian had been deflected in his intention to walk away and seek solitude until he had shaken off the desolate mood that had fallen on him since revealing the thoughts he had meant to keep secret.

'Why did I allow myself to babble on so?' He was feeling angry with himself. 'Why did I show such discontent? Exposing my wounds to my dear friend and causing him to flinch. Was it a need to make him suffer as I have suffered? Am I jealous of him? Jealous of the happiness he has salvaged from his own adversity?'

These brooding speculations flew about in his inebriated head until one stayed fixed, refusing to be brushed aside. Had he always resented the fact that it had been Richard who wed Ysella? That his unhappy life had been of his own making, yearning for her? Suddenly racked with guilt, he allowed himself to wonder if the coldness shown by Kweras had been but a reflection of his own, that she had been unable to give him love because he had been unwilling either to take or to give it, his own heart being elsewhere. His grief cried out within him, but it was too late for remorse, he told himself, wincing. As well to bury it with poor, unloved Kweras.

With his back against the trunk of the lofty tree he stared up through its branches, his tortured thoughts no longer suppressed as they had been for years. Seeing Meralda, the image of her mother, had reawakened feelings previously stifled until this fateful day, swamping him with their intensity. Was he at last being given a chance to lay his demon to rest, he wondered? By wedding the love of his youth? He unclenched his fists as if relinquishing his hold on the pain of yesteryear. If he wed Meralda it would be as if he were espousing Ysella – achieving what his heart had coveted – and all those former, agonising years of despair and desire would vanish forever. Perhaps, he might even convince himself they had never been...Alarm swept through him. Was this Satan's work to tempt him? Could he ever escape the haunting and accusing presence of Kweras' shadow in order to share his life with another? But, enough of this foolishness – he would have no more of it!

Determining to distance himself from temptation and be rid of his maudlin, introspective mood, he brought his mind back to his surroundings, expecting time to have relentlessly sped on after falling into his reverie, but Hicca was still hiding behind Gweniver so it could only have been a moment. The boy's escapade had served to prevent him slipping away to be alone – as yet unknowing that nothing concerning him would ever elude the watchful, loving eye of Lowenna.

She had been keenly observing the discussion between the two men, noting the effect the interaction was having upon them, her father's perplexity and Vivian's sorrow, and her soft heart was rent. She wanted, above all else, to share the grief of the man she had adored since childhood, to hold him in her arms and feel him respond as he relaxed his taut body against hers. Now, violet eyes brimming with compassion, she made to go to him to offer her comfort.

By some mischance Tressa reached him first to thank him

for her rescue from 'that horrid little toad'! She was turning away as Lowenna approached, blocking her path, but was able to see the concern on her sister's face and guess at the reason. Lowenna averted her head and went on towards Vivian, but the moment when she might have offered her sympathy, when he might have realised the extent of her love for him was lost. Richard, thinking he knew how to help his friend, had the intention to set in motion a strategy to force the issue, so bounded up in front of Lowenna and gripped Vivian by the arm, either to prevent him moving away or to steady himself from the uncertain behaviour of his legs.

'My dear fellow,' he said, inebriation giving boldness to his words. 'Your loneliness is threatening to destroy your future life, and I feel, of a certainty, that you should become enamoured of a loving damsel and wed again – no, listen – do not mistakenly judge all maids by Kweras. Besides, you need someone to grace your houses and take to bed, thereby giving you infants to love and to…'

As he was speaking an uproar claimed his attention, caused by Hicca teasing a dog with a joint of meat, making it run riot on a board laden with food. 'Restrain that human whelp in his knavery, Jowan!' he thundered, and waited to see that his order had been acted upon before continuing. 'I have an answer to your need, Vivian. Be pleased to consider my swans.'

He broke off and faced the company, raising his voice. 'Harken to me. We will have a further amusement! Martin…! Prepare to play your music for your sisters to dance in turn and to end by telling what, as a wife, they would offer a husband. Declare it as to a likely suitor, my swans – pretend it to be m'Lord.' He glared warningly at the noisy crowd. 'Let us have silence from those who wish to see the sun rise again!'

His tone brooked no argument. Meralda and Lowenna traded vexed glances, bashfully aware that there would be no escaping this disagreeable contrivance – Father had spoken and that was the end of it. Vivian shrugged his shoulders in resignation as he lowered himself on to a seat, knowing full well that he was being coerced into committing himself and just as determined to parry it.

People hurriedly began to resume their seats as quietly as they could, parents upbraiding noisy children, while Martin conferred with the older sisters about the tune and tempo as Tressa ran to her father. 'Me, too?' she pleaded. 'May I play this game too?'

'Of a surety, my cygnet,' her father agreed, indulgently. ' 'Twould be shameful for you not to take a part. Martin…' he called. 'Tressa will be the first to offer herself, so we await your discretion to commence. Meralda will be last.'

The young priest, unaware that he was aiding an intrigue, sat down on a bench to one side of the space left empty by the entertainers and took out his panpipes. He waited for the three maids to stand poised before starting to play a haunting melody and they began to dance with smooth, gliding steps, moving as a trio, twisting and twirling in time with the music, spreading their skirts, each lifting it high enough to keep her feet free. The effect of the glimpses of shapely legs was provocative without meaning to be so. Greenish-blue, purple and yellow followed one another round and around until, at a sign from Richard, Tressa stopped and curtsied to Vivian as the others paused, continuing to sway.

'If you would marry me,' she said, speaking fast but clearly. 'We would ride our horses in races and play hide-and-go-seek all the day, and at night we would feast and I would sing and dance for you and stroke your weary head 'til you slept!'

Vivian smiled and nodded his thanks as she went to rejoin the dance, but his troubled gaze had not wandered far from Meralda. He knew that he had been wine-imbibing too freely, and that usually when in his cups his eyes had a tendency to play tricks on him – as they were doing now.

'Is that Meralda?' he mouthed mutely. 'Or could it be that other, Ysella, back from the dead as a living ghost? I dearly desire it to be Ysella, but can it be so?'

'Fool, cease your yearning!' his conscience told him, 'for then you would suffer boundless anguish as she would still belong to Richard as before.'

The audience were meanwhile clapping and shouting 'Bravo!' at the way in which Tressa had acquitted herself, Richard fondly agreeing with those around him that his 'comely maid' would soon capture any heart she fancied.

Lowenna held back before coming to a standstill. She was vexed at being included in this public performance, afraid her feelings might become apparent to others, and full of foreboding, almost sure of what the outcome would be but unable to delay the certainty for much longer. At last, she forced herself to curtsy, sinking down into her purple skirt, loose, black hair falling forward. She shook it back as she rose to her feet, willing Vivian to look at her. Briefly he did so, acknowledging her presence before glancing back to Meralda. She nervously entwined her hands, and feeling the ring with the black stone she thrust it before him, speaking desperately, the words inaudible except to those near.

'I vow upon this ring that, were you to be my Lord, I would love and serve and share with you all the days of my life, and do your every bidding without question knowing it to be made with wisdom – and I would be faithful to you always.'

She saw that he did not respond, offering no indication that he had heard her faint voice, so she curtsied again and moved slowly back into the dance. Richard sensed discord. He cast a sharp glance in her direction, but before he could rationalise his thoughts Meralda had halted in her turn. She did not bend to Vivian, merely inclined her head, standing straight and tall before him.

'I have not yet felt the kind of love expected of me,' her voice was clearly heard, 'but if a man declared his unceasing devotion to me and would teach me how to love him, I could learn – and would surely love him unto death – because it is said that swans mate for life.'

Vivian arose, unable to resist the words or the deceptive blending of the dead Ysella with the live Meralda. He went to her, tentatively taking her hand as if this phantasm might vanish at his touch. 'Then you will be my Lady, fairest swan, if I have your father's pledge and hand upon the bond.'

'Gladly!' Richard was overjoyed at his success, too full of delight to remember his momentary unease concerning Lowenna, who was standing numbed as good wishes were proffered to the couple. Again, it was Martin who moved to her side to comfort her pain, placing an arm about her waist to swing her round in order to hide her face from the others. She hid it in the rough cloth of his habit but soon pulled away, forcing a smile.

'I love him so much that I can hardly bear it,' she murmured, 'but I know I must, and though I feel distress I will strive to be truly happy for Meralda. Besides, it gives me joy to see m'Lord and our father so filled with happiness.'

Martin bent and kissed her gently. 'I marvel at your resolve, sweet sister, and will pray to God to help you endure and hold you firm against Satan's ill.'

They joined with the others to toast the betrothed pair, Richard already beginning to make wedding plans. He took Meralda's hands in his own. 'My much loved child,' he said, his voice husky with emotion. 'The gown your dear mother wore when we were wed, and promised for your use when you were yet a nursling lies ready, locked in the chest beside my couch. You resemble her so closely, in face and form, that I am sometimes befooled into thinking Fate was cheated in its intent to rob me of her – and then I thank the good God for you.' He lightly kissed the two hands he held, reviving his memories as he regarded her figure. 'I fancy the gown will need but a modicum of altering, if any, to adjust to your own shape, so see it done.'

Pushing reminiscence aside, his mood changed, brightening. 'Where and when shall we have you joined in wedlock? I would wish it to be here, in Lyonesse, but when? We have to hurry to commence the removal, as little time remains to complete it by Saint Martin's Feast.' He slapped his leg. 'That shall be it! The eleventh day into November, your name day, Martin. Then after the union we will journey together to the mainland, departing well before the rising of the new moon.'

Martin showed added interest. 'I believe the archdeacon will be coming to the church of Saint Berian, which is near the end of the mainland and therefore close to us, for a pastoral visit on the day of the feast. He intends to cross over by the ferry to observe Mass in my church, and mayhap could be asked to officiate at the ceremony.'

''Twould add to my pleasure if you should assist him, Martin.' Richard said, welcoming the idea. 'Tomorrow we will ride out to the church and see what can be done. Now, let us retire for the night.'

The three made their way unsteadily up the outer steps while the remains of the sumptuous meal were cleared away. Meralda went to Lowenna, surveying her with serious eyes. 'I am truly sorry,' she said. 'I did not seek this happening.'

Lowenna shrugged her shoulders with resignation. 'I know it, Sister, but do not charge me with your pity. We have to do what Father wants, and I know that no one desires my hurt.'

Tressa pushed past Lowenna to confront Meralda. 'Why do you have to take him?' she demanded. 'You have no need of him! Why not let Lowenna be his bride? Your only thought is to be a great lady – the Lady of Lyonesse – Mistress of Dinas Ryal and Trevivian over the sea! Lowenna loves him...'

'But he has no love for me,' she interrupted her, sadly. 'He does not even see me before him. He only has eyes for you, Meralda – and I wish you well.' She put her arms around Tressa, kissing the top of her shining head. 'Hush, now, little one. I am obliged for your concern but no blame cleaves to anyone. Go in search of Hicca and take him to prepare for sleep. Mind that he does as you bid him with the reminder that, if he refuses, his father's hand may be laid more heavily upon him the next time.'

After watching Tressa run off she avoided the others, eager to be alone, stacking bowls in a forlorn pretence of not caring. 'I must submit,' she sighed, 'albeit unwillingly to my fate.' Then, with a burst of barely controlled passion, she cried: 'Dear God! Must I forever be condemned to conceal my love – to display a glad face to the world? How can I endure it?'

She glanced around to see if she had been overheard but no one was looking in her direction. Calm returned as she said more softly. 'But I wonder. Will he ever come to guess, though I try my utmost to hide any trace of it, what lies burning in the depths of my heart?'

# 5

---

## *The Glade*

The men at Trevelyan greeted the following day with a certain reluctance to rise and begin the daily tasks. Copious swilling of water down parched throats was evident and a tendency to cringe at loud noises, heads being supported by massaging hands seeking to suppress their incessant thumping. Richard and Vivian were amongst the severest sufferers, Martin having escaped the pangs of over-indulgence by being more abstemious. So, the proposed early start for the church was delayed, the visit to Kellimargh forgotten, and the sun rose high before they set off to arrange for the wedding and afterwards to prepare for their removal to the mainland.

There were few women with a similar problem though, having risen at dawn as usual, a little weary, but eager to make their plans for a new way of life should it become necessary. Both Meralda and Lowenna began their day very early, neither having slept soundly, for this was their regular day for visiting the fish market on the quay of the bay in the south, bartering produce from Trevelyan for fish, the many inhabitants of the mill house being able to consume a fair amount for supper. With difficulty, and much grumbling and resistance on his part, they roused Old Jowan to escort them, bidding him see that the horses – and cart fully laden with goods – were made ready.

'You should be up betimes on a market day with so much to do,' Lowenna admonished him. She was feeling out of sorts and afraid she would easily be upset, a rare occurrence for her. When Tressa and Hicca declared an intention to accompany them for once she refused, ignoring their surprised pleas for her to reconsider and sending them off to do household chores in no uncertain manner. She was sorry, but knew she would be unable to endure their endless bickering.

When the cart was brought they set off, the two maidens riding their ponies. Each young face was shaded from the sun by a wide, flat circle of plaited straw, threaded through with a soft scarf to tie under the chin. The dirt track was dry, throwing up enough dust to discourage conversation, although no one showed any inclination to indulge in it. Jowan moaned at every jolt making a corresponding thump in his skull, otherwise all was silent except for the sound of hooves on the impacted earth of the track and a monotonous creaking made by the cart swaying along precariously, juddering when its wooden wheels hit stones. The sun was warming the air, dispersing the morning mist and promising a brilliant, cloudless day.

It was still climbing up the sky when they reached the bay around which the fishers lived, worked and sold their wares. They left the cart in a dell shielded by trees, tethering the horses nearby, and while Jowan brought out a pitcher of wine – ostensibly to cure his pains – the maids each filled a basket with samples of what they had to offer, flour, vegetables, fruit and meat, then bade farewell to Jowan, already swallowing his self-prescribed remedy, and went off to barter their wares.

Along the quayside the fisher folk displayed their catches on the big, stone blocks that made up the wall. Baskets overflowed with fish of all shapes, sizes and colours – the choice of the fruits of the sea was almost endless. The vendors were constantly chanting, 'Fresh fish – fish as fresh

as the day! Come and bargain! Bring forth your provender!'
as they urged passers-by to stop, each professing to have the
best, each trying to shout the loudest. The noisy clamour
rang out along the quay, in sharp contrast to the peace of the
little boats riding the splashing swell on the other side of the
harbour wall. Gulls strutted about, ready to swoop down on
the viscera from gutted fish as it was tossed into the water,
screeching like lost souls in torment searching for salvation.

Atlan had come in on the tide and beached his boat below,
setting himself at a distance from the others at the far end of
the quay. There were some who did not welcome his
proximity, perceiving that he differed from them, and also
that he was favoured among the priests. Few buyers reached
him, most having bought where the sellers were grouped the
thickest, so this day, finding himself unable to concentrate on
the fish, he pondered the task that had so recently been thrust
upon him. Deep in thought he leaned against the wall, the
cold from the stones striking through his tunic. He idly kept
an eye on Mordon, cropping grass in the shade of feathery
tamarisk shrubs growing on an incline not far distant,
watching the horse tossing his head and swishing his tail in a
futile attempt to dislodge the flies attracted by the smell of fish.

Meralda and Lowenna were wending their way along the
line of baskets, their own seeming to grow heavier despite a
lessening of the contents. Whenever they agreed an
exchange they would hand token samples to the fishers,
sending them with their fish to find Jowan and the cart,
visible among the trees, to collect what had been decided
upon. The sisters moved slowly onward, meeting friends who
had already heard about Meralda and the governor, the news
having spread rapidly, and there was much talk of the
wedding. Meralda remained unruffled during these
encounters while Lowenna became flustered as she tried to
ignore the hurt, longing to return to Trevelyan with her
troubled heart.

'Sister,' she said at last. ' 'Tis hot and I am wearied. The fish look all the same to me, and we could have had a good bargain from that wizened man a few paces back. Also, it seems we have more than enough already and our own wares are well nigh spent. What is the purpose of going on? Let us leave for home.' She dropped her basket defiantly, pushing back the straw brim from her wet forehead, the loose sleeve falling back to her elbow. She was determined not to take one more step so sat down on a stone block, her back turned to her sister.

'As you say,' rejoined Meralda. 'We have ventured so far, and as we have nearly come to the end we may as well be sure that the best has not eluded us. 'Twould be a shame to forfeit a reward that could be waiting ever so near.' She continued to wander along by herself as if drawn by an invisible cord, unwilling to depart, her mind centred on the fish until a well-shaped, bare brown leg ending in a similar foot came into view. She stopped, staring at its perfection – it was as if she had never set eyes on such a thing before.

Atlan, meanwhile, had looked away from Mordon and found himself confronted by what was undoubtedly the most beautiful maiden he had ever seen. He caught his breath in a gasp of genuine astonishment, hardly daring to move lest it was an illusion – to disappear in an instant! Could this be what he had been wishing for?

Meralda's gaze had travelled upward to the body and head of this golden youth, and was deciding that the rippling muscles and strong, handsome face must belong to someone other than a lowly fisherman. The fact that she allowed herself a lingering look at him at all was strange. What would be the point in showing interest? She quickly transferred her eyes to the mass of silvery pilchards before her, asking if there was anything she could offer that he would consider worth the exchange?

Atlan had only one thought now he had heard her speak,

knowing beyond doubt that she was composed of flesh and sinew, bone and blood. This had to be the bride for Poseidon, led to him by the mystic force exerted by the all-powerful god! Tardhamor would say he had excelled in finding his quarry with such speed, and now he would have to play and net her with care – she must not be allowed to escape!

Endeavouring to keep his overpowering excitement in check, Atlan fixed on her question about bartering, calculating his reply. 'Your favour in letting me speak with you is enough reward for a handful of fish.' He waited for her reaction.

She appeared disconcerted by his words, a slight colour staining the transparent skin of her face, raising her head without meeting his look. 'Words are worth nought,' she said. 'Has what you are offering no greater value?'

'Take it all, and I would still be in your debt for the joy of having such beauty before me. You have the grace and loveliness of a swan.' Without her trying to evade his hands, he gently removed her straw head-cover by tilting it and dropping it down, the better to assess what lay beneath. 'Tell me,' he went on, 'what roof shelters this fair head when the sun sinks?'

'Trevelyan – my father is Richard of Trevelyan. He, too, calls me a swan.'

'I have seen and heard him of late admonishing and disputing with the people. What is your given name? And are you already wed?' That was a fact that must be quickly established!

'Meralda – and not yet wed but betrothed.' She felt annoyed for allowing his insolence that, but a brief span ago, she was sure she would not have tolerated. Yet...she had this strange feeling of attraction, a feeling never before encountered. It stirred her blood, arousing a reluctance to leave him. She ventured a question: 'How are you called?'

'Atlan.' He took the basket from her unresisting hand and set it down, wondering how best to entice her away. He began to walk towards the grassy slope. 'The sun's heat is fierce. Let us go over into the shade of the tamarisk.'

She moved elegantly at his side, staring at the ground before her feet, her purpose forgotten. 'What a strange name! Atlan...'tis one I have not met with.'

'Have you ever heard of Atlantis?' he asked.

'Of a truth, once I did...It was a land that vanished into the sea. I was told the tale when a child.'

'Then you do know of it.'

'Ay – but not what made it disappear.'

'Then I will tell you. You see, in the course of time, from being a contented land abiding by its laws, it became a place of wickedness, so Zeus, who is king of the gods, ordered its destruction as a punishment. It was not completely destroyed – merely sank beneath the waves, deep into the ocean, and remains there still – waiting for its children to return whenever their time above the waves is over.' He gazed out in the direction that seemed to call to him, the far-away look in his eyes.

'It does not tell me why you are so called.'

'So I will. Some Atlanteans – perhaps those of a cleaner heart – were allowed to survive in their boats and reach other lands. I believe my ancestors were among those who settled here, so as a direct descendant I was named Atlan. There is a certainty within me that sometime in the past I was there, my own being, and it would explain why I constantly have visions of Atlantis. In the beginning, before it yielded to evil desires, it was a land beyond compare. There is a place near here – a wondrous place – that reminds me of its glory. I would delight to share it with you – will you come with me?'

Meralda felt almost bewitched. She was about to agree when she was reminded of Lowenna. 'Oh, my sister!' she cried. 'I cannot leave without her. May she come with us?'

Atlan was startled, having believed her to be alone. 'Your sister? Where is she?' Meralda pointed to where Lowenna sat with her back to them.

Atlan gathered his wits together. 'She seems at ease – let us not disturb her. We shall be gone but a short while, not long enow for your absence to be noticed.' If he had to tell an untruth in order to snare her, then so be it. His god would forgive him.

'As you will.' Meralda was persuaded. 'Then, how shall we go?'

'My horse is waiting – look, he comes now.'

Taking her elbow Atlan induced her to move forward, and they had nearly reached Mordon when something compelled Lowenna to look for Meralda. Failing to detect her along the quayside she stood up, anxiously turning this way and that. When the greenish-blue gown she was searching for finally caught her eye, she was taken aback. What was Meralda doing so far away? She was without her basket and head covering – and walking far too close to some strange man dressed in a fisher's short tunic! And why were they approaching that white horse?

'Meralda!' she called. 'Come! I need to speak with you!'

They both turned at the sound of her voice, Meralda making as if to obey the summons but Atlan put out a restraining hand. 'Tell her to have no worry,' he urged, 'that you will return while the sun still moves in the southern sky.'

Meralda did as he asked, adding: 'Do not fear for me, Sister.'

But Lowenna had started to run to them, full of misgiving. 'Where are you going? Have you lost your senses? Harken to me…!'

Atlan, fearing to be baulked of his prey, pursed his lips and gave a curious melodic whistle. Mordon understood the signal and increased his pace as Lowenna, in tears, watched with dismay as the man leapt onto the horse and reached down to swing Meralda up in front of him before galloping away.

The distraught maiden tried to find some meaning in this disquieting situation. Had Meralda been abducted? Yet she had appeared to be unconcerned and content, promising to return in good time, so she decided to remain calm and stay where she was. If she went back to Jowan she would have to find a plausible explanation to satisfy his curiosity and, should he disbelieve her, he would feel in duty bound to inform Father so what else could she do? Only wait...and wait...

\*

After a time, Meralda felt the horse slacken speed as they reached a forest, Atlan curbing him when he splashed across a stream. The horse's progress had not been impeded by the low branches or by the men hiding amongst them, as these sentries guarding the grove were used to Mordon as a familiar visitor, so Meralda remained unaware. She was leaning sideways against Atlan, contemplating the silver cross-within-a-circle that hung around his neck, holding firmly to the horse's mane in case she fell. Not that there was any likelihood of that happening because of the way in which those sturdy arms encompassed her, holding her close. She felt some surprise that she was neither repelled by his presumption nor by the silvery scales that adhered to her from his tunic, and the odour of fish emanating from him only served to remind her of the freshness of her beloved ocean.

Meralda had always known the sea to be her friend, more so than any person, aware of its moods, its dark and bright days, but recently there had been a change, a wildness and threatening violence beyond her understanding. She had seen the increasing restlessness of the water while noting a similar turbulence within her inner self, though staying outwardly calm. She had feared this turmoil might burst forth and engulf her, removing every vestige of self-control, and had hoped, since last night, that her forthcoming marriage to Vivian would quell these alien tendencies and return her to her usual complacency.

For Atlan, the elation he felt at his success in capturing this maiden so easily had suppressed his ability to interpret other feelings, although he was finding this intimate contact with her not unpleasant – she had melted into his shape as if she belonged there. As Mordon came to a halt he eased Meralda to the ground before dismounting, becoming aware of a surprising sense of loss when her body was removed from his.

'I see you wear the symbol of our Church around your neck,' she was saying, 'but there is a difference.'

'Because this is the cross of Atlantis,' he answered. 'It was our emblem long before you Christians adopted the form. It was put upon me as a babe to link me to the lost land – I have ever wondered why it should be an object of worship for you.'

'Because ours represents the cross that Christ died upon.' She spoke as if instructing a child. 'He was the son of God who came down from Heaven to be born and die as one of us, that He might save all who believe in Him and repent of their sins and thus be allowed to live forever. Do you understand?'

' 'Tis not so difficult,' replied Atlan gravely, 'since many of our gods have come down to earth, some in mortal form and others in various disguises. Have you been persuaded that this was the true cause of the visitation?'

'Of a certainty – and I could teach you…'

'Then I must avail myself of your kindness when we have more time for discourse.' He grasped her hand, not only to lead her onward but to continue touching her, recalling his prepared words of encouragement should she show resistance. 'Come – just a few more steps and the wonders

63

will be revealed. You have never seen the like before, I know, and you will surely be wiser as to why this is the most wondrous part of Lyonesse...'

He wanted to hand her over to Tardhamor as soon as they entered the glade, and in spite of his doubts she went willingly enough as he led her through the remaining trees. A quick glance sufficed to show that the high priest was not in evidence. No matter, he was never far away, so the pretence would need to be kept up for only a short while longer.

When Meralda stepped into the glade she exclaimed in surprise. She had not known what to expect, but it was certainly not what met her eyes. The temple with its pillars, the altar with a granite post close by, the upright, holed circle of stone, and the two imposing marble statues instinctively appealed to her. The very atmosphere gripped her imagination, fascinating her. For reasons she was unable to explain she felt excitement, a different person in a different world, one she was almost mindful of having lived in before. She began to stroll about, regarding everything with delight. 'Where are we? And what is the purpose of this place?'

Atlan had been watching silently, unprepared for the intensity of her reaction to this centre of his devotions or his own reaction to her. He decided there was no need to be untruthful since she would not return to the outside world to tell her tale. He was ignorant of this proposed marriage rite or what it would entail, but was sure that Poseidon's bride would remain the god's consort here for always, wanting for nothing and with all deference being paid her.

'This is what you Christians call the Forbidden Place,' he answered, cautiously. 'You are in Kellimargh, at the foot of Carrag Uthek which rises above us, though hidden by the trees.' He studied her absorbed face, which showed no fear. 'A place of worship very like this existed on Atlantis,' he continued. 'There was a similar, though much larger temple – and this is the altar where our offerings are bestowed.'

64

Meralda moved closer to regard it more clearly. 'Why, you observe the same custom as we who worship in our church of Saint Ana,' she said, impressed, 'but are more careless with the wine. See, it has spilled over and stained the stone.'

Atlan refrained from giving the true explanation, merely saying: 'There were also two statues akin to these standing in a Sacred Grove of the Horse dedicated to our god Poseidon, but were of a far greater magnificence.'

'Poseidon…' she breathed the name and pointed. 'That is Poseidon?'

'Ay, the all-powerful god of the seas. He protects and helps us fisher folk and so is deserving of our worship.'

Meralda inspected the statue from head to toe, glancing now and again at Atlan. 'He bears a strange likeness to you.'

' 'Tis not so strange, since I was made in my god's image.' Atlan looked at the statue, his eyes trying to imagine what hers were recording, then stared in disbelief as he received the distinct impression that as she studied Poseidon, Poseidon was studying her. Did those blank, sightless eyes have the ability to assess the maiden chosen to be his bride? A shiver ran through him, his thoughts no longer coherent.

Meralda shifted her gaze. 'And the other? She seems to yearn for him.'

Endeavouring to sound casual, he said: 'That is Cleito, his human consort, a mortal maiden who bore him ten sons – all becoming kings of Atlantis.'

'I knew it, I see it, I feel it! I have been here before, or somewhere very like – though either possibility would be impossible. How strange it all is! I have been caught up in a web of enchantment and changed…'

She now believed herself to be no longer confined by anything, reckless and free as the air and began to twirl joyfully and abandoned in a wild dance. Finding her gown restricting, she undid the fastenings and let it fall away, leaving her clad in a thin, loose shift that ended just below

65

the knees. Each movement revealed the outline of her youthful, lovely body as she flung up her arms to pull out the pins that held her hair, allowing it to cascade in a shining veil of pale gold about her shoulders and down her back, where it shimmered like moonlight on the white sands of the seashore.

'Dance with me,' she called to Atlan, as he stared, mesmerised by the unexpected transformation from the reserved and remote maid he had met such a short time before into this thrilling nymph, effervescing with ecstasy. But...had their meeting been so recent? He suddenly thought he recognised this altered and transfigured damsel as one he had often seen in his visions of Atlantis, one he had made his own in some other time...

Then he responded, unable to refrain from sharing in this rapturous demonstration of freedom from the bonds of convention. He weaved and twisted, matching her rhythm, laughing with her, their arms and bodies entwining then pulling apart, until a moment came when his eyes fixed on hers – manifesting intense, unmistakable desire – and laughter died. Hands slipped down from shoulder, to elbow, to wrist, to fingers and beyond, in a slowness of motion that ceased only when the two breathless young people came to rest, each with an arm outstretched toward the other, almost touching, as an awareness came to them both in the same instant. Meralda was first to interrupt that mystical moment, speaking hesitantly. 'I...I will make myself as one with Cleito – if you will do likewise as Poseidon.'

Atlan could feel the blood pounding hard in his body, his manhood aroused by this maid such as he had never known before. It filled him with the total conviction that he was invincible, omnipotent, that he had the infinite power of Poseidon. For the first time in his life he fully understood what he had been brought up to believe by the minor priests of Kellimargh, that some of the children of Atlantis had been fathered by the kings of Atlantis, themselves the children of Poseidon and Cleito. Therefore, though part human they were also part god, and he was a direct descendant. The sudden realisation left him shocked and briefly bereft of words.

Meralda waited fretfully for his delayed response, thinking he might not have understood her meaning. 'You be Poseidon and I will be Cleito!' she urged.

Atlan had understood only too clearly and found his tongue once more. 'You be Cleito and I will be Poseidon!' His voice caught in his throat.

He gathered up her discarded gown before carrying her, with great tenderness to a grassy bank furthest from the temple. He spread the gown where the lush grass grew thickest, already with a scattering of the fallen leaves of early autumn, and gently laid her down and covered her body with his own. He pressed his mouth to her forehead, cheeks, eyes and lips, staying there for a long time. Then he began to pull at her shift as she opened her eyes and her mouth to draw breath – and saw a large sea bird eyeing them from a high branch above. Its very presence brought feelings of guilt, causing her passion to subside. Some birds were messengers, she knew, having been told so from the cradle, and this one could carry the news of what she was doing to Vivian – or Father! The doctrine of chastity, instilled in all his children, enveloped her mind as she pushed Atlan from her. 'Forgive me, I beg you! My senses were mazed! I cannot give myself out of wedlock!'

At that moment they felt a strong tremor accompanied by a rumbling noise from deep in the earth. The bird flew off with a noisy whirring of wings as the couple awaited further disturbance, remaining still, as subsequently did the earth.

Atlan was fighting to subdue his emotion. Aflame with ardour, he wanted to possess this maiden more than anything he had ever desired before, sure he could overcome her opposition if he wished – with strength, if needs be. But should he? Dare he? That shaking of the earth – Poseidon was the god of earthquakes! Was it to show his displeasure for so insolently venturing to take this maiden from him? Surely not. He may have brought Meralda here to be his god's bride but she had not yet been offered nor committed to Tardhamor's care. Tardhamor! He had completely forgotten him! Hurriedly getting to his feet he saw that enigmatic figure standing on the top step of the temple, looking in their direction.

The high priest had been lying on his couch, deep in trance-like meditation when he felt the tremor. Only waiting to cover his head and face, by way of habit, he had rushed outside to be confronted by a pair of lovers seemingly in the act of desecrating the Sacred Grove! He was the sole person to sanction behaviour of that kind in this place, and on occasions when secret rites were celebrated with revelry. Peering more intently, he recognised Atlan rising to his feet and assisting an unknown maiden – and how beautiful she seemed to be, even from this distance! His heart leapt – this must be the promised bride! But – had he defiled her? Is that why he was now ushering her away?

'Take heed – attend me here – this instant!' he shouted wildly, his customary restraint abandoned.

Atlan was hurrying Meralda out of the glade, placing the gown around her shoulders while emitting that strange-sounding whistle. He knew with the utmost certainty that he had to remove her from Tardhamor's authority and was also destined to protect her for as long as he should live. Too much had happened too fast, and he had a burning need to find solitude by the sea in order to cast his chaotic thoughts on the waters until they became ordered. As Mordon came up to them, alerted by the signal, he lifted Meralda on his back and placed the halter in her hand.

'Who called so forcefully?' she asked, troubled. 'And why are you sending me away? Have I angered you? I need…'

'No, my love, you cannot stay here now and never return without me,' he said with urgency. 'Keep your head down and hold the horse's mane – he will take you to the quay. Soon after sunrise I will wait for you there and give you your answers. Tell no one of me – or of this place!' He slapped the horse's flank and they sped away.

He heard his name being shouted vehemently as he walked back, unsure what he should do, unable to understand the momentous events that had overtaken him. He began to feel guilt at his temerity in defying the orders of the high priest and started to run as he approached the clearing, anxious to avoid further delay and thereby increase his wrath. With no reasonable explanation to offer, he decided to tell the truth and throw himself on his mercy.

Tardhamor was beside himself with rage at being ignored for so long by a priest he had thought to be well versed in instant obedience. When Atlan reached him, with all pretensions of godlike mightiness banished by dire reality, he flung himself face down on the ground and for a brief time neither spoke.

It was the high priest who broke the silence, anger held menacingly in check. 'I make no sense of your actions but have great interest in hearing how you propose to explain your situation – and so does our god. Open up your mouth that we may judge the extent of your defiance and fasten upon a suitable punishment!'

Atlan got to his knees, daring to raise his eyes to try to glimpse those others he knew were glaring down at him, but was unable to penetrate the folds of the cloth. 'O Lord High Priest,' he pleaded, clasping his hands. 'Hear me. I came upon that maid by chance this day and brought her here for your approval, only to discover that we were made as one in some far off time, long ago in Atlantis. Since I have grown aware of our past together, she has become my inescapable destiny. You may punish me as you will, but I can never bring her back...'

He lowered his head as he saw Tardhamor begin to pluck at his robe with forceful fingers and begged. 'Have patience with your unworthy and regretful priest! I promise to find our mighty god another lovely damsel, mayhap even fairer, with all speed, and ask only that this one be joined once again to me!'

Tardhamor had stilled his hands and stood musing. 'Have you left her yet a virgin?' he inquired, thoughtfully.

'Indeed, I have!' Atlan felt grateful for a lessening of the tension, 'but only because she refuses 'til she is wed. I will have to win her, biding my time so as to suffer her no more alarm, and try to reawaken further remembrances of a past that she now but dimly perceives. I beg you to intercede for me with our great god and ask his forgiveness, then, should he be merciful and show his benevolence, to remind him of his promise to grant me a favour and for you to wed us at the holed stone.'

The high priest considered his words with care, deliberating on his appraisal and assessment of the situation before answering. 'So be it,' he said at last, 'provided you first present Poseidon with what he considers to be the fairest maiden in the allotted time – before you claim your prize. This is what he expects of you. 'Twould occasion certain disaster for us all should you fail in that endeavour...'

*

While the scene in the glade was being enacted Lowenna waited on the quayside. She had tarried far longer than the time promised by Meralda before her anxious eyes saw the white horse approach and a lone, familiar figure slide from its back. As the stallion galloped away she ran to meet her sister, becoming appalled by her appearance when she came

70

close enough to observe her struggling to fasten her gown, hair hanging loose and dishevelled. Fearing the worst she called, on a rising note of panic: 'Meralda! Has some mishap befallen you? Have you been set upon?'

Meralda ignored her dismay, calmly continuing to adjust a sleeve and smooth her hair without replying, an indefinable smile playing around her lips, her eyes impassive. Lowenna flung her arms about her errant sister, sobbing with relief. 'Meralda! I feared you had been stolen away and harmed, and by your looks you have surely had restraint put upon you. What mischief was wrought by that graceless knave?'

'Nought. Cease your wailing, Sister, no harm has come to me,' and with no further comment she began to walk away, bringing the conversation to an end.

Lowenna stood staring at the retreating back, disbelieving the evidence of ears that failed to match the evidence of her eyes, then hurried to catch up, falling into step beside Meralda, twisting her head askance to glimpse her face in the hope of detecting a reason for this mystery. Never could she recall having seen her sister other than neat and tidy and behaving with seemliness, but today's events showed her changed, the suddenness of which, to her mind, could only be due to one influence. Certainly there was a difference in her facial expression, inscrutable though it was, a softness that belied the austerity of her words.

'Meralda – are you going to confess what befell you?' she inquired, as they hurried along towards the cart.

'My answer remains the same – there is nought for me to tell,' returned Meralda coolly, wondering how she was going to deal with this unwanted curiosity.

Lowenna was apprehensive enough to risk rebuke and held on to an arm, forcing her to stop. 'I beg you to give ear, Sister. I am filled with dismay, fearing you have come under a spell of enchantment in some manner.'

At this, Meralda gave another veiled smile. 'It may be that

71

you are right and I have been enchanted, but if it brings pleasure without hurt I have no need of your concern.'

She made to turn away, but once more Lowenna held her back. 'Any sorcery that causes you to act so strangely must be my concern,' she insisted. 'To betray the trust that Father has placed upon you would have been unthinkable before this day. You must have protection. Let us hasten home and declare you are accurst and ask Martin to free you from the Devil's wiles!'

Meralda was horrified. She knew she had been indiscreet but wanted no one prying into it. She needed time to appraise both the situation and these new, wonderful, exciting feelings. Somehow she had to allay Lowenna's suspicion.

'Lowenna,' she said, as sudden inspiration came to her aid. She linked her arm in her sister's, moving her forward. 'I am under no spell – my behaviour is of my own choosing. 'Tis unwise for me to speak of this to any other as yet, but your persistence compels me to satisfy your querying. I vow, there are things of which you have no knowledge, and one is the right of a maiden who is soon to be wed to discover all she can about the state of wedlock and the needs of the man she will espouse – 'specially one who has already bedded a wife. That is what I was doing today – I went for instruction. 'Twas a misfortune to have a wild ride on a horse which led to my disordered look, though glad I went for I learned much of the ways of men and how best to please them – so let us have no more discourse about sorcery.'

'I had always understood 'twould be one of Gweniver's duties to instruct us in the ways of men when the time came for us to require it, Sister.' Lowenna sounded dubious but wavering. 'Where, then, did you go?'

'I cannot tell the place, but can only say that we have never been there before. The fisherman was my escort to take me for the purpose of guidance, the better to learn how to love

72

the one whose life I will share – who is a person of such wonderment that I must be perfect in serving him.' She had not meant to utter that last sentence but was thinking of Atlan and gave a sigh of pleasure, remembering.

Lowenna drooped her head, her thoughts making her despondent. 'I would have required no such instruction to love m'Lord,' she said softly, adding: 'How did the fisherman know to find you here?'

'I must not tell – 'tis to be kept secret 'til the right moment for disclosure, so have a care not to wag your tongue to anyone at all!' Meralda stared hard at her, trying to see if she had found this unlikely tale plausible. 'I need your promise.'

Lowenna lifted her head and gazed into the intense blue-green eyes, and smiled once again her gentle, warm smile. 'Surely, you have it. Any guidance to bring added pleasure to your betrothed must have my whole-hearted blessing. You will understand that I am so inexperienced in the ways of maturity that it causes me to show doubt when I should accept without dispute. I trust in you, my sister – please forgive my foolishness.'

Meralda felt a momentary qualm of conscience and came close to admitting that she had dissembled the truth, but by now they had reached the cart and the sound of loud and raucous snoring diverted her attention. Old Jowan lay asleep on the grass, empty wine jars overturned at his side, and as it was obvious he would be taking no further part in the day's activities the sisters prepared the horses before trying, unsuccessfully, to rouse him. They had to drag his inert form to the cart, and with much difficulty managed to heave him up amongst the fish.

'He is nought but a bag of bones,' observed Lowenna. 'Now, we must make haste to be home before sundown,' she went on, wrinkling her nose, 'to give Gweniver time to prepare the fish – long expected for supper – lest they decline to await the knife and jump straight into the pot by themselves!'

Meralda tied her small mare and the other pony to the cart, climbed up and took the reins, glancing down at Old Jowan. 'Nought but a bag of bones...' she muttered to herself, adding with satisfaction: '...and so stupefied with wine that he cannot have noted the length of my absence, so there will be no whit in his empty skull for him to apportion out to Father and the others!'

On arrival back at Trevelyan they were beset with questioning as to the reason for their late-coming, Gweniver fussing around in her relief from her anxiety and to get the fish unloaded. This led to the discovery of Old Jowan in the cart, everyone erupting with laughter as the men lifted him out and dumped him unceremoniously into the shallows at the edge of the river, where he lay splashing and spluttering and spitting out weed from his almost toothless jaws. For days afterwards, every child pinched its nose in a rude gesture whenever they ventured near him.

Meralda laid the whole of the blame for their delay on him. For someone who had never before found the need to tell an untruth, she was now finding it remarkably easy to prevaricate. Lowenna said nothing, shocked by the obvious lie. She soon made an excuse to slip away on her own, the incidents of the day causing her to inwardly cringe with mental discomfort as she recalled them.

Fortunately, Richard and Vivian were also late returning, so found the meal ready to be served. Richard questioned Lowenna's whereabouts, accepting the reason given that her head was paining her, as his own had troubled him the entire day. Desultory talk mainly centred on the brief shuddering of the earth, alarming at the time, but which subsequently had been dismissed as a probable fall of rock.

After the meal, released from the cooking pots, Gweniver approached Richard with the news that she had been entrusted with a message, the messenger leaving when she had been unable to say when the master would return. 'Then unburden yourself of it, woman,' he invited her shortly, tired and out of sorts.

She bobbed. 'A brother from Saint Ana came to ask you to consider afresh your decision to leave Trevelyan, Master. He said you are misguided, that as God has not seen fit to unfold a threat of calamity in any of his hallowed churches here then it will not happen, and you have been made the Devil's instrument to beget overmuch suffering. That is what he said exactly, Master,' she ended, shamefaced at having to repeat the words. 'He made me say it many times ere he was content.'

Richard did not respond at once, but sat staring at the table before him while reassessing the facts. Having come to a conclusion, he called for all to come closer, the better to hear his pronouncement, as he feared his voice might falter.

'I address myself to all those who have regarded Trevelyan as their dwelling-place and the means of begetting their daily bread,' he said at last, leaning back informally in his chair, not standing as usual when he made a speech, 'but that is over, and this may be the last time we all sup here together. Tomorrow, some shall hunt to see the larder filled in readiness, lest fewer chances are presented later, and others among you will view the stock and movable goods to be foregathered on the coast prior to being carried across by boat. The millers and tinners will continue working for as long as possible, so Meralda and Lowenna will remain here to care for them and their kin 'til they finally leave, departing themselves on the day of the espousal. Martin has offered to visit oft-times to render aid, guiding you through your prayers and Mass on the Sabbaths. Some must go shortly to prepare the hillfort and take the children there betimes – Hicca and Tressa will journey over with Gweniver and stay with her 'til the ceremony has taken place here, when the couple will remove to Trevivian. After a suitable time, the remainder of my family will join them there.'

He ceased speaking, noticing Tressa jump to her feet and come towards him. He waved her back, weariness on his face, saying: 'Seat yourself, child, there must be no argument. Overseers will be chosen for each undertaking, and I will only return here as dictated by necessity. I trust that will not be oft, as it will grieve me deeply to see decay begin to clutch at this home that I love. I have nothing more to impart, except to ask God to bless every one of you and keep you safe…'

He rose to his feet and strode away into the darkness to hide his tears as the subdued company began to clear the tables and disperse in silence. The enormity of the impending changes having been made very clear, it now hung heavily upon their drooping spirits. Even Tressa and Hicca went without a word, though Tressa was greatly upset that it had been manifestly made clear that she would be excluded from the ceremony she so much wanted to take a part in, knowing it would be useless to entreat her father – he had spoken with such finality.

Only Vivian felt talkative, trying to engage Meralda's interest by discussing their future plans, but she pleaded fatigue and begged leave to retire. He showed his disappointment. 'Tomorrow I must return to Dinas Ryal, and thereafter my days will be taken up by the move. Though I will try, I may find difficulty in visiting you often to have further converse ere we are wed.'

'Opportunity will present itself should it choose,' she said, longing to hide herself away in order to explore her secret thoughts and emotions, 'so, 'til then, I bid you have a good night, m'Lord.'

He reached for her hand, holding it firmly in his own. 'I beg you to pleasure me,' he said, earnestly. 'My name is Vivian and I give it to you to keep and to hold as a token between us. The other I would give you is the jewel the Vivian brides have ever worn by custom at their espousals – when I can to bring it to you.'

'You are gracious, and I have no reason to dissent as 'tis your tradition – my Lord,' she answered, stressing the words and disengaging her hand as if to fan a moth away from her face, 'but, as you can see, concerning your name I will have to learn to rid myself of the previous habit. For now, I trust you fare well as you go about your matters of importance.'

Vivian gave a slight bow. 'And for you, my love, my Lady of Lyonesse, my wish is that God will always go with you.' He watched as she made her way up the steps and along the wooden platform to disappear through a door. Tonight she had seemed even more like Ysella, the softness of her expression being more pronounced than he remembered previously, and he longed to hold and possess her. He consoled himself with the thought that, after the passing of this moon and before the next, a time which he hoped would fast hasten into oblivion, she would be his wife and his life would begin anew!

Darkness lay sombrely upon the cheerless atmosphere of Trevelyan that night, many finding sleep eluding them. Among those affected was Vivian who, though his heart told him he would share his new life with Ysella, his head insisted that this was another, Meralda, and the twain could never be one – or could they…?

Then there was Richard, suffering the sadness of having to abandon the land of his ancestors and his home, blaming himself for failing to discover the source of the alleged wickedness. How had he erred? If only he had searched deeper and prayed harder he might have succeeded in his quest to meet the expectation of God…

And Lowenna, who lay staring into the impenetrable dark, tormented by her desires and suspicions. She had a growing disquiet that Meralda had not been entirely frank – that she was hiding something. Was it possible that she had indeed suffered enchantment? But what could be done about it? Who to be told? Not Lord Vivian – he must not be alarmed unnecessarily. Suppose she was mistaken? Martin was away and would probably laugh at her fears – he might even think jealousy to be at the root of them! Father, then? He had so much else to worry him, and if Meralda really was under instruction he would surely know of it and show impatience with her unwarranted interference. Besides, she had promised silence to her sister, so sleepless, tossing and turning, she decided to say nothing.

For Meralda the cloak of darkness was a blessing she had craved since returning home. She tried to gather her thoughts, to make up her mind whether to defy convention and return to the harbour or accede to it and attempt to forget this day had ever been. She felt overwhelmed by the memory of Atlan's kisses, the pressure of his arms around her, and lucid reason was put to flight. She could hardly restrain herself to wait for the dawn to break, to take the earliest opportunity to ride out unobserved to be with him again. He must surely take her back to that wondrous Sacred Grove…

It was curious that neither maiden associated the hidden evil, once foremost in their minds, with the unusual events that had occurred earlier, so could that have been due, in some measure, to enchantment?

# 6

---

*Betrayal*

As October merged with November the days passed in quick succession. Gweniver had gone to the mainland with Tressa and Hicca so Lowenna had the extra task, together with routine activities, of planning meals, cooking and generally providing for all those left working in and around Trevelyan. She had some help from the women and found the pressures upon her gradually decreasing as the numbers lessened with the departure of each family, but during the nights she had time to wonder about Meralda, where she went and what she did as soon as the sun arose. It was losing its fierce heat and there were many grey days, evidence that autumn was advancing apace. At first, she supposed her sister was still going for instruction when she packed food and drink into panniers and rode out on her little mare at daybreak, even now refusing to describe the day's happenings on her return at sundown.

Lowenna did her best to make allowances, but found herself resenting the fact that she lacked another pair of hands to lighten her burden. Besides, she was having difficulty in finding different excuses whenever Martin, or Father with Old Jowan, who rarely left his side, called at the mill house with news of the children. Some of Martin's visits were for prayers, and at such times Meralda would stay until he had gone, but others were unexpected and surprise was expressed at her absence. On these occasions, Lowenna could only say her sister was away comforting the sick or taking food to those in need. It could be that was true, but it grew increasingly obvious to the worried maid that her father knew nothing of this 'instruction into wedlock', which heightened her unease.

Lord Vivian visited, too, once arriving in the kitchen to discover her on her knees vigorously scrubbing the floor on which a mash of fruit and honey had spilled, not that he stayed long enough to note her discomfiture, neither seeming to see her hot and blushing face nor the water dripping from her hands as she scrambled to her feet. She flourished the hand bearing the ring with the black stone, deliberately flinging droplets of water on his sleeve, hoping he would notice and remember how precious it was to her and remark upon it. At the very least he could have made a light comment, she thought, but he hurried off to search for Meralda in the marketplace of the Town at Breonseyth, where Lowenna had said she might possibly be found.

'She could be intending to look for me at Dinas Ryal, then,' he had said eagerly, 'as it lies close by.'

'Ay, she might well do for all I have been informed, but I have some doubt upon't!' she had replied, annoyance being tempered with regret, as she carefully dried the ring on the cloth about her waist while gazing at his retreating back, though the words were uttered in a tone not quite loud enough for him to hear.

'Why am I put in this plight where I have to fumble with the truth?' She flung the query at the unresponsive walls. 'And why can he not find me of interest enough to be civil?' With no answers forthcoming to these pertinent questions, she lifted the bucket and in one swift movement forcefully tossed the water out into the courtyard, thereby drenching from head to toe a kitchen maid bringing fresh vegetables. For an instant she sincerely wished it had been Meralda's ill fortune!

That elusive creature, as yet unaware of her sister's growing rebellion, was reposing in Atlan's boat lying offshore in the shallows, fingers dipping lazily in the water as she awaited his arrival. He was unusually late in keeping what had become an established rendezvous, when they would spend the days bathing, eating, drinking and loving. She looked forward to the intimacy of his company, which offered little need for talk because, in the same way that he and Mordon communicated, they had discovered a similar telepathic understanding. She was the one who actually talked the most, describing her home and family and how she felt bound to them by her love – bonds she was loath to see broken. Their kisses and caresses had intensified, as had their longing to be together for always, but she still would not yield to him although the idea of sharing her life with Vivian or any other man was now unthinkable. Her fancied memories of an earlier life in another time with Atlan, and the remembrance of her joy in the glade, filled her head to the exclusion of all else.

'Can we not be wed?' she had asked the previous day, then continuing, intense desire overcoming common sense: 'My brother Martin, being a priest, might be persuaded to join us as one.'

Atlan had kissed her tenderly, cajoling her with 'we will think on't', and 'mayhap', and while realising the impossibility of the idea, beginning to feel desperate. The time was near for him to fulfil his obligation to Poseidon, Meralda's proposed espousal to Vivian and their departure to the mainland were nigh, and he was just as eager for their own nuptial bonding to be realised. When that had been achieved he intended to take her to a place of concealment, a tiny bay accessible only by boat; it was only her reluctance to sever her family ties that had prevented him from already doing that, and also her insistence upon a ceremony before their union. He knew she had convinced herself that if she behaved in a conventional manner, even though acting against her father's wishes at the outset, Richard might find it in his heart to forgive her when he observed her happiness, but Atlan had no such expectation.

He had not yet explained his intention for them to be wed by Tardhamor at the holed stone – she would demand that he take her to the Forbidden Place at once if he did. She had already made clear her disapproval of people calling it by that name, aware of the reason but erasing the logic from her mind.

'They told me it was filled with the spirits of the dead, sacrificed to pagan gods on the Fire Rock, but that happened so long ago they must surely have settled to rest by now. Anyway, I found no such thing – I was falsely told. To me, the Sacred Grove is a marvellous, magical place!'

Despite her entreaties to return there Atlan had firmly refused, knowing it would be unwise before finding another maiden. His search for one had not yet begun, partly because he was spending most of his time with Meralda and partly because of his certainty that none other as fair existed on the island. He feared a rejection of what could be considered a lesser choice and the effect it could have – the high priest might have Meralda taken from him unless an equally satisfactory offering was made. On the few occasions when he had ventured into the grove he had sensed the high priest's unseen eyes boring into him. Nothing had been said, but when Atlan had shaken his head he knew by the way the restless fingers plucked at the robe that Tardhamor was asking himself why his young priest was idling here then, should that be the case.

This day, in the early light of dawn, close to despair with the situation and well aware there were but seven dark nights left before the new moon rose for the third time, Atlan had gone to Kellimargh, not caring that he risked another meeting with Tardhamor but determined to pray to his god, beseeching his help. As he knelt before the statue, a sudden revelation had come in a flash of perception. He had cried aloud in his joy and hurriedly sought the commanding figure that appeared at the temple door seeking the reason for the unexpected noise.

Atlan prostrated himself at the foot of the steps. 'Most worthy priest, I humbly ask you to show your mercy.'

'What mercy do you expect if you are about to tell me that you have failed in the task entrusted to you?' Tardhamor's voice was curt. He had been kept informed by his spies of Atlan's liaison with Meralda and was now unsure of her purity. 'Our god grows ever more impatient, as you can witness from the increased agitation of the seas!'

'I bid you hearken to me!' Atlan's passion engulfed him. 'My quest is over! Poseidon has minded me of a certain circumstance. The maiden I love has a sister that I once set eyes upon. She is of a different colouring, true, but fair of face and form – and also a virgin. I can foresee no obstacle in bringing her here.'

Tardhamor's interest was caught. 'Poseidon demanded the fairest maid,' he said regally, pleased with the confirmation that Meralda remained pure.

Atlan clasped his hands, willing him to consent. 'They are sisters – who is to say which is the fairer?' Further insight came to him. 'Lowenna is younger and of a rounder, fuller cast, more of the shape and outline of Cleito.'

Tardhamor hesitated, staring thoughtfully over Atlan's head for a long moment until he snapped his fingers. 'Bring her to the temple this day for me to observe these qualities and decide upon her fitness for the sacred rite.'

Atlan stood and bowed. 'It shall be done as you say, O Keeper of the Grove. Then, will you join Meralda to me as soon as the sister has been delivered? With our union sealed we will leave for some secluded place, the better to prevent my bride's awareness of her sister's disappearance. Once the rest of her family, and the governor, have repaired to the mainland as they plan, any threat will be past.'

Tardhamor nodded in agreement. 'And Richard of Trevelyan will be repaid for his iniquity, in some small measure, by the loss of two daughters! I am told he struts around Lyonesse, his lips spouting forth about an evil that he seeks, yet proposes to act the coward and flee from it to the mainland. He could find it under his very nose in his churches if he was not blinded by his own pomposity! It is manifest in their pervading, intrusive belief in someone so-called a "Saviour", which was brought here and thrust, uninvited, upon this unsuspecting land! Our faith in Poseidon was in evidence long before, but was condemned, forbidden and cast out without redress. You mark my words well – our god will continue to survive long after this other has been wiped from the face of the earth!'

He ended his bitter upbraiding, and forcing his attention back to Atlan relaxed the ferocity of his anger. 'Now, go carry out what you have proposed and I will get word to our followers. We shall make all necessary preparations and await your coming with the maidens, but I warn you – do not fail us – or your god!'

Atlan lost no time in riding off to where he knew Meralda would be waiting, and waded out to the boat. She held her arms wide when she saw him approaching. 'I feared you had forsaken me,' she said, laughing, as he scrambled over the side. ''Tis already near the middle of the day and I have lacked your closeness, to feel the touch of your skin against mine, to breathe the air you breathe and…'

Before she finished speaking he had swept her up, holding her to him, both soon breathless with the ardency of their kisses. When he set her down he continued to hold her, gazing into her face, adoring her, until he found he could contain his news no longer, guessing that she would be puzzled by his burst of exhilaration.

'What affects you so?' she asked, trembling with expectation.

'Meralda, my love – I have contrived a way for us to be wed!'

For a moment she was silent with the unexpectedness of the surprise, then: 'How? Where? When?' Questions tumbled out until he called for her to end them.

'Hold! Softly, my dearest one – leave me space to satisfy your inquiring. First – how? Because I am a clever fellow, much given to inspired thoughts!' He swerved away, grinning gaily as her hand came up to pat his boastful mouth. 'Next – where? Why at the wedding ring – the holed stone in the glade of the Sacred Grove you have so desired to revisit, where the high priest has agreed to join us as one. And – when? Would you consent to this very day when the sun begins to sink and night awaits its turn?' His fingers traced the contour of her upturned, delighted face.

Meralda was ecstatic. 'So, the waiting time is really over and our espousal come upon us! Then you will play Poseidon and I will play Cleito as we were that day in the glade – you must remember…'

He held her tightly. 'I have not forgotten.' He put his lips to her ear and whispered with loving emphasis: 'I will be Poseidon and you will be my Cleito!'

'And what will you give me as a wedding gift?' she teased him.

'I possess no chattels to give,' he answered regretfully.

She was resting her head on the warm flesh of his chest and her cheek touched the cross-within-a-circle. She lifted it up. 'You may give me this bauble.'

He hesitated. ''Tis no bauble, but a talisman to lead me back to Atlantis one day. I cannot recollect a time when it did not hang at my throat.' He kissed her again, pondering. 'But since I would never again wish to be anywhere without you – I will bestow it with gladness and it can lead us both there.'

85

He made as if to remove it, but she held his hands. 'Wait 'til the moment we are wed,' she said, and pulled away reluctantly. 'Now I must hasten home.'

Atlan laid a hand on her arm. 'There is no need for you to venture there again.' This was something he had not foreseen – he needed to keep the sisters apart for his plot to succeed. He had intended to leave Meralda alone on some pretext, ride to Trevelyan, entice Lowenna to go with him by saying her sister was in trouble, lead her to Tardhamor and then return for his loved one.

'Why go?' he continued, alarmed. 'Is it your desire to fetch honey cakes? Though I am forgetting you know nought of those – that they form a part of our ritual. But do not fret, the fishers will bring some for the ceremony.'

'Honey cakes?' she queried.

'Ay, small, round cakes to resemble the main island of Atlantis, each with a cross at the centre to show how straight the roads were made – the same as this talisman. Whenever I think in solitude I recall them stretching out afar…'

'Oh, I surely know of them but not as honey cakes,' she broke in. 'We bake them to mark the day when Jesus was crucified. The cross we put on ours is for the cross he died upon. Let me tell you of…'

'Then yours have a different meaning,' he interrupted hurriedly, more concerned with her proposed departure. 'What matters it now? You may tell me the tale when we have nought else to do but for you to teach me what you will. Consider again, my adored one. Remain here in safety, so that none may interfere and try to sway and hinder you. Once we are wed I will take you to a place where we cannot be found unless we wish it, though many moons may wax and wane.'

'But my family will soon be gone away! Shall I ever be able to find them again to tell of my happiness?'

Atlan kissed her eyes, stroking her hair, soothing her fears.

86

'You say they are going to the mainland on the word of some Seer on Scilly who has predicted disaster here because of the increased turmoil of the waters. You must trust me in knowing that Poseidon has the power to calm them whenever he chooses, and as soon as one of his desires is satisfied, peace will once again be evident. When your kin discover they have been misled and had no reason to flee they will return, and you can be reunited. Does that pleasure you, my sweet maid?'

'I'faith, it calms my foolish heart!' Meralda accepted his argument and returned to hers. 'But now, I must return to Trevelyan.'

Atlan was disquieted at her insistence. 'For what purpose, pray?'

'Why, to fetch my bridal gown, you simpleton!' Meralda was laughing but she was also emphatic.

'You need no other gown.'

'I intend this one to clothe me – 'twas my mother's which I promised to wear. Am I so feeble as to break my word?'

Atlan found himself helpless against her determination and had to submit, thinking that perhaps his scheme need not be abandoned, merely adjusted. He agreed that she should ride alone to the mill house and return with the gown to the boat, when they would go together to Kellimargh.

When she left, full of anticipation, Atlan let her travel some distance before starting to follow, as Mordon galloped much faster than her small mare. He espied her as she reached the big gates, then concealed himself and Mordon in a coppice, watching. He had no idea of the number of persons inside, but hoped the men would be elsewhere, helping with the move, the mill itself having been shut down. The sight of Meralda emerging would be the signal for him to tarry, to give her time to get well away before he entered to confront Lowenna with a plea to come and give aid to her sister, fallen from her horse or some such story, then take her to Tardhamor and finally ride back to the boat and Meralda.

He waited with impatience while the shadows lengthened imperceptibly, having been sure that Meralda would leave at the earliest moment. Suddenly a disconcerting flurry of dust in the distance, that signalled the approach of horsemen, caught his eye. Three riders were heading in the direction of Trevelyan – with the intention to pass by – or stop?

*

When Meralda arrived at the mill she had walked her mare quietly into the courtyard, leaving it loosely tied and ready to depart. She peered into the stable to ensure that no visiting horses were inside, before creeping into the large kitchen so as not to startle Lowenna – but proceeding to do so, just the same.

'Lord ha' mercy!' The violet eyes opened wide as her body jerked, her hands sending flour flying. 'You were not as yet expected. What determined you to steal in like some pirate from the Northlands intent on raiding our home, Sister?'

Meralda glanced swiftly around. 'Are any others expected to arrive?'

Lowenna shook her head. Heedful of her sister's flushed and unusually animated face, she immediately sent two young kitchen maids, who were observing and listening with interest, away on errands.

Meralda had flung off her cloak and swung into dancing, rhythmic steps around the kneading-trough, where Lowenna had resumed pulling and pummelling the dough with vigour. 'What? Is the bread not yet baked?' she asked idly, unwittingly tempting Providence, unaware that the quicksand of her sister's annoyance was already under her dainty, prancing feet.

Lowenna had fashioned her black hair into a plait that hung down her back, some curling strands clinging to the sweat on her hot face. She smote the dough with her fist, likening it in her mind to some part of Meralda's anatomy, but her voice stayed low and controlled. 'Not quite,' she said, 'though the green-stuff is prepared, the fruit sorted, the meat jointed, the oatcakes ready for the griddle, the eggs beaten, the poultry and livestock fed, the wine jarred, the floors swept, fresh straw laid, the clothes washed and water brought from the well! I would have done more, time lying heavy on my hands, but I see that your only concern is for the bread, and for which I am greatly afeared you will be forced to wait, Sister!'

The sarcasm was initially lost on Meralda, her worries being not the bread but retrieving the wedding gown secretly, while hoping the key was still in the lock of the chest and also if she should divulge her plans to Lowenna. However, as she had dimly perceived an accusing, impertinent tone at the end of her sister's utterance, she felt she should counter it. She stopped twirling while she considered whether she should bother to repay this waspishness with a retort of her own or remain silent, but she misreckoned.

'I have no especial care for the bread,' she said, forced on the defensive and speaking haughtily, 'and am not lingering overlong – I must be on my way. But I note that you have acquired some airs and graces and think yourself equal to discharging the household duties without the guidance of Gweniver or myself!'

Lowenna's patience suddenly melted like fat dropped in a heated pan, and slipped from her control under this provocation. She flung down the dough and faced Meralda, placing hands on hips in a positional, combative manner.

'You!' she exclaimed. 'Whenever have you guided me in anything of late? Or helped when I most needed it? You have been away every day since Father left to oversee the move, and refuse to tell me where you go or what you do – apart, that is, from naming it "instruction" – which I have long since ceased to believe! You remain here when Martin is due, only to vanish when he leaves and before his horse has passed out of sight! I have been sick with worry, yet you have failed to spare a thought for how I feel or for the untruths I have had to tell in order to protect your probity! Lord Vivian has visited several times though unable to find you once, and his sadness made my heart ache for him. You are betrothed to him, Meralda – or have you found that it adds to your comfort to forget that seemingly unwelcome reality?'

She calmed herself and began to speak in a more moderate tone to her startled sister. 'You know you must be prudent in what you do – there are but few days left 'til your union. I have been greatly afeared of Father discovering your shameful deception, as I now realise it must be, and assume that I had a part in it. What has caused you to be so disloyal and hurtful towards us? Why are you unable to tell me the truth?' She ended by striking her hand on the floured board, starting to sob with exasperation, tears falling down her cheeks.

Meralda was appalled. She had been completely unaware that Lowenna had suffered so much on her behalf, having not given a thought to anything other than her own selfish desires. She threw her arms around her sister, tears welling up in sympathy, and kissed her fondly. 'Dearest!' she whispered. 'How could I have distressed you so? I have been thoughtless and unkind only because…'

She stopped, undecided. Should she confess the true reason for her inconsiderate conduct or continue with the pretence for a while longer? Lowenna's stifled weeping bade her choose the former – her sister deserved the favour of her honesty. Besides, what harm could it do now? She would soon be leaving for a new way of life, departing from Trevelyan – maybe forever. Strangely, the thought gave her no pain or regret but rather an immense feeling of joy.

'Dry your tears, my sweet one,' she continued, moving away again with dancing steps, her feet unable to stay still any longer. 'Forgive my seeming folly and lack of courtesy, but at this moment my headiness will not allow me to dwell upon't! I have tidings that may shock, but I beg for no fuss. I have come to carry away Mother's gown and kiss you farewell!'

Lowenna had made no sense of the words and so her expression remained unchanged. She faltered: 'But you are mistaken – you will not need the gown for several more days yet...'

Meralda could contain her news no longer. 'There you are in error, my dear, for I will be wed this day at sunset!' Her eyes shone with gladness. 'Please say you are happy in my rejoicing and promise to care for Father as I have ever done, filling Mother's place as best I could to ease his loneliness.'

Lowenna had been splashing water on her tear-streaked face and was patting it dry, only half-listening because still not comprehending. 'My head pounds and feels as solid as a turnip,' she said. 'How can I grasp this silliness with which you try to fill it when there is no room inside to allow it to enter and make some kind of meaning?'

'Lowenna – give ear to me! Why will you not attend?' Meralda curbed her irritation with an effort. 'Do you recall the fisherman with the white horse?'

Lowenna nodded. 'Well, he and I were together once before, on that vanished island called Atlantis, lovers in that other age, that other time! It seems we still love each other more than life itself – and he is the one I will wed once again at sunset!'

At last, Lowenna, looking into that bright face eager for approval, fully grasped what she had said, and the reason for all these singular happenings instantly became clear. Became clear, certainly, but brought her no solace, so shocked that words deserted her until anger welled up and flooded over in a torrent. 'Meralda! How could you be so shameful? What

91

mischief have you done? And what is this nonsense you are saying? I am bewildered and mazed by your falseness! And who, in our Church, would wed you without Father's given word?'

'There is a priest...' Meralda began to give reasons, make excuses. Voices were raised, one against the other, one reproaching, the other defying so hotly that neither heard the hooves in the courtyard – nor the footsteps that approached inside. Both maids were totally absorbed in their impassioned altercation.

'There is only one for you to wed,' Lowenna was saying. 'Father will make you – you must obey him – as we all do for our own good!'

'But I love another,' Meralda was firmly insisting. 'I can never become Vivian's bride – never!'

'What is this treachery?' thundered a voice from behind them, and silence dropped like a curtain, quelling the clamour. 'Both turn to me,' the voice roared again. 'I demand your early response.'

The sisters slowly twisted around to face their father glowering in the doorway, Martin at his elbow. The quietened mouths opened and quickly closed again.

'Well? In what disgraceful place have your tongues taken refuge? They were working well ere now! Meralda – will you do me the favour of repeating the avowal you just made to your sister? I must be sure I heard aright and was not mistaken in your sentiments!' He came further into the room, seating himself on a bench in a surly manner, his whip beating against the leather on his leg.

Meralda stood before him, head bowed, unable to meet his fierce, brown eyes. 'Father...' Her voice faltered, gaining strength as she realised she must be plausible and unafraid if she was to persuade him of her earnestness. 'Father, I spake truth – I cannot wed m'Lord. I beg you not to be so pitiless as to try to force me into a union with him because my heart is given to another – whom I love as dearly as you loved our mother…'

'How dare you compare my love for Ysella with your own capricious dalliance! And who is the philandering cur who has brought shame upon me and my house?' Richard's rage was increasing rapidly as the full import became clearer.

Meralda fell to her knees, submissively. 'I beseech you – be not hasty in your judgment, Father!' she pleaded. 'He is an honest fisherman – and loves me truly. I will not tell his name for fear of your anger and vengeance upon him!' Her gaze fixed on Martin. 'Brother, join me in my plea! He wears a cross about his neck to show his faith in the same manner as you, though he prays to the god Poseidon as do all the fishers, craving aid and safety from the perils of the sea!'

There was a second's startled pause when everyone, except the speaker, held their breath, before Martin began to accuse her with his own vehement condemnation. 'If true, 'twould seem the Devil has a hand in this affair, hell-bent on reviving old pagan customs that were suppressed centuries ago. 'Twould be better had the earlier worship of fire been resurrected on Carrag Uthek, the flames carrying a warning to all on Lyonesse! But, I suspect you magnify the extent of the infidelity of these fisher folk to God, Meralda, in order to deflect us from your own misconduct.'

He was unwilling to believe that the fisher folk had re-embraced paganism and, therefore, were not united in their faithfulness to the Church, but if Meralda was to be believed, there must be some place where they gathered and his father had searched every portion of the land without finding such a site. Surely something would have been apparent to his eyes, as this might well have been the evil that was sought. Now, it was too late to begin searching anew with nothing more definite, and there was a plenitude of other things to concern them, notably this latest and most pressing problem with Meralda that had to take precedence. If the ravisher who had led his sister astray with tales of other gods displayed a cross upon himself, then he thought the rogue must have been paying lip-service, at least, to the Church, even though not wholly observing its dictates. Meralda had said the fisher folk prayed to Poseidon, and again Martin assumed these would merely be fitful mutterings, lacking worship and therefore of no consequence. His thinking had become so confused by this calamity that he failed to recall that any form of prayer, anywhere, constitutes worship.

Somewhat sadly he said: ' I am benumbed by your defiance of Father's wishes and your rejection of our traditions. You were raised with us to believe and have faith in God – has all that gone for nought?'

'To be sure – I believe! But I am in love and bewildered. I know God will understand – he is loving and merciful. Can you not show me mercy, too? I am filled with such sorrow and anguish...'

Richard's heart was also filled with anguish – to the exclusion of all else. This lovely daughter, his adored swan, secretly special to him because of her likeness to Ysella, was opposing his express wishes, unheard of amongst daughters and rarely amongst sons, flouting convention, disobedient and tarnished. In his pain, one thought came uppermost, and he cast about for the words to express his anxiety.

'Have you coupled with this...this...unholy wretch?' He feared her reply and what his reaction would be.

'In no way! I refused to give myself until we could be wed, knowing it to be against your teaching and that of the Church. I have observed my chastity and done no wrong!' Meralda could feel panic rising within her as she remembered Atlan awaiting her. 'I beg you, Father, relieve me of my bond to Vivian! You cannot keep me burdened with it – the weight would be unbearable – too great for me to carry!'

His mind momentarily eased, Richard ignored her appeal,

shifting his attention to Lowenna, standing rigid, eyes downcast, awaiting the moment when her turn would inevitably come.

'And you, Daughter. What have you to add to the deception to which we have been subjected? Why were we used like children at sport with a cloth tied about their eyes so they have no knowledge of what occurs around them? What part have you played in prolonging this cunning game?'

Lowenna was at a loss as to how to answer. If she owned to the half-truth of knowing nothing about Meralda's secret meetings, she would be blamed for failing to notice and report her absences. If she admitted to the half-truth of knowing that meetings were taking place, then she would be equally guilty of concealing it. Either way, she could not escape censure. 'I have played no part in any game, Father, simply done what I saw fit, to occasion the least harm, and if I was mistaken in my efforts 'twas because I lack the wisdom of years. I crave your forgiveness – for us both.'

'Humph!' snorted Richard. ''Tis easy said, but I wonder if you have smiled upon, and helped to advance, this betrayal. Ay, you may well start and look askance and shake your poll, Lowenna, but I had already heeded you making sheep's eyes at your sister's betrothed! 'Tis plain to me that you desire him for yourself!'

He sighed deeply, striding up and down, marshalling his thoughts. 'It might hap that not too much damage has been done if m'Lord is kept in ignorance of your perfidy,' he went on. 'This lapse in your conduct must never be revealed, Meralda, and I claim the pledge of all here to observe it. I will not have my friend endure further needless vexation – he has suffered enough in the past from an unchaste, loveless female, and now has the misfortune to be besotted of another!'

Meralda, meanwhile, had risen to her feet, staring into

95

Richard's face unable to believe she was hearing aright. 'Would you make me an unwilling bride for no other reason than that?' she cried. 'What about my torment? Do I have to pretend I was lost in a dream these past days? That 'twas a fancy conjured up and can as easily be dispelled? Asking me to deny my love? Then I refuse – I will never consent to it!'

Richard drew himself up to his full height, looking down on her. He had regained control of his temper and was displaying an almost regal dignity. Everyone was aware that this was a man who directed his household and their lives and would tolerate no dissent. He was the rock they could cling to for protection, and against whose rugged strength any adversary could batter himself in futile opposition without it shifting or crumbling one iota.

'I have given my word – and yours, Meralda – to my old friend, and nothing can alter that,' he said quietly. 'The time is too short for me to find some acceptable means of compelling you to confess where this knave may be found that I might cut out his liver, though should I chance upon him I will surely give myself that satisfaction. I am minded to allow you to reconsider your refusal to obey me until the day of the espousal, and as for now, I have no recourse but to put you where you can cause no further harm and have no distraction from your reflections. We will escort you to the Priory on the Rock to be kept restrained by the Holy Sisters, and then if you yet refuse to fulfil your obligation to your lord, you will be taken to the mother house of the Sisters on the mainland, there to spend the rest of your life amongst them.'

Meralda was struck dumb, but Lowenna let out an audible gasp that made him turn upon her. 'And you,' he continued, his wrath still visibly lurking beneath the surface, 'you, for your duplicity in not alerting us to the circumstance, will keep your sister company until the wedding day...' Then, as Lowenna showed signs of beginning to plead, he went on, 'and, if she is not persuaded to honour her bond, Daughter, then you, too, will spend the rest of your life with the Sisters!'

'Have pity!' Meralda cried. 'You cannot shut us away!'

'You will comply with my wishes or take the consequences – both of you!' Richard glared from one to the other, saddened by what he saw as the necessity to place a guard on the daughters he so dearly loved, who had been given his implicit trust – only to betray it.

He looked around for Old Jowan, left to secure the horses, and saw him hovering just outside the room uncomfortably shifting his feet, held back by the contention within. 'Jowan – saddle Lowenna's horse – I saw Meralda's already awaiting her...' he said, but broke off as that maiden made a dash for the door.

Jowan, showing surprising agility for a man of his age, flung himself across the entrance, blocking her way. 'I will not go!' she was crying, trying to evade him. 'You will never keep me from my love!'

'Let us see what a few days in the priory will do for your resolve,' Richard answered grimly, holding her fast. 'The Sisters endure an austere discipline, I believe. Come, Martin, we must hasten off with this graceless pair in order to deliver them before sundown. Jowan!' he called. 'Forget the other horse. I have need to keep a tight hold on this swan lest she fly away!'

They left at once, heading off rapidly in a northerly direction.

# 7

## *The Priory*

The Priory on the Rock was situated on a tiny isle, barely separated from Lyonesse, at the end of a spit of land jutting out from its northern coastline. Known as an island of women for centuries past, it was inaccessible except at a single point of entry, an impregnable, and therefore, ideal refuge for self-sufficient women who felt no need for men. Thus, it presented a suitable locality in which to establish a priory to house a lady prioress and the Sisters of her order. Perpendicular rock surrounded it, but from a small beach, entrance could be found through an opening cleft leading into a passageway that meandered upward between outer and inner rock, the upper part of the outer side open to the elements. It was so narrow that only one person could pass along it at a time, which enabled the doughty Sisters to easily keep intruders at bay, being as well versed in the use of arms as they were in their religious responses for the protection of their immortal souls.

A thin rain fell as the travellers, cloaked and hooded, made their way northwards to the coast, and when it lessened a mist blew in off the sea, blotting out all but a short length the road ahead. Eventually, they reached the spit of land and began to rein in the horses, the men alone glad to be approaching the end of their journey, and were forced to come to a halt when they came to the narrow strip of water which separated them from the isle. They could just make out the cleft that would gain them access directly on the shore opposite, and also see that the tide, far from being low as expected at this time, was high enough to be surging around the rocks, throwing up spray and spume. The horses stood steaming, stamping their hooves, while the men considered the situation.

'The waters have taken on a determination of their own,' muttered Jowan.

'Perhaps they help to keep the pirates from our shores,' rejoined Martin. ''Tis many a day since we heard the bells ring out in warning – mayhap the men on watch will grow careless as they scan the seas, searching for sails that never appear.'

'And the animals, too, shun our land.' Richard was thoughtful. 'D'ye keep in mind, Jowan, how yester-morn, when we sailed to the mainland the sea was full of them, the prow of the boat cleaving through? There were deer and boar and all manner of creatures seemingly frantic to swim from these shores – I cannot 'member the like before. Be still, Daughter!' as Meralda tried to struggle from his arms. 'A fall from the horse may give you hurt.'

'None so much as you give me!' she cried. 'I entreat you, Father, do not deny us our freedom!'

He disregarded her, his attention on the obstacle in front of them. 'We must test the depth ere we risk crossing.'

'I will be first to go.' As Martin made to move forward, Old Jowan spurred his horse and was halfway across before the other could enter the water. When he reached the further side he turned, holding an arm aloft. 'It can be done,' he called, 'and the current not swift enow to pose a danger!'

When the others followed, they could see more clearly through the mist exactly what was facing them. It was as if the isle had been thrown straight up out of the sea like a dead volcano. The priory, its buildings and land concealed, was

99

well hidden within the centre of the isle, surrounded by a sheer, high crag, with no break anywhere other than the cleft leading into the narrow passageway that led upward, cut out of the rock itself. Even pirates had failed to gain entry here.

The men tied the horses to iron rings set in the rock, unknowing that the action sounded an alarm bell somewhere in the interior far above, and leaving Jowan on guard the others went into the passageway and began to ascend single-file. Meralda resisted at every step, causing Richard to exert himself to the utmost, red-faced, breathing heavily and hitting his elbows painfully against the rock. He was thankful when they reached a wider, more open and level space, but found a massive double door blocking their way, so set into the rock that it prevented ingress into what, in all probability, had originally been a cave. A smaller door had been cut into one of the main doors, giving the impression of a blank picture in a frame. Richard seized a rope hanging by the side of it and they heard the muffled clanging of a bell.

The shutter of a spyhole in the small door was instantly pulled aside, and an inquisitive dark eye examined the visitors with care. It fixed on Martin who had put himself forward, the cross on his breast visible from beneath the cloak.

'You are not our usual priest, who comes to provide us with the Holy Sacrament from where you stand outside this door, but surely you must be aware that no man sets foot beyond it, so will you state the purpose of your visit?' The voice was impassive, considering the vigilance of that alert eye.

'Ay, Sister,' he replied, surprised at the extent to which the sounds reverberated and echoed, ''tis well known, but we men have no desire to gain entry, and would not have chanced bringing displeasure by our unexpected arrival were it not an exceptional necessity. I beg you inform the lady prioress that we are of the family of Richard of Trevelyan who stands at my side. I am Martin, his son. My sister Meralda

– here,' he indicated the struggling maid, hood pulled over her face to drown her cries, 'is pledged to wed our governor on the day of Saint Martin's Mass, when the archdeacon observes it in my church of Saint Perran during a pastoral visit. I hear that your Sisterhood has been invited to attend this rare event.'

The eye blinked. 'Ay, 'tis so. We are familiar with your tidings – and the hearsay that you intend to desert Lyonesse.'

'That may be true for my family and the governor,' Martin answered quickly. 'I believe my Father has already tendered his reasons and pleaded for your aid in seeking out a place where wickedness is hid – without the benefit of any further word from you. He also appealed for you to leave this threatened land, which it seems you have also seen fit to disregard, but there...' He hesitated. 'There is another matter at issue. My sister has become a victim of the Devil's wiles, refusing to obey Father and observe his bond to her betrothed. We beg you to keep her for chastening, aided by her sister Lowenna, who will be able to tell you more. If you should succeed in exorcising her from Satan's snare by the day of the espousal, we request that you will convey both sisters in your procession to my church, ready for the ceremony after Mass. To requite you, I will bring food and cloth on the morrow, having been marked as go-between to come daily for tidings of your progress.'

Richard, having had no respite from Meralda's struggles, was losing patience with this long speech. 'I crave an early response to our request – before I am forced to deliver a beating to this unruly and graceless wench! Will you take her and do whatever you can to bring the vixen to her senses?'

The dark eye vanished from the spyhole, to be at once replaced by a watery blue one. 'Have a care for the heat of your mind, my rash fellow! Calm yourself! I am the lady prioress and know of you and your over-haste, Richard of Trevelyan,' came the quavery words. 'Your daughter is, like you, wilful and determined. So, you have been unsuccessful in finding evil on Lyonesse, of which we have no particular knowledge other than it would, for sure, be found in the dark soul of some man. Could not what you seek be conjoined in some way to the Devil's sorcery that seemingly afflicts your daughter?'

Richard impatiently refused to consider this idea for a moment. 'The evil is one thing and the Devil's sorcery quite another, m'Lady,' he retorted, provoked by the waiting, the strain of holding Meralda, and what he thought to be an unjustifiable sharpness in the lady's speech. 'But what is of consequence is that this ungrateful maid...' – he gave Meralda an angry shake – '...is destined to become the governor's bride!'

The watery blue eye closed briefly as if in prayer for the apparent foolishness of this man. 'To my mind,' the prioress retaliated, opening her eye again, 'they run hand in hand – evil and the Devil – they cannot be separated. Where you have one you can be certain t'other lurks.' She gave an audible sniff. 'As for the so-called governor – he has neglected to govern for many a long year without causing us to suffer ill, so has not been missed overmuch. We will continue to thank the good God that the people of Lyonesse obey his laws without recourse to the rules of man. But I grow weary – let us have done with this discourse. Your request is granted, Richard of Trevelyan – prepare to hand over the maidens when the small door is opened to you!'

Bolts were heard drawn back and the small door creaked open, revealing a glimpse of white-robed figures dimly seen in the torch-lit gloom of a long tunnel, like wraiths waiting to attend upon the bodies of the dead.

Richard thrust Meralda forward, lifting her over the raised door-case when she stubbed her feet firmly against it in her determination not to go inside. Gone was her regal, self-contained manner as she sobbed and screamed in despair, having the semblance of an unwilling soul being cast into the flames of hell and bringing grief to those responsible. Then other hands took her away.

Lowenna, hood pulled forward to hide her distress and offering no resistance, stepped with a newly found dignity over the wooden frame without a backward glance, fearful that if she lingered and dared imagine what lay ahead she might become as uncontrolled as her sister. As the door banged shut, the two left outside heard the bolts shot across, and the faint sounds of Meralda wailing in torment followed them briefly as they hurried away, hastening to pass out of hearing, both appalled by the cause and effect of what had been done.

Rejoining Old Jowan, they forded the strip of water and fast disappeared into the hazy landscape, each with his own unhappy thoughts and anxious to reach shelter before nightfall. They were so intent upon leaving the priory and what it contained with all possible speed, that none noticed the white horse blending into the mist not far off the road.

*

Atlan had been watching, with increasing anxiety, for some indication of the progress of events inside Trevelyan when he saw four horses leaving, one carrying two people. He had no idea where they could be heading or who was in the speeding party, but sensed that it included Meralda, who had not emerged in the interminable time since he saw the horsemen enter, and possibly Lowenna, so he began to follow at a safe distance. When they neared the Priory on the Rock he had no further doubts – Meralda must have been trapped into disclosing her secret. He waited impatiently in a patch of scrub after seeing them cross over the water to the further beach, until he saw three riders returning through the mist leading a riderless horse, to gallop away along the route to the south-east.

103

Then he left, riding with bitterness and apprehension towards Kellimargh in some alarm as to how he would be received by Tardhamor. By this time, with day fast passing into night, the high priest must be aware that something had gone very awry and would be exhibiting mounting anger at Atlan's failure to produce the two maidens into the expectant, festive assembly awaiting the espousals, and thereby bringing his own carefully planned preparations to nought.

As he rode onward, Atlan began to wonder if he was being wise in rushing headlong into a meeting with Tardhamor with no new constructive solution to offer, but his immediate thoughts were centred upon the necessity to return to the priory before dawn to await unfolding events there. Nothing had gone aright for the two lovers as yet, though, he reasoned, that must surely be reversed, as surely as the tides, enabling him to somehow succeed in satisfying his god, the high priest and his own passion. It had at first appeared to be such a simple task, but was proving to be as evasive as an eel in the mud – almost under one's hand but gone again in a trice! For the moment his sole desire was to hide himself and his aching heart, so let Mordon take him to the shelter and comfort of his boat but even there found no peace, as the sea – or was it Poseidon? – tossed it about with increasing violence.

He lay with searing, burning desire inside him. Meralda, his love, who should now be enclosed in his arms, had to be freed and would be relying on him to rescue her. He imagined the lovely tear-stained face and the rising panic that would be filling her breast, laying a hand over his own heart in an effort to quieten the thudding that sounded in his ears. If she were to be taken away from him abidingly he had no doubt she would kill herself, and he would do likewise, unable to endure the idea of being unabe to see, touch or kiss her – or to lie with her as his body yearned to do. He beat his head with his fist in desperation. He must find a way to release both her and Lowenna for Poseidon, so he could accomplish what he had set out to do before this terrible hindrance had been forced upon him.

He groaned aloud. Rapture had been within their grasp, but what was happening to her now in the confines of that secluded priory?

*

When the small door slammed shut it had sounded like the crack of doom to the sisters. Meralda continued to fight against the restraining hands, defiant and voicing her anguish, but as fatigue overtook her she went limp and silent. Lowenna had stayed motionless during this uneven contest, robbed of any desire to feel or do anything, temporarily deprived of emotion and movement until she was herself urged forward through the torch-lit tunnel. Fear returned and gripped her – this was the first time she had been separated from the comforts of home. Scared and helpless, she was lost in a world over which she had no control, knowing that Meralda had submitted, been defeated, and that she could no longer draw support from her sister's strength. Having been unwittingly thrust into this strange environment, she would now have to rely entirely upon her own resources.

They soon came to the end of the tunnel and emerged into the open air, moving along paths skirting well-cultivated plots while being guided towards one of several long buildings. The light was beginning to fail, everything appearing hazy in the mist, vague impressions of the surroundings barely registering on their minds. In their humiliation they had no volition and as the nuns forced them onward, they evinced no interest in this awful place.

Once inside the building, they were taken the length of a

corridor past a row of closed doors along one side, the last door standing open where they were pushed inside. The nun leading the way held a lantern containing a lighted candle, which she placed on a crude board supported on a frame for use as a table, two stools as seats beside it. Against one wall was a smaller board holding a bowl and pitcher of water, and straw surfaced the rough floor. This nunnery cell was kept for persons needing a period of restraint, self-imposed or otherwise, so was larger than others used merely for sleeping and had been hastily converted for the use of the visitors. Two straw palliasses lay on the floor as beds, thin coverlets flung over them, and a three-legged stool put in a corner, a round hole in the top with a pot beneath. On another wall hung a plain wooden cross above a row of pegs to hold garments, and a narrow slit in a third served for a window.

Lowenna and Meralda stood looking about them, hardly believing what they were seeing, forlorn and appalled, staying close together as if afraid they might be torn apart. A nun of small stature with a young face slipped past the others into the room carrying a tray holding a jug of water, two beakers and a platter of dark bread with a modicum of meat. She set it down by the lantern and turned to go.

Lowenna was very aware of the oppressive silence, the only sounds being the shuffling of feet and the swish of skirts as the nuns moved through the door. She put out a hand to touch the small nun's shoulder. 'I entreat you,' she said faintly. 'Stay to offer us a word of comfort. Is this place ever so cold and cheerless?'

The little nun hesitated momentarily, regarding Lowenna with sympathy in her eyes but no smile on her lips before putting a finger to them and, following the others through the door, pulled it sharply closed behind her. The two left inside heard the latch click and a bar pushed across.

'You cannot leave us so!' Lowenna ran to the door and tugged at the handle, which did not give an inch. She turned to Meralda, who stood listless, gazing down. 'The door is fast!' she cried. 'We have been made captive in here! Where do they think we would escape to?'

She saw that Meralda had begun to shake and shiver as with a severe ague, so took the damp cloak from around her and shook it vigorously. She then offered the food and drink provided, but her sister merely grimaced. Finally, she persuaded her to lie on a palliasse, wrinkling her nose at the malodour arising from the straw filling, and swathed her as best she could in covers that proved sadly inadequate. Then, in her turn, she rejected the unappetising provisions and lay down beside her without having recourse to kneel for her prayers as usual. She did not dare douse the candle and be left in the fearsome dark and thought she would never close her eyes for the night but, within seconds, both the spent and weary maidens slept soundly.

They were awakened, in some alarm, by the loud tolling of a bell sounding as if it was in their very room. They both sat up at the same instant, startled, not remembering where they were, unable to see properly by the light of the guttering candle. When realisation came, Meralda sank back with a long drawn-out moan, but Lowenna arose and poured cold water into the bowl, sluicing her face and hands and drying them on a rough cloth. Her first concern, as always at the start of a day, was for Lord Vivian, and while carefully wiping the black stone of her ring she wondered whether he was at Trevivian, the hillfort or Dinas Ryal. Wherever he was he would be unaware of their miserable condition, assuming, if he had been informed of their admission to the priory, that it would have been with their consent.

Her daydream was interrupted by the bar being drawn from the door, a brighter light showing through as it opened to reveal three white figures standing on the threshold, their lanterns aglow. Lowenna eyed them nervously, pressing back against the wall as the tallest, having a pointed and prominent facial outline, though not of an unpleasing appearance, stepped forward.

'I am Sister Columb. The lady prioress extends her hand in greeting and hopes that the night's rest has lessened your weariness. She requests that you come to prayers to be said for you in the chapel before joining us in the refectory to break your fast.' She glanced at the recumbent Meralda. 'I would advise that, for your own regard, you both attend upon her wishes – she is unused to refusal and waywardness.'

'Of a certainty – my sister will ready herself on the instant.' Lowenna was grateful to hear another human voice. 'Why would no other address us before this? Are you hostile to our presence?'

The tall nun allowed a half-smile to soften her lips. 'We may only speak when given leave to do so,' she replied, 'and that applies to but a few. Most of our Sisters have not used their tongues in years – apart from eating and singing the Lord's praises – so do not read hostility into silence. We have no quarrel with you, only sympathy for your unhappiness when we have such joy in our devotion to God.' She exchanged the spent candle in their lantern for a fresh one. 'The two Sisters here will await outside to escort you to the chapel, but do not tarry. You must be on your knees before the bell ceases to toll.'

When she went, Lowenna tried to raise Meralda, encouraging her with a promise of possible hot food, but to no avail. Then, having recalled that prayers said by many together can sometimes result in miracles, and also beset by hunger, she resorted to a threat. 'You fill me with scorn, Meralda,' she rebuked her. 'Why this retreat into oblivion? Can it be the shame of having been so false with us? Of begetting disgrace upon our family, as you seem determined to do? Then I will leave you to your thoughts of perdition alone – and in the dark!' She seized the lantern and made for the door as Meralda cried out in terror.

'Wait! Do not scold and leave me! I am assailed by demons without and within! Help me to rise and I will come and pray with you.'

Having donned their cloaks, they were led outside into the grey light of dawn. Everything looked grey, Lowenna was thinking, the faint, lifting mist, the sky, the earth, the buildings – even the white habits of the nuns. Had the material become so coarsened with usage, she wondered, causing dirt and grime to be held in an inexorable grip within the fabric that no amount of cleansing water had been able to remove the tainted residue to render it pure white again? Is that what happened to some human souls? She felt her legs shaking, fearful of the effect this grey, unknown and remote region was having on her. Did purgatory, where souls went to be purified from venial sins, resemble this awful place?

Inside the chapel the brightness of the lamps and candles lifted her spirits, aided in part by the warmth generated by so many kneeling bodies crowded together. They had fallen to their own knees just as the bell ceased its commanding call to worship and the lady prioress made her stately way forward to stand facing them. She ordered that prayers should be directed towards casting out the Devil from Meralda, to that maiden's mortification and Lowenna's embarrassment, while the two maids were praying for an early return to life beyond this daunting place. The silent prayers completed, all rose to their feet as one Sister produced a pitch pipe to blow a single note to guide them into the lusty singing of a hymn of praise, after which they all walked a short way to the refectory.

Finding no benches, the two sisters stood before a long board that Lowenna believed must have been fashioned from the tallest tree that ever grew, straight and without visible join. The nuns ate and drank diligently without lifting their eyes from the board, mute, using their mouths solely for the purpose of chewing. Lowenna followed their example, feeling refreshed and more relaxed from the fare, simple as it was, and glad, too, for the peaceful atmosphere and lack of the harassment from which she had recently suffered overmuch. Meralda remained withdrawn, huddled in her cloak, still refusing anything offered.

When the prioress rang a handbell everyone bowed their heads for thanksgiving, and with the close of the meal the two maidens were taken outside for exercise and fresh air. Lowenna observed vegetables and herbs growing in neat rows and white flowers tended for their strong perfume to disguise odours. The nuns toiling there wore black work aprons over their habits to protect against soiling, girded about the waist with a knotted cord from which hung various implements required to be at hand, while others tended the beehives that supplied them with honey, all appearing happy and contented – in sharp contrast to themselves.

She glanced at Meralda, seeing her tense, trembling with violent spasms, her eyes darting this way and that until, impulsively, she broke from those about her like a boiling sea which, having been confined, surges forcefully through any opening in whatever impeded its flow. She fled towards where she imagined the entrance to the tunnel lay, but was unable to get far before being seized by several nuns, habits all a-flying, and brought back crying and protesting for both to be locked in the cell once more. Such was the penalty for trying to escape the inescapable.

Sister Columb was kindly, but serious, when she visited them later that morning. 'Your brother has brought us gifts this day and enquired as to your health and bearing. He will return on the morrow to hear of any change in your present disposition,' she said, addressing Meralda, who lay prone on the palliasse on which she had thrown herself when thrust back inside. 'It sadly seems necessary to keep you constrained in here as, while it would not be possible for you to leave, we cannot allow any disturbance to disrupt our daily pursuits. We are praying for a change in your demeanour so you may be able to travel with us to the church of Saint Perran, as time hastens away and departure is nigh upon us.'

Lowenna arose from her stool with an apology, gesturing towards Meralda. 'Forgive my sister's ill manners – she is compelled by some graceless spirit within her. I have never before seen her behave in such a despairing, unseemly way.'

'Ay, I was to ask for a fuller account of the reason for your enforced stay with us – the holy Mother desires it in order to direct our prayers.'

Lowenna found difficulty in answering, deeming it an act of disloyalty to disclose such personal family details to outsiders, but after glancing at Meralda she said, speaking low. 'My sister agreed to wed Viv...' – she bit her lip – '...the governor, but now refuses, having fallen in love with another – not of our faith. My own sin is that I did not hinder and betray her, and unless she complies with Father's demand to submit to his will, we shall remain within nunnery walls for always.' Having put her fear into words, the enormity of it was made more obvious and she paled.

'There would be nought to dread if 'twere your own choice but that, seemingly, is not so.' Sister Columb's voice had an edge to it. 'You know your Father must be obeyed, just as we all obey our Father in heaven who guides and keeps us from evil, and if your sister thinks she loves a heathen then the Devil is in command of her soul and must be cast out by the most expedient means.'

Until then Meralda had been lying still, listening. Now, unable to contain her anger at this apparent condemnation of Atlan, she got to her feet in a rage, tearing off her cloak. Lowenna was disconcerted by the extent of her disarray, uncomfortably aware that this was how the nun saw her, too, and must be equally shocked by her disordered appearance. Her gown had been severely ripped as she struggled with her captors, her long, fair hair hung lank and matted, her face was dirty and streaked with tears and her once clear, beautiful eyes were reddened, blotched and wild.

She approached the nun, standing insolently before her, hands on hips. 'And have you appointed yourself chief torturer in this prison, may I ask? Eager to prick and torment any tender, defenceless creature that you light upon whose views disagree with your own? You – in your ignorance – you can have no idea how wondrous real love is!' she taunted her. 'Have you ever lain in the arms of a lover and had his kisses and caresses send you swooning? Love, not the Devil, fills my heart and will never be cast out by any means at all!'

Sister Columb quietly regarded her with a superior air of equanimity, displaying no overt emotion. 'I would have it that your heart was filled with the love of the Lord Jesus, as is mine. The wonder of it is far greater than any other love and brings me peace and contentment – which yours evidently does not! Be mindful that I have been named for Saint Columb, the Christian maid who repulsed the attentions of her pagan suitor, and when he demanded that she renounce her faith she refused, so he killed her. You obviously lack her courage and steadfastness and must discipline yourself – or have it done for you. Victuals will be brought anon.' She turned, and had put herself on the other side of the door before Meralda could reach it and beat on it with her fists.

Her desperation began to affect Lowenna, who pulled her away. 'That will achieve nought. We must use the brains we have been blessed with to consider what the end will be if a miracle does not occur to make you obedient to Father's wishes. I trow I have no fervent desire to remain forever captive within walls like these, which impress me as the stalls in a stable solely for the use of mares!'

'Nor I!' agreed Meralda, vehemently. 'But I have no fear of that as, of a certainty, Atlan will rescue me!'

Lowenna gave a wan smile of disbelief. ''Twould be easier

112

to call upon Joshua to blow his trumpet and make the walls fall down than for any man to gain entry as they stand so solidly now, but I doubt the likelihood of either happening!'

Neither could settle, pacing up and down the room, facing opposite ways, each immersed in her own thoughts and each confronted by her own predicament. Meralda was bitterly regretting having refused to take the talisman Atlan had offered her. If only she had it to bring her solace! She flung wide her yearning, empty arms.

'Oh, I love him – I love him so much! I miss both him and the sight of the sea before my eyes. I cannot endure this captivity – I am dying inside of me!' She paused. 'I' truth, I *would* rather die than be wed to Vivian!'

'And *I* would rather be dead if unable to be near him, to see him, to touch his garments – even though he disregards my very presence. But what chance have I? If you fail to wed him we will both spend the rest of our lives as prisoners, and if you do…?' Lowenna covered her face with her hands. 'If you do, I fear the jealousy that might overcome and destroy me! You know I have always loved him – there will never be anyone else, so if mayhap you do submit, Meralda, my heart will break and 'twould be better were I shut up 'til I die!'

They continued pacing, one soundlessly praying to God and the other to Poseidon, until Lowenna cried out: 'I beg you, dear Lord above us! Is there no manner by which we can be saved this hopeless anguish? How can our discord be resolved? It seems I shall be the loser any one way or t'other!'

'You only consider yourself,' exclaimed Meralda, her tone reproachful. 'Should I not be a loser also? Nay, this must not be the way of it…' She suddenly stopped pacing. 'Stay,' she went on. 'Mayhap there could be a chance…'

She had been listening to footsteps outside and ceased speaking on hearing the door unbarred, watching the young nun carry in a tray with their meal. Putting it on the board, she retreated to the door while shyly offering them the same look of sympathy. Meralda stared after her for a long moment then, as if awaking from a deep sleep and with an amazing return to her previous decisiveness, whipped the cloth from the tray and sat down.

'Come, Lowenna,' she said, calmly. 'Please to join me – I am famished and faint from lack of nourishment. We must make every effort to conserve our strength and alertness should they be required of us. See, try a portion of the meat as I do...' She chewed hard. 'Not what we have been accustomed to, stringy and gristly, but edible if swilled down with water.' She gave the surprised Lowenna an encouraging smile. 'Be of good cheer, Sister – do not lose heart. Eat your fill, and afterwards we will discuss a possible way for us to escape.'

Lowenna was astonished by the sudden change in her, and when they had finished the unappetising meal and the nun came to remove the tray, her previously hostile sister politely requested another pitcher of water for washing. Cleanliness was not usually considered important and so not widely practised, but Richard's children had regularly bathed in the rivers and sea and enjoyed the freshness and vigour generated by a clean skin. When it was brought, Meralda washed the grime from her body and hair and begged the loan of a comb to free the tangles. This was not forthcoming, no one seeming to possess such a thing, so she had to make use of the teasels offered in its stead. Then Lowenna cleansed her own self, finding her spirits much improved by the discipline and less overburdened by their plight.

Meralda was her confident self once more. The failure of her plan to elope had brought such inward pain that her rational mind became impaired, giving rise to her contentious and resistant behaviour, then the anger induced by Sister Columb had jolted it back to sanity again. She completed her toilet by tying up her long, pale hair with a strip torn from her already torn gown, then regarded her sister.

'My dearest Lowenna,' she began, fondly. 'I ask forgiveness for the added burden with which I realise I have, without intention, overladen you. I never thought for you to suffer so.' She knelt by her side, taking her hand. 'Nothing can douse the flames of my love for you and our family, but they have been lessened by the desire I feel for Atlan. Both you and I need to love – as well as to be loved. Just think how you often reflect upon, and dream about, Vivian.' Closing her eyes, she envisaged her own ardour as she said: 'Can you not feel his arms around you, willing you to submit to his passion? Could you resist his advances as I have resisted Atlan 'til we can be wed? I have had to suppress my yearning until wedlock, a chastity ever taught as necessary for our honour, thus bringing no further hurt to Father.'

'So, in that way did God put a stop upon your lusting,' murmured Lowenna, 'with the hope that, given time, you would be induced to return to the fold.'

Meralda continued, unheeding. 'I could not sustain the guilt should I disregard what we have been taught, although I believe, having had my inner eyes opened, that for Atlan and myself other principles take precedence, as they did on Atlantis. They are forces which stem from long ago when God, having created everything in the beginning, created the lesser gods on Mount Olympus to act on His behalf over their limited dominions, such as Poseidon, who rules the seas. Therefore, God must be held responsible for them and what they do.'

Lowenna pulled her hand free from Meralda's grasp and held it across her sister's mouth. 'Hist!' she whispered. 'I fear your thinking is sadly awry – you could call down retribution with your blaspheming! Have we not enough to trouble us without that? You and Martin were ever quick-witted with your easy reasoning, and I the simple dullard to whom words mean little. I beg you to have a care!'

Meralda shook the hand away with a laugh that faded the

contemplative frown on her brow. 'You and I, no whit the same as my nature resembles Father's. I can be as ruthless and relentless as he, swayed by my determination to do what I think is right. Martin is from the same mould and so is Hicca, but Tressa and yourself resemble Mother with your soft hearts and kindliness. Though I mirror her outwardly, you reflect her innermost beauty – why, you have not ceased to be gentle even though I plague you constantly with my pettishness! But, I know who and what I am – I am *me*, and sure of the direction in which my future lies.'

'How fortunate you are!' Lowenna evinced her annoyance as she stood up suddenly, knocking over her stool, and began pacing again. 'But, what about *me*? Do not be forgetful that I am *me*, too. Once, I had a hope for my life, that m'Lord might somehow enter into it again, but now that he has, the only future I can see lies trapped within these bare walls – or others very like them – with no likelihood of ever setting my eyes upon the one I love or our family ever again!' She brushed tears from her cheeks and faced Meralda. 'You lately spoke of escape. Have you a plan whereby it could be brought about or was it said merely in bravado? 'Tis a foolish thought in any event, for where would we escape to?'

The young nun interrupted them by entering to remove the washing water. She tipped the bowl into a bucket and, as she passed Meralda, their eyes met and lingered, pity and esteem in one pair and calculation in the other, and as soon as she left, nuns outside closed and barred the door again. Meralda arose and moved around the room, lost in thought. Presently, she said: 'That little nun has sympathy for me. Perhaps she could be persuaded to exchange her garments with mine to let me walk free from this place.'

Lowenna considered before commenting. 'I fear she would be thrown into confusion if asked, being unable, because forbidden, to argue her case with you, and the two who stand without the door might hear your plea and be

116

aware of it. Besides, changing clothes would take time and they would wonder what was afoot.'

'Then mayhap I could stand unclothed behind the door and we could strip her of her garments, as she could not call for help, and tie her with pieces of my gown. I would don the habit and be away before anyone knew!' Meralda was excited.

'I perceive one insurmountable obstacle to your escape plan. As you rise head and shoulders above her the habit would barely cover your knees. Methinks that would be unlikely to go unobserved by the others!' Lowenna's sense of humour overcame her solemnity in a burst of half-suppressed laughter.

Her sister irritably stamped a foot, not sharing her amusement. 'Can you do nought else but mock?' she snapped. 'Whatever befalls, I cannot continue in these rags. Would Father expect me to be wed in such a poor condition?'

They both drew in a deep breath, enlightenment spreading across their faces. 'The wedding gown!' they cried in unison.

'Does it still lie in Trevelyan?' Meralda was intent.

'Why not? Father gave me the key to the chest to enable the gown to be tried for fitting when he left to begin the move, but you were seldom there. It was to be lifted out to clothe you on the wedding morn, then the chest shipped to lie in m'Lord's Trevivian home, awaiting its return.'

'So it has been forgot but should be here, ready for my use when I wear it to church. A better plan begins to form in my head – it must be fetched! Where is the key now, Lowenna?'

''Twas large and awkward to keep about my person,' she confessed, 'so I hid it away for safety.'

'Where? Will its container have been taken to the mainland?'

Lowenna shook her head. 'There is a small split in the tree in the courtyard, just above my head and only large enough to put a hand within, where I have always hidden things secret to me and told none other of the place. It lies there.'

'Ah – so you have ever kept things from me? No matter. Now – I have the scheme hatched – 'tis perfect to carry through. Mind you hearken to me well!' Meralda was sparkling with enthusiasm. 'You have to request the prioress to bid Martin bring an additional horse when next he visits, to enable you to ride with him to Trevelyan to fetch the gown at Father's behest, a necessity – you must insist – for the ceremony. It has to be you to propose it – they would never allow me to go with him. You can make it known that you have forgotten where you put the key and must search in divers places – thus being sure that Martin does not travel there alone for it.'

'I am following your words but cannot see how this can aid us. I find the key, unlock the chest, remove the gown and bring it here, then Martin departs and we remain as we were.'

'You goose!' laughed Meralda. 'You will not venture out at all! With my cloak wound about me and its hood over my face, *I* will be the one to escape! Martin will not suspect until the door is shut behind us, when I will tell him that I was let go after all. I have no doubt that Atlan lingers nearby to avail himself of any means to effect my release – I feel him close to me – then we can ride away and fetch the gown for our union. Lowenna – this is the chance I have prayed for!'

Lowenna was gazing at her sadly. 'So, you would abandon me here, alone? I had not once imagined that I would be deprived of your company – since none of this vexation has been of my contriving.'

'Oh, come, Lowenna!' Meralda showed impatience. 'It has happened, so why must we both suffer? By your own words, you have no expectation of achieving anything, while I have everything – to meet with the fulfilment of all my hopes. You cannot be so selfish!'

Lowenna was staring at her, open mouthed, collecting her

muddled thoughts, then settled on the one uppermost. 'Have you spared no thought for Martin?' her voice showed her concern. 'Should your lover be lying in wait, d'you think our brother would easily give you up to one he regards as a member of the Devil's fraternity? He would fight with all his strength – and mayhap suffer hurt – even death. Could you abear that?'

Meralda dismissed such a possibility with a toss of her head. 'Atlan would have the benefit of surprise and snatch me from my horse before Martin could recover from his usual reverie. There is no stallion that can outrun Mordon – he flies along as if borne up by the wind. Let your mind cease its useless wandering for mine is made up. It only remains for you to instruct the prioress of the importance of Mother's gown, mistakenly overlooked 'til now, which Martin will confirm to be in accordance with Father's wishes and make no demur.'

Eventually, under the pressure of Meralda's insistence, Lowenna reluctantly let herself be persuaded into a course of action she regretted having to follow, but one in which Meralda brooked no refusal. And so it was agreed.

# 8

## *The Chastening*

Although greatly distressed, Richard applied himself to matters affecting the other members of his family and his many dependents. He had at first viewed the hillfort with misgiving, regarding it as austere and primitive compared to the habitation his workers had enjoyed, then reminded himself that it would only be temporary whatever happened.

It was built on a hillock, set back above a cliff, and could house a number of men engaged in its defence. Circular and mainly uncovered, it had roofed areas built into the walls for sleeping quarters, off-watch places for rest, food preparation and stores, the largest holding the hearth for the fire, with a hole above it for smoke to escape and a shield suspended beneath to avert rain. There was also an all-important well for water within the thick, solidly built walls that provided a walkway around the top for those on lookout. This was edged by a parapet with archer's slits at intervals and reached by steps constructed against an inner wall. Entrance was gained through a heavy double gate.

The whole fort was surrounded by a palisade of pointed wooden stakes, and surrounded again by a wide ditch spanned by sturdy structures which were removed nightly and swung into position again by means of ropes and pulleys. The seaward side of the grassy hill sloped down to the edge of the cliff overlooking Perran Sands, Lyonesse visible in the distance. The Mount of Saint Michael dominated the view looking toward the farthest end of the Cornish mainland, the grey rock rising out of the forest.

When he had first made an appraisal, Richard ordered that the greater part of the fort should be roofed over to provide extra shelter, and as he approached it now with Jowan, riding across one of the bridges over the ditch, he was cheered to see that more than half had been covered. As only a few of the workers and their families could be accommodated inside, some, and in particular those responsible for the animals, were to be housed within the palisade, their huts already being erected.

Having dismounted, he found his way to a bench to rest his tired limbs, being immediately greeted with enthusiasm by Tressa and Hicca. Although it had not been many days since he had last set foot there, their hugs and kisses were repeatedly interrupted by many questions, demanding answers to satisfy, not only their curiosity, but also a need to establish some stability in this vastly changed environment.

'What have you brought us?' was asked simultaneously. After a necklace of shells and a small hunting knife had been handed over and examined carefully, Hicca was eager for news. 'What tidings have you of Martin and our sisters and when can we go back to Trevelyan? Does Lord Vivian even yet drool over Meralda? Shall it be long ere they are wed and we can all be together?'

Tressa was sitting on his knee, her arms about his neck, hoping to cajole him. 'Father, I beg you to let me see them wed. 'Twould be a sight for me to think on all my days. Meralda has told me how beautiful is Mother's gown, and I have such a desire to lay my eyes upon it! Will you not grant me this favour?'

Wedlock was not a subject that Richard was prepared, or willing, to discuss with anyone just then, and certainly not the children. He stood up, standing her on her feet in one swift movement. ''Tis not the outer covering that matters but what lies beneath – in the heart. That is what counts, child!'

Gweniver had come by to call them to sup, chancing to hear Tressa's plea and her father's short reply, and knew that something had occurred which troubled him deeply. She comforted his youngest daughter with the explanation that it was natural for him to be sad at the thought of losing Meralda from his household, but wanting to content herself and find out what was amiss, found and confronted Old Jowan. 'The master is disturbed. What has happened? Come, tell me, old man! You know I love the family dearly.'

But Jowan loyally kept his counsel, refusing to be drawn.

Meanwhile, Lord Vivian had been carrying out his affairs concerning the move with diligence, but though presenting a calm face to the world he was sorely troubled. He had not set his longing eyes on his beloved since the night following their betrothal, and the wedding was now due in three days time. He had thought at first that it was tricks of Fate keeping them apart, resulting in Meralda's absence from wherever he sought her, but as the hours passed his frustration increased and he looked for some other reason, with no success. He rarely met Richard because of the divergence of their destinations, one taking the ferry to the end of the mainland as being nearest to Trevivian, the other using boats in the south-east for Perranuthnoe and the hillfort, but whenever the occasion had arisen for their paths to cross, he found Richard behaving as if he believed the courtship to be proceeding well.

To add to his worry, he had a wavering doubt that this whole move could be in error, that he should not have so readily agreed to desert Lyonesse. His steward, servants and retainers were all in an ill humour, showing rancour at having to leave, and he found he constantly needed to remind them to pack their belongings and set off for the east coast. The chief landowners, too, were openly voicing their disapproval that the governor, so recently returned, was in the manner of a mouse turning tail to scamper off again, presumably afraid for his skin, calling him craven and faint-hearted behind his back, yet still refused to listen when he said it would be wise to heed the Seer's prophecy. Besides, he had daily to overcome his own incredulity as he observed the peaceful days of early autumn and the serenity of the people going about their usual tasks.

At Trevivian, too, he found resentment at the influx of men and beasts, though overcrowding was unlikely in the extensive compound sheltering those who lived and worked there. As he wandered through the bleak and bare rooms of the house he had once shared with Kweras, he wondered at his audacity in thinking to bring his new bride here to usurp her place, tempting her shade to revile them both. He resolved that Meralda would stay only fleetingly under this roof – he would build a new residence elsewhere.

On this day he hopefully went once again to Trevelyan, and was saddened to sense the desolate, empty atmosphere pervading it. The few remaining servant maids, busying themselves in a desultory fashion, could give him no answer regarding the whereabouts of Meralda and Lowenna, except they were gone away with the master and with no likelihood of return, suggesting he betook himself to Martin's church to make enquiry, and Vivian hurried there to discover that he, also, was absent. Close to desperation, he set off for the hillfort determined to meet with Richard along the way, and finally reached the small bay from which the boats transported the stock and contents of Trevelyan across to Perran Sands. Some of the men manhandling goods were encamped along the shore, where a rough shelter had been erected for storing provisions and as a place for apportioning out refreshment.

As Vivian dismounted there he saw Old Jowan in the distance, and being the middle of the day when it was customary to take a short rest, went inside to corner his quarry, soon espying Richard and Martin set apart from the men and huddled together in conversation. He could not guess that Martin had just arrived from the priory to report on the health of his sisters, bringing the news that Meralda yet showed obstinate defiance. He did note that, as they became aware of his presence, Martin seemed to give a guilty start and Richard at once ceased speaking, as the latter, having previously concocted an account for such an eventuality, was hurriedly gathering his wits to give plausible answers to the inevitable questions.

'Vivian, my dear friend!' he cried. 'You are well come – be pleased to join with us.' He indicated a place beside them on the bench where they had been leaning their backs against a support. 'Bring more wine!' he called, turning again to Vivian, correctly guessing by his solemnity that he was overly concerned about Meralda, that he would not be kept in suspense a moment longer and that his temper, usually equable, was dangerously inflamed.

'I demand to be told where you hold Meralda!' Vivian began contentiously, without preamble and displaying a militant stance. 'In what hidden place has she lain concealed these many days since we plighted out troth? Why do you keep her from me?'

Richard was both wounded and shocked by this unexpected attack, not realising until now the length of time that Meralda had played them both false in avoiding her betrothed. He was angered with himself for not having extracted more information from her, and hastily sought to improvise upon his rehearsed account.

'I? Keep her from you?' No one could doubt the surprise in his voice. 'But my earnest desire is to bring you, and keep you both together! I take no blame for your long separation – which I had not guessed at 'til this instant!'

Vivian regarded him with suspicion. 'Then why has she

124

been absent from Trevelyan whenever I called there, and Lowenna never able to help me gain a sight of her? Now she, too, has been spirited away and my forbearance is being sorely tried!'

Richard had risen to his feet and attempted to put an arm across his friend's shoulders, only to have it shrugged off in Vivian's anxiety to forgo courtesy for candid speaking.

'Do not excite yourself unduly, there is no occasion for alarm.' Richard gently tried persuasion. 'It could have been pure chance that brought about avoidance of each other, not intention. Meralda has had many outside tasks to engage her time, thereby giving rise to this elusiveness, whereas Lowenna has kept entirely within the household and so been excluded from her movements. Are you agreed, Martin?'

Martin nodded his tonsured head uncertainly, as Richard pushed a drinking cup toward Vivian. 'Would you have had her neglect her duties? To refrain from visiting the sick and needy or bidding farewell to her friends, simply to languish at your gates or the mill in the faint hope of you neglecting your own duties to come riding by? To thus play hide-and-go-seek with each other? My friend, come and seat your self and drink while I give my tidings. See, the frown already leaves your brow.'

Vivian slowly lowered himself, passing his fingers through his thick, brown hair as if drawing out the vexation that had been circulating in his head. 'Your chiding is well deserved. Forgive my impatience, which brought fanciful reasons for the absence of the one I love, and is why I have behaved in such a churlish manner. I am contrite – but have still not been made privy to her whereabouts so that I may place the Vivian Jewel in her hand to further adorn her when we wed.'

Richard lifted a foot and put it on the bench, leaning a forearm across his bent knee. 'Ah, the Vivian heirloom – I mind it well. I noted its beauty as it hung between Kweras' breasts...' He broke off, annoyed at his error, and re-embarked on his untruthful tale while hoping that God would understand his wish to prevent hurt to his friend and so forgive him.

'Let us return to our former discourse, Vivian. I'faith, 'twas not made known to me that Fate had kept you both apart in such a shameful way, but be that as it may, I have been eager to meet you to disclose that only yester-morn I deemed it prudent for the maids to have more protection in their separation from us. The notion would not leave me that, although the pirates have spared our shores for some time past, what would result if they return to assail us yet again? We might be with our men on the mainland, so who would guard my daughters? None but Martin, who might be committed elsewhere...'

He cast a sideways glance at Martin, who sat motionless, mouth slightly agape, before continuing hastily, '...and there was ever the chance of other adversities befalling them, so conscience smote me for having left my dear ones alone, vulnerable to any malign influence that came prowling.' He was very mindful of the fact that that was exactly what had happened. 'I would beg to remind you – as I myself was reminded,' he ended, 'that the Seer spoke of evil abroad on the island so, not losing any valuable time in seeking you out to gain your approval, Martin and I conveyed them to the Priory on the Rock for their safety and our easement.'

Vivian was silent for what seemed an age, then rose to his feet and pressed Richard's shoulder. 'I ask your pardon, my dearly loved brother,' he said gratefully, 'for that is how I have always regarded you. My very dear "older" brother,' he added, a faint smile playing around his lips and making a brave attempt at the raillery they had once both enjoyed. 'Will you ever be able to forgive me? How could I have doubted that your intent was to bring about nought but good? I feel such shame as can hardly be borne. Will you acquit me?'

126

Richard was moved but discomfited. 'Of a certainty – but there must be mutual forgiveness. I was careless in my regard for the safety of my kin, blind to any danger 'til I beheld the possibility, but am consoled that harm cannot reach them now and Martin visits daily to enquire upon their welfare. The redoubtable Sisters are on guard and have agreed to bring them safely to us when the greater part of the body of the priory present themselves for Mass on the day of the feast, so that Meralda will be able to stand at your side. Afterwards, we will all leave together for the mainland.'

Vivian sank back on the bench, relief softening his taut features. 'I live for that day,' he said. 'Without Meralda my life would go for nought.'

Richard gave a nervous glance at Martin, saying: 'I have just had a worrying thought. 'What if she finds life in the priory so much to her liking that she chooses to remain? 'Twould be impossible to remove her by force from that fortress, and the lady prioress would doubtless be unwilling to give her up.'

Vivian's face stiffened once more, his eyes flashing with anger. 'What devilry! How can you so cruelly profess to jest? You do me no kindness with your waggishness! Should I allow myself to entertain that thought for an instant I would affirm that my life would be forfeit, taken by mine own hand!'

Richard was startled by the violent effect his words had produced, having intended only to instil into Vivian's head the possibility of her staying there, and tried to lessen his friend's misgiving. ''Twas but surmise on my part and never said to grieve you. Let us have done with such maudlin ideas and drink to the fulfilment of our hopes and wishes!'

But despite Richard's efforts to cheer him, Vivian was unable to throw off his melancholy and soon announced his intention to depart. 'I am relieved to learn that Meralda is safe,' he said, adjusting his sword belt and fastening his cape, 'but I shall not rest 'til we are met and I am able to keep her forever by my side.' He transferred his attention to the young priest. 'You have kept strangely silent, Martin. Are all the arrangements for the ceremony ordered?'

Martin assumed a wooden expression. 'Ay – all is made ready.'

'Then I will bid you farewell.'

Richard followed behind him into the open air. 'Preparations at the fort are about done. I cannot thank you enough for your kindliness and neither can Hicca and Tressa, who grow restless to greet Meralda and yourself when you have been made as one – but I have enjoined them to wait 'til afterwards. As soon as the wedding party arrives at Trevivian, you newly-weds will be left there in seclusion while the rest of us travel on to meet up with the children at the fort. Later, when betimes you have bedded your bride, we will rejoin you.'

'We will do whatever Meralda desires, Richard.' Vivian took the reins from the lad holding his horse. 'This may well be the last time we see each other until we meet, God willing, at the ferry to greet the archdeacon, then on to the church to celebrate Mass and the union of our houses.'

The two men briefly held each other close before Vivian swung himself into the saddle, a pensive smile lingering on his drawn, tired face, then with a wave of the hand he galloped away.

'God go with you, friend!' Richard called after him, now even more determined that Meralda must be made to fulfil her commitment without causing Vivian further, even fatal, hurt.

Martin and Old Jowan were standing by his elbow. 'Father, I am afeared for that good man,' said his son. 'I regret but realise the necessity for your straddling of the truth. You did well in setting him at ease at the start, but later…I suppose 'twas wise to prepare him for a reversal of his hopes, though he is so far gone in passion I doubt he will accept anything other. Meralda is set fair to resist to the end but, should she be made to surrender to persuasion, what kind of pretence would she make of the marriage? 'Twould be obvious to a man without his senses that she was acting double-faced.'

'Mayhap he would even settle for that, he is in such thrall to his ardour. I rue the day I put my trust in those foolish maidens!' Richard ended fiercely. He lifted his face to the sky, silent for a moment. 'I pray to You, God, for some miracle bearing upon Meralda, but am unsure whether You would care to waste one upon such a deceitful maid! I also beseech You to aid and take pity on my dear friend Vivian.'

He looked to see that Martin and Old Jowan had bent their heads and put their palms together. 'Have You given ear to our prayer, God?' Richard accentuated every word. 'Then I thank You for listening. I know, indeed, that You always hear me but I speak also for these others who stand with me who beg this one especial miracle of You, that m'Lord Vivian will at last find comfort in the arms of the one he loves, having been denied my beloved Ysella in her lifetime!'

There came no flash of lightening, nor did the clouds part to reveal angels and celestial visions, but Richard's plea had been spoken with such intensity, willing it to be heard, that the three men had no doubts that God, and all the company of heaven, had been attendant upon them. Each returned to his duties feeling less anxious and more hopeful of the outcome.

*

The two sisters in the priory were sharing similar feelings, and on the morning appointed for Martin to accompany Lowenna to Trevelyan their cell door opened and the small nun entered to escort Lowenna to the gate. She saw two cloaked and hooded figures, one peering through the slit window and the other, nearer the door, venturing to pass her and move through it. Being short, she was able to look up into the hood – to find herself staring into Meralda's large, luminous eyes. Neither made any sign though both held their breath, but Meralda felt no restraining hand upon her as she continued on through. There, her progress was checked by a flurry of skirts coming along the corridor effectively barring the way, and from the centre of the group stepped the lady prioress, her clear intention being to enter the gloomy, unlit cell. She was followed by her escort, with Sister Columb, who seemed to be next in importance, at her shoulder, and Meralda was forced to retreat until she stood back inside, ending her regression almost beside Lowenna. The small nun's gaze had remained firmly fixed on the floor.

The prioress, her swiftness of movement belying her age, stood peering about her. 'Why is the lamp dark? Someone put a flame to it. Now, I have come directly from the gate,' – the old voice was brisk – 'having been called there to hear a request, and am undecided whether or not to grant it. It was agreed for Lowenna to ride out for the gown, but I am not yet convinced that you, Meralda, will consent to don it. My Sisters inform me that the Devil still holds sway, my child, and there remains much resistance to your father and to God. What have you to say? And why are you both cloaked?'

'Against the cold...' The muffled utterance could have come from either figure, the silhouette at the window having swung around in surprise at the presence of visitors. '...And, of a surety, the gown *will* be worn!'

''Tis good to hear.' The old head nodded, pleased. 'I ask because our governor stands with your brother at the gate. 'Tis he who has begged a sight of you, Meralda, destined to become the future Lady of Lyonesse, as I understand it. He brings a wedding gift to place in your hand, and wishes to be assured of your health and happiness before you meet in church on the morrow.' She was wondering if her ears had heard, or only imagined, twin gasps. 'Meralda?' she queried, and as no sound came from either: 'Why d'ye keep silent? Which of you is Meralda?'

At her gesture, Sister Columb went to pull back the hood of the figure nearest the door and met with resistance. In the brief scuffle that ensued, an arm became entangled in the chain holding a crucifix around her neck, causing it to break and drop into the straw at her feet, just as the hood fell away to reveal Meralda's angry face, her dream of escape smashed into sherds. Sister Columb, with a look as of stone, stooped to retrieve her treasured crucifix without bothering to search for the now useless chain.

Meralda's thoughts were centred on herself, her rage at being thwarted blinding her to all else. 'The fool! Why did he have to come? I want no sight of him now, on the morrow, or ever again – and the gown can stay where it is!' She threw off the cloak and flung herself down on her straw bed, burying her head in her arms.

'I see you are fevered about this.' The prioress held her own anger in check. ''Tis very plain that we have failed to cleanse you of your sinful conduct.'

Lowenna uncovered her own face, aglow with joy at the nearness of Vivian, but fearing that the chance of a longed-for, perhaps last, encounter with him could fast disappear. She fell to her knees, pleading: 'Holy Mother, let me yet go to Trevelyan for the gown, and on my return I will renew my prayers and do my utmost to change Meralda's heart back into the ways of uprightness so she will be content to wear it – I entreat you!'

The prioress considered, knowing her to have been party to the attempted deception but rightly suspecting that she had not been the instigator. To her surprise, she found her heart softening, held by the manifest aura of love surrounding this maid, outpouring from the eyes in the young, eager face. She recognised it as being akin to the pure, spiritual and selfless love that she ever hoped to see but rarely witnessed, though according her profound bliss when she did.

'My earlier decision stands, and we must trust that the gown *will* be needed, Lowenna,' she said, her voice husky, deeply affected by her rare sentiment, and reminded she had been taught that God himself is love – not merely a stern dispenser of divine judgment on righteousness.

'Sister Adwen – escort her to the gate,' she ordered the small nun. 'You have permission to speak to those who wait beyond it, to say that Meralda is overwrought by the approach of her espousal and unable to appear but sends greetings to her lord. You, hold your tongue and show agreement with these words, Lowenna!'

'You have my pledge upon't, holy Mother!' She glanced at her sister's prone figure. 'While I am gone, Meralda, think well on the hurt you could bring to all who care for you – and pleasure me with a change in your demeanour when I return,' she called over her shoulder, Sister Adwen at her heels.

When they were out of earshot, the lady prioress brought her thoughts back from the sublime, transferring her attention to the form that lay twisting its body and beating its fists in frustration, and her heart was hardened once more. 'I see the Serpent writhing within you, Meralda, and it must be cast out without further hindrance. Sisters,' she bade her attendants. 'Take her to the cell of correction and whip her 'til that Thing from hell inside her cries out for mercy!'

\*

When Lowenna arrived at the gate she was tense and breathless, feeling that she could have been heedlessly running towards a destination she might not want to reach. The small nun, supposed to be preceding her, had found

132

difficulty in keeping up with her headlong rush and lagged behind. Unsure of her welcome from Vivian, the anticipated presence of Meralda being denied him, Lowenna determined to make the most of this brief moment of freedom no matter where this day would ultimately lead. She stood anxiously by the gate until Sister Adwen arrived panting, her wimple askew. After making the appropriate sign to an obviously disapproving gatekeeper that she was permitted to speak to those waiting, the slot was pulled aside and she tried to peer through, teetering on the tips of her toes. Lowenna heard the message uttered slowly with a high, lilting clarity.

'Our holy Mother bids me say that Meralda is too overcome by the nearness of her espou…espousal to attend upon you, but sends greetings and…her sister awaits to join you!' She ended on a quick, rising note, dropping her heels with evident relief, cheeks flushed, eyes bright, having enjoyed her moment of importance and the rare use of her voice.

Lowenna had a brief glimpse of the blankness on Vivian's face before the gatekeeper closed the slot. She heard muffled argument from without as the door was opened and she stepped over the door-case into her brother's welcoming arms. 'Oh, Martin!' She clung to him, hiding her head in the familiar roughness of his habit.

He held her thus for a while before lifting her chin to kiss her upturned face, sure he knew the real reason for Meralda's non-appearance, and hurriedly said: 'We cannot tarry with idle discourse here, and must have a care not to stay overlong at Trevelyan lest the tide strand us on the beach.'

But Vivian was not to be deterred from obtaining immediate news. He grasped Lowenna's hand, holding it so firmly that her ring bit into the flesh. Seeing her wince and realising what caused her pain, he at once released it. 'I meant you no hurt, Lowenna,' he said gruffly. 'My clumsiness was due to unease for Meralda. Did she send word of her goodwill and hopes for our future? Is in good spirits? How did you leave her? My disquiet torments me with none able to allay it. You have just left her side so I have no recourse but to trust your account. I plead for your answers!'

'My Lord,' Lowenna spoke softly, sympathy engulfing her as she realised the extent of his disappointment and unhappiness. 'Her converse consists solely of her hopes for the future and how she longs for the time when she will depart this place, and there is nought amiss with her well-being except having been wearied by the events that have occurred of late.'

Vivian took her roughly again by her upper arms, forcing her to look into his eyes. 'Swear it!' he demanded. 'Swear that she has met with neither sickness nor harm or been laid down by death to steal my beautiful swan from me!'

Lowenna kept her gaze steady, thinking that while it was true that swans were beautiful, they could also be fitful and well able to inflict grievous hurt. Face to face as they were, she knew he was not registering who was standing before him, his thoughts drawn firmly within the priory. She studied the deep lines etched into his anxious features and noted the first sprinkling of white hairs that had so recently made a showing amid the rich chestnut. How she longed to touch them and kiss him and care for him – to smooth his path through life and give him ease!

'I'faith – I speak nought but truth,' she said faintly, knowing that indeed it was so, but hating the deception and the fact that she was misleading him with false hopes. 'I swear that I left her laid upon her bed, alive and reflecting on the future!'

Martin was watching them, wondering how Vivian could possibly fail to notice the love flowing from Lowenna, while hoping she would not let slip that they were held in the priory against their will.

134

He had earlier been discomfited by Vivian's unexpected arrival in the stable adjoining his church, saying he remembered Martin making mention of his daily visits to the priory and wished to accompany him this day to ask for a sight of Meralda. He had been too surprised to think of a way of avoiding it and had no recourse but to agree, remarking that he was choosing a mount for Lowenna to ride with him to Trevelyan to retrieve a gown, trusting that might deter him. Instead, it had the reverse effect, Vivian expressing the hope that it would be Meralda who would go, and as he lingered over his selection Martin tried to explain that it was Lowenna who had to go to find a key, and supposed Meralda would wish to stay resting before confronting the important day ahead.

Standing now outside the priory, he was pleased that both Lowenna and the nuns had confirmed his surmise. 'Come,' he urged, bringing his concern back to their present situation. 'There is little time to be wasted or we miss the tide for our return. What is your intention, m'Lord? Will you now be about your own affairs?'

As the vehemence of his emotion evaporated, Vivian appeared to be drained of all colour and volition. He stepped back, looking askance as if uncertain of what to do next, finding himself without direction, finally saying: 'Love is making a mockery of me. I will join with you. Let us go to Trevelyan.'

\*

Meralda had been right in her assumption that Atlan would stay close at hand, waiting for any opportunity to present itself that would secure her release. He had remained hidden within the stunted trees where he could observe both the island and the road, subsisting on the plentiful supplies of nuts and berries that surrounded him and slaking his thirst with water from a nearby stream flowing to the sea. Plan after plan had been considered and quickly discarded as unfeasible. He noted the short daily visits made by Martin, and thought perhaps to rob him of his habit and take his place but suspected the ruse would be unlikely to succeed. There was also the pressing matter of a bride for Poseidon.

But this day, the day before Saint Martin's feast by his reckoning, there was a change in the routine, for apart from being later in the morning there were two horsemen approaching, one richly caparisoned and the other leading a riderless horse. As they drew nearer he recognised Martin, so in all probability the unknown second man would be the governor, but what of the third mount? Had Vivian come for Meralda already? Then why leave Lowenna? Or was it t'other way about? Atlan fingered his talisman as he attempted to grapple with these questions, glad only that something to break the tedium was about to happen.

He had a longer wait than usual before he saw the horses returning to make their way back through the surf, then his heart leapt! Martin was in the lead, with the man he supposed to be Vivian coming last, and between them a cloaked and hooded figure that might be...? It was all he could do to prevent himself from riding out to snatch her from her horse, but managed to hold back while considering the wisdom of attempting such a rash action.

As the three rode along the spit of land, Lowenna suddenly remembered what Meralda had said about her possible rescue by Atlan, that he would ride in and take her, so threw back her hood, releasing the long, black hair that streamed out behind her, hoping it would act as a signal to him to refrain from making any impetuous move.

When he saw it his thoughts were again plunged into confusion. Why had Meralda been left behind? Was it conceivable that she had already been removed under cover

136

of darkness – perhaps by boat? His heart pounded uncomfortably, though knowing it was only supposition that fuelled his anxiety, there also being the problem of delivering Lowenna to be the bride of Poseidon, and here she was, close at hand and ready to be stolen away to placate Tardhamor. He could ride in swiftly now and lift her from her horse, but that would engender the certainty of a skirmish with her escorts when he might receive a thrust from the governor's sword before being able to put his own dagger to good use, a risk he would surely have taken had it been for Meralda. But for Lowenna...?

He reminded himself he must take care in everything he attempted until he had established Meralda's exact whereabouts and bring her safely out of harm's way, but for the present he would try to discover the reason for Lowenna's journey, so began to follow at a safe distance. Thus quarry and stalker finally neared Trevelyan.

\*

When they arrived, Vivian reined in his horse while Martin and Lowenna rode on into the deserted courtyard, Martin helping her dismount before looking back.

'Come and refresh yourself, m'Lord – Lowenna has to search for a key before she can bring the gown into the light of day,' he suggested cheerfully, as she walked away. 'I can but offer water from the well – though it tastes as sweet as any other liquor.'

Vivian stayed in the saddle, regarding him with sad eyes. ''Twould bring me no refreshment. I am mindful of the feast and your decision not to depart out of danger. Can you not be induced to come with us – to ease your Father's fretting?'

A smile lit up the ingenuous face. 'It might give him comfort that I stay where Mother lies buried.' Then, wondering: 'Are you desirous of seeing the place?'

Vivian shook his head, sharply. 'I cannot believe she is there.'

'You speak truth – her soul is elsewhere, and as for my remaining – who knows what the morrow may bring? My faith in God enables me to trust Him to make clear His plan in His own good time. Now, heed what I say. D'ye remember I once confessed I had been granted a vision in a dream?'

'Ay, but not of how 'twas composed.'

'It may be as well to explain. The scene was dim, but I was in a place with flickering candles crowded with frightened people craving my comfort, as if only I could give it and lead them to glory. Then there came a great, rushing wind and a light far brighter than the sun and I felt myself lifted by strong hands. I looked into a face close to mine and saw 'twas the face of Jesus Himself. Since that day I have been His most fervent disciple and will remain so, waiting to see what beckons. 'Twould aid you to adopt patience and also have faith in Him and His compassion…I entreat you not to divulge my confidence to anyone.'

Vivian leaned down and pressed his shoulder. 'Of a surety. I give you my word and my thanks for disclosing what is concealed within your heart and will endeavour to match your faith, you have my word upon't.' He glanced about him. 'This desolate mill house, once joyous, fills me with sadness. I must leave you, but first…' – he reached into a saddlebag and produced a small, finely fashioned pouch. 'For many days I have tried to find Meralda to give her this token – 'tis a jewel passed down through my female forebears. She is to wear it at the altar, as has been our custom, and I beg you to contrive this for me. Now, I must go.'

Martin took it from him. 'I have heard many a tale told of the beauty of the Vivian Jewel and will see your errand done.'

Lowenna had approached, having pretended to search for the key for Martin's benefit, and finding the two men talking earnestly was just in time to hear Vivian's final words.

Anxious to keep him there, she said: 'M'Lord, be pleased to dismount – you are not refreshed – and do you not wish to cast your eyes upon Mother's wedding gow...?' She stopped, realising by his attitude that she had erred.

He had turned his horse sharply but stayed, unsmiling, to say: 'The last time I saw Ysella's gown it clothed her in beauty, and when next I see it, it must clothe m'Lady or stay lost to my sight forever!' He urged his horse away without a farewell, leaving Lowenna crestfallen, with no expectation of ever seeing him again.

Brother and sister stood motionless until Martin grew aware of Lowenna's silent distress and took her arm in his, trying to distract her with questioning. 'What news have you of our miscreant sister? Are our prayers holding sway over her? Is she disposed to be amenable to her intended?'

Lowenna shook her head miserably. 'Her determination to defy Father and her lord, whom she still despises, increases if anything. I cannot conceive of a way to ensure the relief of his suffering unless it be by God's intervention. Whenever my eyes alight upon him it wrings my heart.'

Martin held her to him. 'If only he could be made to see how much you care for him,' he said softly, his cheek resting against her head, 'and thus quench his passion for Meralda. 'Tis sad that, unless it be by a person's own accordance, only old age – or death – can efface memory.'

He felt Lowenna shudder and regretted his words, at the same time remembering the pouch and holding it out to her. 'M'Lord requires this token, an heirloom, to be given to Meralda to wear as they are wed, otherwise it must, in all honour, be returned to him – I place it in your care. For the present, cease your maudlin worrying and allow yourself to trust in God's wisdom by not seeking to have your own desires gratified over His greater understanding.'

Her tolerance was again overcome as she flung herself from him. 'Then why does He not spare a thought for how I feel? Why did He arrange for Meralda to have two men adoring her while I have none? I will have attained seventeen years on Christ's Mass day, well past the age when I could be wed, and each time I see m'Lord my pain increases when he looks through me, as through a ghost. Failing to see that I am a child no longer and how much I love him – how much I have always loved him! I foresee that I shall go to my grave and he remain unknowing that he was loved as much as any man could be!'

Martin tried to pacify her. 'Do not despair, Lowenna – look to your strength. Believe that everything will happen for the right reasons in the final resolution. Once I had a love like yours and thought nothing could surpass it. I lived in torment 'til I found a greater love, so I know what you are enduring…'

She stamped her foot in anger. 'I have no sureness that you do, Brother, and neither has anyone else!' Then her fury was spent, leaving her forlorn, guilty. 'In my self-pity I have neglected to ask the condition of the others – Father, the children, Gweniver, Old Jowan…' her voice wavered.

'I have no adverse tidings of them,' he answered, gently.

''Tis well – now I must fetch the key,' she said, moving towards the tree.

Martin felt the need of respite from this charged atmosphere to clear his mind, and thought of a way to accomplish it. 'While you are thus occupied, I will ride out to the church of Saint Ana to say prayers over Mother's grave – and try to make peace with the Brothers for one last time. I have not laid eyes upon them since Father's vexed visit to the Seer.' He went to his horse. 'The time will barely advance 'til I return, little Sister, while you are sure to find things to occupy you,' he said tenderly, and set off at a gallop.

# 9

## *The Jewel*

Left by herself, Lowenna retrieved the key and climbed the steps to the gallery, opening a door into one of the family rooms. Clouds had blanketed the sky since dawn but it remained dry and warm, so she unshuttered a window to banish the mustiness before making her way to the chamber she had shared with Meralda, loosening her soiled attire as she went in search of other clothing. Her hopes were dashed on finding that everything of that nature had already gone to the mainland, and all she could discover were a few hairpins, which she decided to take with her.

Going to her father's room she opened wide the door leading out above the courtyard, not only for fresh air but to let in more light. She found the chest where it had stood for many years and gently caressed its carved surface while reflecting on her mother, wishing she was here to advise her. With a sigh of regret she put down the pouch and inserted the ornate key into the lock, but found it resisted all her efforts to turn it. She looked around for something with which to bind the haft to enable her to increase the pressure, espying a length of cloth lying on the floor that her father had worn around his neck, and with it managed to turn the key and free the heavy lid. Raising it released fragrant and aromatic perfumes of dried herbs and spices, smelling as fresh as the day they had been placed inside to thwart any insect damage to the precious material. She lifted out a large, closely woven linen bag and laid it on the floor, pulling the fastening ties apart and folding it back to reveal the gown, catching her breath in wonder as she gazed at it.

She retained a vague remembrance of having seen it when she was very young and her mother had shown it to Meralda, making her promise to wear it at her espousal when she found her true love. Then she had smiled at Lowenna, who was visibly disappointed, saying mayhap it would be her – it depended on who first became betrothed. She had told them it was fashioned in Cornouaille on the mainland of France over the sea, where she had been born, and brought to Lyonesse for her union with Father.

Tears pricked her eyelids and were hastily wiped away before they could fall on the unusually delicate, filmy material that Lowenna had never seen elsewhere, also unusual in that it was white – brides generally favoured a colour – and there was an accompanying length to cover the head, some brides veiling themselves for modesty's sake. Holding the gown against her, she looked for some means to mirror her reflection, finding a sizable sheet of metal leaning against a wall which, though somewhat dulled, had once been burnished until it shone and used by her mother for the same purpose. She moved to stand in front of it, entranced.

Below the high neck was sewn a small, gathered cape that extended over the shoulders and dipped at the back, the sleeves flouncing out into fullness, one edge resting on the wrist whilst the lower edge touched the ground. The bodice was fitted to the figure down to the tiny waist, then was joined to a voluminous skirt which also dipped at the back. At each movement the diaphanous fabric seemed to float with the lightness of swan's-down, and was loose-lined with cloth barely more substantial. Staring at herself in admiration, she was minded of her mother's words that she might be the next one to wear it, and decided to take this opportunity to make it so.

'Since it becomes more and more improbable that neither Meralda nor I will ever wear it in church, I must – I really must – see how it beautifies me!'

She let her clothing drop to the floor and stepped, naked, into the mass of whiteness, wondering if it would feel the same as entering a fleecy cloud, being brought sharply down to earth when she found that the front fastening of the bodice would meet only when pulled together with difficulty. Her bosom was fuller than her mother's, but she knew the gown would fit Meralda like her own skin. Determined to overcome this setback, she wrapped the cloth used to hold the key tightly around her breasts and managed to do up the fastenings. Though her breathing was restricted, that was forgotten when she saw herself and marvelled at the reflected vision, her black hair accentuating the whiteness enveloping her.

As she moved to swirl the skirt her foot touched the pouch lying on the floor and, curious, she untied the top. Her searching fingers pulled out a golden chain attached to…She could hardly believe what she saw – a huge pearl held in a delicate cage made of fine strips of gold – like a full moon seen through a latticed window. She had never imagined a pearl could be that size! She held it to the light and swung it, marvelling at its milky, phosphorescent lustre of soft blue, grey, pink and green. She slipped the chain over her head and settled the pearl on her bosom, wishing with all her heart that Vivian would enter, and finding her thus arrayed, fall madly in love with her, unable to resist this tempting creature he had hardly noticed for weeks past.

As the thought formed in her mind, so the room darkened as the open door was filled. She turned quickly, a smile lighting her face, believing for an instant her wish had come true, but it was soon replaced by fear as she sensed this was no friend, realising by the silent approach that she had reason to feel threatened and knowing it would be useless to scream. She put a protective hand over the pearl and turned.

Atlan had held back when within sight of Trevelyan until he saw what he thought to be the governor ride away, shortly followed by Martin in his distinctive habit. The mill appeared deserted but others might be there – or had Lowenna fortuitously been left alone, defenceless, unknowing that it was in his mind to take and deliver her to the Sacred Grove and Tardhamor?

Cautiously entering the open gate he had sought until he found her and, stepping into the room, caught her by the wrist as she shrank back. 'Do not fear, Lowenna,' he said, without menace. 'I mean you no hurt – I merely look for tidings of Meralda.'

Lowenna found fright giving way to a timorous calm now she knew the identity of this unexpected visitor – but was he really unexpected? She should have guessed he would come. Endeavouring to keep her voice steady she said, haltingly: 'She is kept in the priory – your plan to wed was discovered by Father. She remains in good health, but I am the only one permitted outside the walls. We attempted to change places this day so she could leave and be free to escape – but that came to nought – though I was yet allowed to come to fetch this gown for her to wear on the morrow for the…'

Her words trailed away as he bent to touch it, his blue eyes ablaze. 'Hah!' His laugh was derisive. 'So this was the reason for her return here, allowing herself to be caught like a fish in a net! Is that the truth of it?' He flung her arm down.

Lowenna could now take time to observe him, seeing what a truly powerful and handsome young man stood before her. She found she could understand why Meralda was so attracted to him, though believing that the allure should have been resisted, and no longer felt afraid as she

144

recognised the same pain behind his blue eyes that she had so recently seen ravaging Vivian's brown ones.

'Ay, that is the truth of it!' She spoke quickly. ''Twas decreed by divine Providence that she be caught for her own good! I might find it in my heart to feel pity for you had you not been the cause of so much turmoil for us, and there is nought you can do for her now. If she refuses to wed Lord Vivian, as she continues to do, we will both be condemned to remain prisoners in some nunnery 'til our final breaths!'

It was Atlan's turn to show disquiet, regarding Lowenna as if considering her a person for the first time, as previously her sole use to him was to become the bride of Poseidon. He had yet to decide how to further that end but, in the meantime, her words gave him pause.

'You also?' And when she nodded, he went on: 'You are too comely, as is your sister, to have to endure such a dire fate spread over the years – better swift mortal pain and soon done with. For Meralda and I, death is of little consequence as we shall reawaken to life in Atlantis, but I must prevent her further distress here.'

Lowenna was experiencing discomfort both from the tightness of her bodice and a fresh anxiety. 'You must go – I should not converse with you at all! My brother will come at any time and I fear for what might happen if he finds you here.'

Atlan seemed unperturbed by this disclosure, standing with arms folded across his broad chest, deep in contemplation. 'There is no occasion for your concern,' he said at last. 'My horse is wise and senses other hooves approaching through his own. He will warn me in time to avoid your brother, who took the road to the north and will return from thence as I go south. Now, I see you could not resist a sight of yourself in what looks to be an ocean of white foam, which has given me a notion by which to save your sister from the

145

imprisonment promised her – and mayhap yourself as well. Let me explain…'

Lowenna did not want to listen – she wanted him gone. How could he possibly help either of them? Besides, her bosom was feeling so confined she thought she might lose her senses. 'You cannot save us. I will not speak further with you!'

He loomed above her, persisting. 'Tell me exactly what measures are planned for the morrow? And what is your brother's intention on his return here?'

Lowenna cowered back from his vigour. 'He will escort me back to the priory then go to his church, leaving me to spend the dark hours with Meralda who will, everyone hopes, at last accept Father's ruling. Should she do such an unlikely thing, then just before dawn the lady prioress, most of the Sisters and we two will begin journeying to the church of Saint Perran where the archdeacon will celebrate Mass, and after…' Her voice faltered, before she continued in a whisper, '…he will wed…'

'Never!' Atlan's violent reaction caused her to feel another stab of fear. He moved around the room, eyes fixed on the floor, concentrating on forming his plan into a viable scheme that would have a good chance of a successful outcome.

Lowenna, having little faith in the ability of Atlan's horse to warn him, was straining her ears for Martin's horse, dreading to hear the sound. She had not the slightest doubt that, were it to come to a confrontation, which man would emerge the victor – she had only to glance at the muscles rippling on Atlan's body to be certain of the result. But, what if he delayed much longer? The bodice was constricting her so severely that she felt she must tear it open to rid herself of the constraint, and that would be impossible with regard to her nakedness beneath. Unwisely, she clutched at her bosom, freeing the pearl. Its lustre caught Atlan's eye, his

146

body stiffening as he took a step forward and Lowenna, believing he was about to seize it, drew away. But he was merely astonished, knowing it for what it was.

'It has been given to Meralda to wear with this gown,' she said hastily.

'There is no fairer neck for it to grace,' Atlan replied, absently, 'but it belongs to the sea and Poseidon and should be restored to the place from whence it was stolen. However, it has brought me the answer I sought.'

He began to speak in a deliberate manner, holding her eyes in an hypnotic stare, forcing her to attend to his every word, to remember and obey them. ''Tis the idea you gave me 'bout changing places and for you to attempt again. On your return, you will induce Meralda to play her part, and agree to wed Vivian.'

Lowenna attempted to shake her head, but his gaze still held hers. 'She will never agree…' she said weakly.

'She will, when you explain fully,' he insisted. 'Listen to me. When they come to escort you to the church, *you* will wear this gown and this jewel – be sure you are not parted from it! You will pretend to be the bride, covering your head in some manner, whilst your sister hides herself in her cloak. You will be the one they guard so that Meralda is able to move unnoticed. Tell her that on the beach beneath the priory crag are many tall rocks, so she must slip away in the darkness and conceal herself behind one of them. When you have gone on your way, I will find and carry her off to be wedded to me – her rightful spouse.'

Lowenna was listening in disbelief. ''Tis not possible – you do not know how we are watched.'

'Then make it possible,' he urged.

She demurred. 'I have often helped Meralda and each time regretted her artful persuasion – now I harken to yours. Nay, I could not be so disloyal to my father or to m'Lord; they would never forgive me. How could I continue to live knowing that every day they would curse me for my deceit? I cannot abear to think on't!'

Atlan had prepared himself for argument. 'Imagine, if you can keep up the pretence 'til after the ceremony, you will be wedded to the man you love.' He glanced askance at her, knowing the falseness of his words. 'Why, he might even have to accept you as his bride and keep you by him. Anyways, you are certain to be discovered and questioned as to Meralda's whereabouts, so you will tell them she is in the Town, in Breonseyth, for the men to go in search of her there and leave you alone. Then, should you suffer rejection by the governor and your kin, you will find my horse waiting near the church to carry you to where Meralda and I are biding. Your future care will then be assured…'

He was thinking that would be true when she was delivered to Tardhamor and he had found a plausible tale to satisfy Meralda. '…But, should you betray me,' he continued aloud, 'and she is forced to wed the governor – and even if she does not – Poseidon will aid me in seeking him out through water and fire to slit his gullet, and I shall find and release her from wherever she is held, do you understand?'

Lowenna nodded forcefully, now fearing for Vivian's life – which had been Atlan's intention – wondering if she was being tempted by Satan in the guise of this comely youth or offered heaven-sent grace. Then a warning whinny came from the courtyard below and Atlan was going to the door.

'Your brother is not yet nigh, but I shall leave now.' He faced her squarely, his intense blue eyes burning into hers. 'You will do as I bid – there is no other way – and will contrive to confound those about you, for you are sick with love and ready to do whatsoever you can to protect your beloved. I shall expect my horse to bring you to me on the morrow – and be certain to have that jewel with you!'

He ended by saying, deceitfully: 'Unless, perchance, your lord finds you have been firmly tied to him in wedlock and he

148

cannot abear for you to leave his side!' With that he was gone, and she heard the same melodious whistle as she had heard once before on the quayside.

Following after him, she leaned over the balcony to be sure Martin was not in sight, but saw only the white horse at the foot of the steps and Atlan, halfway down, spring outwards and on to its back. Before they disappeared through the gate, he looked back, pointing with an index finger as if to fix her with the dart of his intent, then threateningly drew it across his throat.

She went inside, thoughts disordered, opening the bodice and breathing deeply to quieten her wildly beating heart. 'What am I to do?' she asked herself aloud. 'Should I lay this burden on Martin? To make him warn m'Lord of this threat that even then he might not escape, although thus forewarned he could find Atlan and run him through. But, should I cause this to happen, I doubt I could bear living all my life with Meralda in a cell, a daily witness to her anguish. Then again, if I stop my tongue and attempt this deception and it succeeds, she at least will find happiness with Atlan and m'Lord's life will be safe. I cannot think, though, he would wish to set eyes on me ever again once made aware of my treachery. Oh, this is too much for my poor head! Is there no one I can safely tell to advise me in my dilemma?'

An answer came to her as soon as she had stepped out of the gown, returned the pearl to its pouch and re-dressed in her discarded clothing. How could she have been so foolish as to think herself alone in her distress? God was ever there to guide and help those who sincerely asked for His aid in the way they should go. Kneeling, she prayed: 'Pity my confusion, dear God. Show me how to resolve my plight. Should I confess to Martin or keep silent and follow Atlan's bidding? Which would ensure protection for m'Lord? I beg for a sign to guide me.'

She waited, but nothing unusual occurred, and on hearing Martin's horse enter the courtyard she arose, shook her head in frustration and went to pick up the gown. Before she could reach it, a shaft of brilliant sunlight broke through the clouds and into the room, pointing like a radiant spear at her objective, enveloping it as in a flame. She held back in wonder, fearing the cloth might be consumed, and then raised her head as if listening. 'Ay, thank you God,' she whispered, just as Martin called up to ask if she was ready to leave.

'Ready, indeed,' came her cheerful reply as she folded the gown into its protective linen bag, then more quietly: 'Now I know which pathway I must take!'

They rode hard and reached the priory before the tide turned, the crag not presenting the forbidding aspect as it had on Lowenna's first arrival, no longer appearing as a prison but simply a resting place for a few short hours. Martin had soon noticed her lightness of spirit and found his own gloomy mood, since he had not been overly welcomed at the church of Saint Ana, lifting to match hers. He was surprised and gladdened by her joyous acceptance of whatever the future should hold.

Outside the priory gate Martin held her to him. Looking into the fresh young face, the bloom of innocence still upon it, he believed there could be no further secrets behind its bland exterior. 'It pleasures me to find you happier than you have been for many a day. Did something happen to change you during my absence?'

Lowenna lowered her eyes. 'I must confess it did.' Her reply was careful. 'I was troubled I could find no riddance from the wretchedness that tormented me 'til I recalled your counsel to ask God's aid, and was rewarded with a portent. Even if I misread the sign I could not mistake the words I heard in my head – that I am destined to dedicate my life to the service of m'Lord Vivian, even to forfeiting it if needs be, so am now at peace within myself and can do none other than what I was bid.'

'Thanks be! Lowenna, I believe that love, in all its forms, is really the only thing worth living and dying for – perfect when souls merge – and now nothing remains but a melancholy for Meralda. What can be done to curb her defiance?' He held her at arm's length while he searched her face. 'What news am I to carry to Father? If I report her case as hopeless you will both be taken to the mainland priory at once, and if I bring him hope…'twould be a cruelty for him to await by the altar and then, denied the presence of his daughter, be unable to witness the union.'

Lowenna managed to meet his eyes. 'You must tell him I have no doubt of it. I shall try further persuasion on Meralda, and if God wills her heart be turned from its waywardness then it must be so.'

Martin beamed. 'You have me believing that a miracle may yet occur, as m'Lord's prayers can only be met by the acceptance of his love by the one he loves. I had thought that impossible 'til this moment. Sister, you renew my faith in miracles! I would have hoped to escort you on the morrow to learn the outcome, but am required to welcome the archdeacon when he sets foot on Lyonesse at dawn.'

He rang the bell and kissed her fondly before transferring the linen bag to her arm and the pouch into her hand, watching as she stepped over the threshold. He smiled as she looked back, wondering that it was so wistfully returned and stayed gazing curiously at the closed door for a moment. He was thinking that everything was now approaching a conclusion and his times of trial and distress for his family were almost over, so with a feeling of peace and contentment of his own he began to make his way to Richard's camp to impart his news.

Lowenna hurried straight to their cell without awaiting an escort. She unbarred the door and entered the bleak room, carefully laying the linen bag and the pouch across the two stools. She heard the bar put back as she turned to Meralda, surprised that her sister remained inert on the palliasse exactly as she had left her. 'Meralda,' she said, then raised her voice at the lack of response. 'Meralda! Rouse yourself. I have fetched the gown and have tidings for you!'

When there was yet no movement or sound from the untidy, heaped bundle, she gave a tut of irritation and sat down heavily on her sister's resting place with the intention of jerking her into wakefulness. This had an immediate effect – but an unexpected one. There came a sharp intake of breath followed by a moan that froze her heart with its anguish, and jumping to her feet she demanded: 'Meralda – what ails you?'

She put out a hand to touch her, to find the garment was not clothing her at all but appeared to have been carelessly thrown on top. Lifting it, she was horrified to see Meralda sprawled naked, her back a mass of raised and reddened weals. 'Oh, my sister!' Lowenna was too shocked for an instant to know what to do or say. 'Oh, my sister – what have they done to you?'

Meralda made no answer, her throat swollen and sore from her screams. She had sobbed until there were no more tears left to wet her cheeks then sunk into oblivion, becoming aware of Lowenna's presence but with no desire to awaken fully to suffer the stiffness and pain blissfully suppressed when she fell into unconsciousness.

'Meralda – tell me! I must know what happened!' With nothing forthcoming, she moistened a piece of cloth from the pitcher of water and dabbed at the parched lips. A blind rage suffused her, rage that this could happen to someone who had never known anything but the kindest treatment. 'God, why have You let her be used in this pitiless way?' she cried. ''Tis becoming ever more evident that You desire me to save her from further hurt and have given me the means to

152

see it done. Should I feel any doubt or wavering I will be 'minded of this cruelty, and my resolve will be strengthened anew!'

Meralda moaned again, opening one eye to mournfully regard her sister, licking dry lips. 'They took me as soon as you were gone – to drive out the Devil, they said. They pledged to scourge me 'til I agreed to espousal or constant refusal brought about my death.' A wry smile twisted her mouth. 'I did not oblige by yielding to either blandishment, but they will return anon to try again.'

Lowenna tried to calm her anger, the better to help this poor, hurt creature. 'I warrant they shall not take you again! Now, 'tis pressing that you hearken well to what I tell you, which is to have courage – courage enough to say you were in error, that they have broken your spirit, and that you will be docile and agree to travel to church with no further denial of espousal.'

Meralda managed to twist her head and turn her blazing eyes on her sister. 'Never!' She spat out the word, albeit with difficulty. 'Are you bereft of reason? They may strip all the skin from my body and still not hear me beg for mercy!'

'Hush, quiet yourself whilst I make known the purpose.' Lowenna soothed her by stroking her hand until she noticed the raw chafing around the wrist where she had been tied, the bonds becoming tighter as she struggled against them. She held back tears, incensed once again.

'I plead with you to do as I ask, which mayhap will enable us to flee this place and you to gain your heart's desire. I have been long in the company of Atlan this day – 'twas he who advised the means by which we may free ourselves, and if you comply you will be saved future torture…' She broke off, hearing footsteps approaching, then whispered: 'Later, I will fully tell of Atlan's plan to escape. Remember, you must bite your tongue and agree to go willingly to church with them,' she ended, stressing the necessity for her sister's compliance.

The door swung open and she rose to her feet, praying that Meralda would bend her pride and do as she had been bid. Three nuns entered, led by Sister Columb. 'We have come for the one who is possessed by the Devil – you are doubtless wise as to the purpose,' she said, addressing Lowenna, prepared for her opposition.

Lowenna forced a smile to her lips. 'Truly, I am wise as to the purpose, and must applaud you upon the method which has brought about the desired result.'

The tall nun was already on her way to the palliasse and did not at first grasp the significance of the words. She was brought to a standstill as Lowenna stepped in front of her.

'You will inform the holy Mother,' she said, in a tone designed to dispel any dispute, 'that my sister agrees to her espousal, and will leave at dawn content to meet with her betrothed.'

Sister Columb was obviously taken aback by this sudden and unexpected change from Meralda's previously fierce resistance. Flustered and uncertain, she pushed past Lowenna, bending down to try to peer into the woebegone face. 'Is this truth?' she queried, forcefully. 'Speak, then – I have to hear it from your own mouth. Have you acceded to God's wishes and abandoned the Devil's and your own?'

Lowenna held her breath, willing Meralda to show her submission. She slowly released it when she heard the faint, but definite, reply: 'It is truth.'

Sister Columb, her countenance a mixture of disbelief and displeasure, ushered the others outside, calling over her shoulder. 'Prepare yourselves for a visit from our holy Mother. She will need confirmation – and is not easily duped!'

Left on their own, Lowenna did what she could to make her sister comfortable, saying she would unfold the plan when there would be no fear of interruption, and all the time endeavouring to think of ways to improve on it. Then, unsure, she asked: 'Did I imagine that Sister Columb was disapproving because further punishment would not be inflicted on you?'

Meralda closed her eyes. 'You were not mistaken. She stood by and counted every stroke as it fell. I could see her pleasure before I lost my senses.'

Lowenna shuddered, seeking a reason for the nun's malice. 'Did you ask her pardon when you broke her chain, Meralda?' With no reply forthcoming she was sure that was the answer. 'Then, of a certainty, my unfortunate sister, you have made a spiteful enemy.' She searched in the straw and picked it up when she found it, hanging it over one of the wall pegs.

Her thoughts were soon distracted by the arrival of the prioress and her attendant nuns, all exhibiting a marked air of excitement. The aged lady approached the prone form. 'My child,' she said. 'Is what I hear really so? Do you truly repent of your wickedness and promise to alter your ways? I would be filled with such joy could I but have your confession that the chastisement cleansed your soul!'

Meralda opened one swollen eye, fixing it on her as she fought back a terse retort. Then: ''Tis so,' she meekly agreed.

But that was not enough to bind her to her word. 'She who bears the holy casket – bring it forth!' demanded the quavering voice, directing it to be placed under Meralda's hand. 'Now swear, swear upon our holy relic that you have rejected your evil intent, and will submit yourself to espousal with your betrothed.'

Meralda had no hesitation in transferring the image of one betrothed to the other in her mind. 'I do so swear.' She spoke decisively, leaving no one in doubt.

The prioress beamed, well pleased with the outcome of her treatment of this difficult brand that she believed she had plucked from the Devil's fire. She lifted the covering gown to observe the extent of the injuries to the mortal body

155

of the soul she had done her best to save. 'See what care they took to draw no blood!' she enthused, 'to heal the quicker, so as not to offend the eyes of her spouse in the event of her repentance. Such mindfulness has proven justified.'

Looking about her she espied the small nun who had stayed in the background. 'You, Sister Adwen, will bring a poultice of herbs which aid the swift healing of sore flesh, and after that has been removed you will anoint the tender parts with a balsam to ease stiffness. Now, hasten to your task – there is much to be done ere we leave in the midst of darkness.' She turned to Lowenna. 'I will order two litters to be made, one for myself and one for the bride – she will yet be suffering discomfort. Sister Adwen and yourself will attend upon her during the journey.'

'Stay! I beg you to linger a moment.' Lowenna had used the time to decide upon her own needs. 'I crave a twofold favour, m'Lady, as I am shying away from facing my father and the congregation in my soiled cloak, and my sister will need another to keep her from the chill of night.'

The prioress, flushed with the success of her imagined victory, nodded. 'I see no reason to refuse. As I shall be wearing the precious ornamental mantle, as befits a meeting with the archdeacon, I will permit my usual cloak to be worn by Meralda.' Then to Sister Columb she said, 'And as you are being left in charge during my absence you will not be needing yours, so see that Lowenna has it.'

'You have our gratitude, holy Mother.' Lowenna was conscious of the glance of resentment cast in her direction by a reluctant lender. 'My other request is for you to allow me to gather some of the flowers that bloom outside to enable me to fashion a wreath to adorn the bride's head.'

'Granted!' With a nod, she and her attendants were gone on their way to the chapel, there to sing their thanks and ring the bell for rejoicing.

Lowenna heaved a sigh of relief as the door closed behind

the fluttering skirts. 'You did well to counter her probing without resorting to deliberate falsehood, but ask me no questions 'til I have acquainted you with the details of the plan,' she said, noticing Meralda's enquiring frown, 'before Sister Adwen returns to tend you.' And she began to outline the steps they were to take.

*

An air of hushed expectancy had hung over Kellimargh all that day, as if forewarned to hold itself in readiness for some impending event. No leaf stirred, and birds nesting in the trees had inexplicably flown away to other preferred habitats.

When Atlan had departed from Trevelyan he made directly for the Sacred Grove and Tardhamor, and having crossed a boundary stream he jumped down from Mordon and ran to the glade, coming upon the devotees in a rite of silent obeisance to Poseidon. Tardhamor stood in the centre of the circle, head thrown back and arms stretched forward in a beseeching gesture, until some mysterious sensitivity seemed to alert him to Atlan's presence.

'O great Provider,' he suddenly intoned, facing the statue. 'Within your sight approaches one who dares to scorn you, who should be cowering with fear at his failure to complete the task entrusted to him. This dishonest knave has been foolish enough to incur the wrath of all your faithful followers by his unkept promises. We have to decide upon his punishment – as if any punishment devised would be adequate for his neglect of you!' He swung around, towering above the rest, his straggly beard quivering below the folds of the concealing cloth as he pointed an accusing finger at Atlan. 'Seize him!' he ordered.

Atlan saw several men move out from the shelter of the trees, clearly having been told to let him enter but not escape. He ran forward, intending to throw himself down in front of the high priest, but before he was able to reach him he was set upon and handled with violence. There was no possibility of him freeing himself, there were too many strong arms to prevent it, and he was pushed to his knees. He tried to speak, but Tardhamor drowned his voice with his own, silencing him.

'There is nought you can say by way of any feeble plea that will appease us. Your mouth is full of lies – which 'minds me of an appropriate penalty for breaking your given word – you shall suffer your tongue to be torn out! Bring him!' he commanded, indicating the altar.

Atlan had known he risked retribution when he came to face the high priest's vengeance, letting himself be ensnared in the waiting trap. As he was dragged along he shouted with all the power of his lungs: 'Then you will never take possession of the treasure I have planned to be brought here – a jewel fit for our great god to wear – one I believe belonged to him long ago but which was passed to others and lost!'

Tardhamor tried to ignore the words forced on his ears but curiosity and greed proved irresistible. 'Stay – let him speak while yet he may,' he ordered, and to Atlan: 'Now, wretch, make known the meaning of what you say concerning this treasure – or was it uttered in a vain attempt to save your miserable self?'

Atlan licked blood from a corner of his mouth and dared to glance upwards at the shielded face, being rewarded with a glimpse of a fiercely intense, pale eye. ''Twas not said for that but, if I am wounded further, I swear you will never have this marvellous jewel under your hand!' he said, thickly.

'I refuse to bargain with a traitor to our god,' Tardhamor said imperiously, before deciding he should not act too hastily before hearing what was being offered, 'but I will give ear to your confession of guilt, since you seem eager to make amends.'

Atlan, believing in his powers of persuasion, pulled from

the men and kneeled. 'My revered high priest, I am only guilty of tardiness in completing the task committed to me, though that is about done, but it is imperative that you listen to the amazing tidings I have to impart! This day I set eyes upon a most wondrous jewel, and knew by its size 'twas the perfect pearl I once saw in a vision adorning a king of Atlantis – a graceless descendant of his forebears – as he took it from his neck and cast it aside saying it brought nought but misery and sadness. It has been held by the governors here and passed down through their line, but should be returned to its true guardian, Poseidon.'

Tardhamor was motionless, his attention rapt. 'Where is it now?'

'Held in the Priory on the Rock where none can reach it, but do not fear. 'Tis to be brought here on the morrow by Lowenna, the maiden I offer as Poseidon's bride, and am wishful our god will forgive me by accepting them both. If not, I fear the jewel may be lost to us forever, as the governor plans to take it to the mainland.'

Tardhamor studied the ground before his feet as he slowly approached the statue, then lifted his gaze and stared at it intently as if communing with the god it portrayed before facing the waiting knot of men. 'The mighty one has given approval for the twin gifts of the bride and the return of his treasure. He also agrees to show this penitent priest, seemingly anxious to show contrition, the forgiveness he seeks. Let him go,' he said in a flat voice.

As the men drew away from Atlan, he staggered to his feet, supporting himself against the altar. 'I thank Poseidon for his favour – and you, high priest. Soon after sun-up I shall bring Meralda to become my bride, and during our ceremony Mordon will leave to bring Lowenna, delayed by events 'til then – and the jewel – you have my word upon't.'

Tardhamor sniffed, contemptuously. 'Your word has been worthless of late. Make very sure that all goes as you say, as we grow weary of preparing for your promised appearances only to find you are as bodiless as a puff of smoke when the time comes for you to present yourself. I warn you, there will be no more chances for forgiveness. Fail this time and you will suffer Poseidon's unspeakable wrath. Go!'

As he rode thankfully away, Atlan gloried in the spectacular sunset that was turning land and sea into solid and liquid fire, hoping it was infusing Meralda with the same ecstasy that filled him, sure Lowenna would have unfolded his plan to her and his love would be preparing herself to play her part.

When he reached his boat, he resolved he would rest as well as his exhilaration and a gathering storm would allow while he waited for daybreak, the time for departure. He gave his impassioned thanks to Poseidon for leading him to the pearl – it was exactly what he had needed to ensure that Tardhamor would not be tempted to rob him of Meralda. The high priest, having already wedded them, would be forced to curb his impatience and await the arrival of her sister and the jewel, after which they could get safely away.

Sleep eluded him as the boat was violently tossed about in the stormy sea. He could not resist anticipating the joyous events to come, guessing that Meralda would be doing likewise, able to think of nothing other than him, their love and future life together. Then, as the storm subsided he slept, deeply and for too long.

\*

Meralda's thoughts earlier that evening had been centred solely upon herself, the poultice seeming to inflict as much pain as the scourging, but later she had to admit that it had eased the soreness. When the time came for the little nun to remove it, Lowenna gave her sister a knucklebone remaining from the meal she had attempted to eat, deeming it

160

necessary to put some victuals inside her to increase her strength and ability to be equal to the stresses that the morrow would undoubtedly bring. Meralda clamped her teeth hard on it to relieve the hurt as the poultice was lifted, and as Sister Adwen began to tenderly apply the balsam she gave a sigh of relief and released the bone from her mouth, letting it drop into the straw beside her.

While they were thus occupied, and before the light began to fade, Lowenna had gone outside their now unguarded door to gather the white flowers she wanted. She viewed the vivid colour of the sunset with uncertainty, hoping it was not an adverse omen when she noted the redness resembling blood that was reflected on the dew forming on the blossoms. When she brought them into the cell, their white-ness restored, perfume filled the stale air and blended with the smell of herbs that helped to dispel other, less pleasant odours. Their presence introduced a festive atmosphere into the dismal surroundings, softening the faces of the three young women into smiles.

Lowenna sat on the straw, busying herself with the wreath, using more flowers than was usual in order to cover her hair, fashioning a chaplet to lie low on her forehead and hide any vestige of black eyebrow. It was almost completed when Sister Adwen collected up her bowls and unguents and covered Meralda's back with a linen cloth, then rinsed her face and hands, giving special attention to the wrists, tidied her hair with a teasel and pinned it up with the pins Lowenna had brought from Trevelyan. Then she went, a look of sympathy on her silent face.

Left by themselves once more, Meralda was eager for the hastily imparted plan to be repeated, which Lowenna obliged by doing as she put the finishing touches to the chaplet, twisting it around and pushing in a sprig here and there until she was satisfied. ''Tis, in effect, what we contrived to do this very morn, Meralda. We change over the clothes we should be wearing so that I will be the one they guard. 'Twill still be dark enough for you to slip away at the foot of the crag and conceal yourself behind one of the larger rocks and wait for Atlan to find you. Can you now move with ease despite your hurt?'

Meralda's smile gave answer. 'The pain diminishes by the instant, and I shall soon be able to cast the assault put upon me into the oblivion it deserves. From now onwards, Atlan will protect me for always.'

Lowenna was regarding her, pondering. 'There is a notion persisting in my mind that gives me great concern. Father is so sure that the threat of disaster here cannot be averted that the possibility fills me with dread. I would not fret for my life were I to lose it as a result of my own conduct, but I could nevermore find peace if I became the cause of your demise by aiding you in this venture – thus keeping you on Lyonesse soil. Can you not persuade Atlan to take you, and mayhap myself, to the mainland before the new moon rises, should we all meet together on the morrow?'

Meralda was now indulging herself with thoughts of complete optimism, and was prepared to agree to any request to please the petitioner. 'Of a certainty I will plead your case for you,' she said, then, continuing in a puzzled voice: 'But in what wise would you be able to travel with us? You will be afar off in the church of Saint Perran with the others and set to travel away from Lyonesse with them.'

''Tis not what Atlan has planned.' Lowenna, at last content with the chaplet, laid it aside. 'He has offered to send his horse to enable me to escape the anger of the others when my treachery is known, should it be so bad that I wish to go, and bring me to where you both will be. Oh, and something more.'

She went to pick up the pouch and placed it in Meralda's unresponsive hands. That maiden was trying to absorb the unwelcome news that Lowenna, while participating as the

162

decoy in the church ceremony – which was warranted – was also intending to participate in the aftermath of her own union, which was, most definitely, not! Surely Atlan did not imagine that the three of them might dwell together?

'Are you certain you were not mistaken in his words?' she queried, sharply. 'And did you find both them, and himself, agreeable to you? You, who have shown such aversion toward him 'til now. So, why are you doing this for us, Sister?'

'I was not mistaken,' answered Lowenna, 'and the most agreeable words I heard was when he suggested that I might be bound to Vivian when the ceremony is over, even if my name was called differently. Should he openly despise and deride me for the trickery, he might yet allow me to enter his house to serve him, though denying me his name. That is why I am doing this – not for you, but for me – though if, as I fear, I will prove offensive to his eyes and he cannot abear a sight of me, then I shall flee away on the horse he calls Mordon.' She decided not to divulge the true reason for her change in attitude, the threat made by Atlan to pursue and kill Vivian.

Meralda considered the alternatives in silence before lifting up the pouch. 'What is held in such a rich purse?' she asked, 'and how came you by it?'

''Tis a token sent you by m'Lord to be worn at the espousal – nay, spare a glance for it,' she said, as Meralda made as if to fling it away, 'it has such beauty!' Lowenna loosed the strings and waited for her sister's small hand to enter and withdraw the gift.

Meralda stared open-mouthed at the pearl hanging from the chain she held aloft. 'The Vivian Jewel…' she breathed. 'I had been told of its perfection but discounted the tale as boastful. It has been stolen from the sea that gave it birth – I must take it to my love – he will never have seen its like.'

'He saw it this very day,' said Lowenna, 'and appeared to esteem it highly. He enjoined me, in a forceful and positive way, to be certain to take it to the church, and from thence, when all will be confusion, to secrete it about myself and bring it to him when Mordon should fetch me. Atlan believes that will be the way of it, and I profess I also have no great expectation that Father, or m'Lord, will welcome my being in their company once they are aware of my deception, but should I be in error, and be forgiven by some miracle, then I will be able to return it to his hand.'

'But that would be folly.' Meralda swung the pearl to catch the light from the lantern. 'We cannot rely upon you to deliver it surely or safely. Nay, 'tis mine now and I shall carry it with me,' she ended with finality.

Lowenna felt annoyance rising within her, annoyance that her sister was unable to trust her to implement Atlan's plan, interfering in its discharge and also assuming a right to the Vivian Jewel, a right she did not have since unprepared to wed its owner. After all she, Lowenna, was the one who had been assigned the task and was determined to carry it through. 'That you will not!' The vehemence of her reply surprised them both. 'I will take it as I was bid!'

Thus rebuked, Meralda made no further demur, though quietly seething at this rebellious mood in her sister, and reluctantly put the pearl into its pouch.

Lowenna had another important concern – the wedding gown. She lay the linen bag on the straw and began to open it. 'Sister, lighten your countenance, I am begging your aid. I was tempted to don the gown at Trevelyan and nearly swooned away with the fit of the bodice. What can be done to relieve the tightness?'

Meralda resolved to hide her ill-feeling and concur as well as she could, aware that her freedom depended on Lowenna but also determined that Atlan would have to revise his scheme, should it include her joining with them. 'Bring it hither – and the lantern,' she bade her in a more gracious tone, scanning the bodice with care.

164

'There is no problem here,' she said at last, taking a pin from her hair and starting to unpick the stitches. 'With the lining undone at the sides, the fine cloth on the outside will stretch and give, allowing you to suffer no further discomfort. See, the little cape falls low enough to conceal any gaping of the lining that might show through the sheerness of the outer cloth.'

She worked on at her unpicking until satisfied with the result, while Lowenna tried on the chaplet to make sure it covered every vestige of hair. Before very long though, weariness halted their labours and, after saying prayers, Lowenna carefully prepared her sister for rest. Finally, she loosened her own hair and garments and lay down on the adjoining palliasse, full of apprehension as to what the new day might bring, which was increased by the disturbance brought about by the sounds of a rising gale and noisy storm growing in intensity, until awareness was temporarily suspended for them both.

# 10

## *The Unexpected*

It seemed no longer than it took to close an eyelid before the strident, insistent clanging of the bell roused the two sisters into reluctant wakefulness. For Meralda, reluctance vanished the second she realised that the day of Saint Martin's Feast had arrived, the day once dreaded but now the day that would end her separation from the one she loved.

'Come, Lowenna,' she said, stretching her arms. 'Let us make ready. I have less pain but am suffering a troublesome stiffness, so shall need your aid.'

After they had washed, Lowenna helped Meralda into her shift, then merely draped her ragged gown over her shoulders as she would soon be obliged to remove it again. She twisted her black hair into a rope, and wound it closely round her head to form a shining cap before trying to assist Meralda, who insisted on fashioning her own, coiling and pinning it up high into a topknot. They hesitated about what to do next, wondering when they could safely don the gowns intended to reverse their roles.

'I doubt we shall be visited 'til they expect us to be ready to leave,' said Lowenna. 'We can hope for no food to break our fast, as nought may pass our lips 'til after we have partaken of the bread and wine at Mass, so we can only wait for the cloaks to be fetched and clothe ourselves hastily afterwards.'

She had no sooner spoken than the door opened and

Sister Columb entered, bearing but one cloak. 'Our holy Mother desired me to bring this for the bride.' Her face was impassive, her voice without tone as she addressed Meralda. 'As you can see it differs from ours, the cross on the back being worked in raised stitching. You must realise that this garment merits your care. Fortunately, the weather has calmed.'

The bell began tolling to give notice of the impending departure, and the nun's eyes swept around the room, falling on the bridal gown draped over the table. Realising that it should be adorning Meralda, she pointed, saying: 'I trust you intend to attire yourself in that wanton covering in all haste. The procession is now forming at the gate – mind you do not delay it!'

Meralda, already resentful that Sister Columb had not brought her own cloak at the same time, and further offended by the scathing reference to her mother's gown, could not prevent herself from delivering a tart response to the nun whom she blamed for causing her excessive physical pain. 'Of a certainty, 'twill soon grace a worldly bride for the avouched purpose of passionate and carnal love between a man and woman – so do not fret that I shall be tardy!'

Lowenna intervened in what promised to develop into a verbal duel and hurriedly took the cloak. 'We are grateful for this, and I shall have more gratitude to offer when I can feel yours about me,' she said, hanging it on one of the pegs next to the broken chain, which reminded her of the source of the nun's hostility. She spoke softly to lessen the tension. 'Will you now be gone to fetch t'other?'

Sister Columb faced her with an unfathomable expression. 'When the bride has been arrayed in her sensual finery I shall return with both the garment and Sister Adwen as escort.' She went with a baleful look, leaving the door ajar.

Lowenna breathed a sigh of relief. 'You could have had us in a parlous way with your tongue, Meralda,' she complained, 'and you have not yet asked her pardon for your clumsiness with her chain.'

'Nor will I! She was baiting me – can you not see it? She would take any measures to keep me here, scourging me daily!'

'Do not misjudge her – she affirms what she believes to be right.' Lowenna was prepared to benefit everyone with the best of intentions. 'But what are we to do? We can hide no longer. Mayhap it would be best to clothe ourselves and for you to don the cloak we already have. I shall be veiled, my face hid, ready to receive t'other when it is brought.'

'That will not serve,' returned Meralda, going to where the cloak hung on the peg. 'The hellhag said this one is markedly different and for the bride's sole use.'

'Then the only way to overcome this hindrance…' – Lowenna had her eyes on the half-open door – '…is to ready ourselves and for you to cover your head while we wait in the passage. When they arrive, I will take Sister Columb's cloak from her and put it around you, pulling the hood over your face before they get a sight of it.' She let fall her purple gown. 'Now, step into that and hand me your own.'

Meralda made a grimace of distaste. 'Could you not have fetched clean clothing from home? You only brought pins for our hair.'

'And not to be despised – they are proving of use to us, and all else was gone. Your gowns await you at Trevivian and mine at the hillfort, m'dear.' She fastened her purple garment around her sister, pulling the sleeves down to hide the chafed wrists, then tore a piece of cloth from Meralda's already torn skirt. Do not fuss so, and tie this round your head,' she directed.

Meralda took the length of cloth, and ignoring what she had said, dropped it carelessly on the table amongst the clutter laying on top and went to sit on her palliasse, watching her sister step into the voluminous white skirt and raise up the bodice. She saw her give a sigh of relief as she closed it with ease.

'You have skilful fingers,' Lowenna said, gratefully, 'to amend it thus without visible altering. I would now be able to breathe in comfort were it not for my coming meeting with Lord Vivian, coupled with the uncertainty that hangs over our setting forth.' She turned to face her. 'How do I look?'

Meralda gave a quick glance, a trace of envy in her eyes. 'Well enow, though I would it were clothing me. I do not doubt 'twould favour my person a great deal more.' She got to her feet, wincing as she did so, moving with care to the pegs to take down the white cloak belonging to the prioress and laying it over her arm.

Lowenna chose to disregard this ungracious remark, busily adjusting the chaplet of flowers and pushing up stray strands of hair. Then she shook out the square of fine fabric and threw it over her head, pulling one corner down in front to hang below her waist. A few pins served to hold the veil in place. 'I can see well enow through it, but is my face visible to you?' she asked. 'Could my looks betray me? And is every vestige of hair hid?'

Meralda was moving backwards, eyeing her attentively until the table intervened, so she put her disencumbered hand behind her to rest upon it as she studied the vision in white. Before she moved away, she picked up the cloth for her head that she had tossed on the top then walked carefully around her sister, inspecting her closely.

'I can see no trace of blackness nor would I know what face lies beneath the veil.' She swung around sharply, hands clasped together as if in prayer beneath the cloak on her arm. 'We must hasten – I shake with unease. What next?'

'Place the cloak over my shoulders, and be quick now to cover your head with the cloth in your hand.' This time Meralda hurried to obey, and after tightening and tidying her golden topknot she hid it beneath the torn strip. 'Now,' continued her sister, 'we will leave the lantern here and go into the passage-way, where there is but a dim light, and await the arrival of the nuns – they cannot be long a-coming.'

So saying, she cast a last look around the cell, thankful that the moment had come for their departure from these mean surroundings – and espied the pouch lying on the table. 'Oh, Meralda! Look yonder at what so nearly slipped our thoughts! I must deliver it – aid me to place the jewel around my neck.' She picked up the pouch and was starting to pull it open when Meralda clutched her arm.

'Soft! I hear them coming – we cannot delay. In any wise, it might be prudent to carry the pouch with you for safekeeping 'til you reach the church.' With no time to demur, Lowenna wound the strings about her wrist, clasping the soft pouch as she hastened out, conscious of the weight and outline of the pearl and its chain.

They were barely through the door when pattering footsteps warned of the nearness of the nuns. Lowenna, moving in front of Meralda, saw Sister Columb carrying her cloak by the light of the lantern she carried, closely followed by Sister Adwen. The tall Sister did not halt in her swift stride until she reached them. 'I now find you of a pressing impatience to be gone,' she said curtly, deftly impeding the bride in her attempt to grasp the cloak she was being obliged, unwillingly, to lend.

'We have no desire to cause hindrance,' came the muted voice of the other figure, turning around. 'My back awaits your cloak.'

The nun made to do as she was bid but seemed to find difficulty in spreading it out. She gave a tut of annoyance. 'My lamp is hampering me – I must set it down on the board. Come with me, Lowenna.'

She clutched Meralda's arm, drawing her back into the cell, and when she had rid herself of the lantern, suddenly flung her around so roughly that the cloth slipped from her

170

head, to disclose Meralda's pale hair and startled features in almost the same unmasking as the previous day.

Sister Columb's eyes flashed in triumph. 'I knew it!' she exulted. 'I knew you might try to repeat your trickery! The Devil has his talons in you yet, causing your mouth to spew forth lies and falsity, but once again your deception has been revealed and this time you cannot escape the punishment you deserve – to forgo your pagan lover and remain with us within these walls for always!'

Meralda gave such a cry that the two outside crowded into the doorway in time to see her tear the cloak from Sister Columb's arm, forcing her off balance, then, her pain forgotten, she lashed out to hurl the nun across the room where she fell in an untidy heap against the furthest wall. As the observers quickly backed away from her fury, Meralda pushed outside and had the door shut and secured before they could register her intention. She stood silent, facing her horrified audience, clutching the cloak and pressing her back against the door as if daring them to try to free the prisoner behind it. For a brief spell no one moved, becoming aware of muffled cries and thumping from within, then Meralda took a step forward, eyeing Sister Adwen, who rapidly crossed herself.

'Adwen – said to be the saint of lovers – does that still hold with you? Will you aid me by doing nought to warn the others of this? Or do you intend to denounce me? If so, 'twill be my pleasure to give Sister Columb your company!'

She searched for a hostile expression on the little nun's face but saw only a confused forbearance mixed with a generous portion of surprise, and thought of a way to be sure of her conduct, so continued: ''Tis well that you are agreed. You have been kind and I am prepared to risk my trust – but bear in mind that I shall be walking behind you all the way to the church, and if I see you weakening in your resolve I will put a tie around your neck and strangle you without any scruple!'

171

She could not see Lowenna's face beneath the veiling but heard her indrawn breath of shock, knowing how horrified she must be by the unexpected violence used on Sister Columb, and also discomfited at hearing her words of intimidation. She hoped she would come to realise that the first had been born of necessity and the other a threat that could not be fulfilled, since the plan was for her to leave the procession soon after it began.

She flung the cloak about her, pulling the hood down as the bell ceased to toll. 'That must be the signal to start. Dearest Lowenna, ready yourself – we must hasten,' and so saying, Meralda urged the little nun to walk in front and grasped Lowenna's hand, giving it an encouraging squeeze as they stepped out into the night, abandoning the fading clamour behind them. They took the path to where they could see a cluster of flaming torches and flickering lanterns, reaching them as the head of the procession was moving through the tunnel. A few uncloaked nuns waited at the open main gates, remaining as custodians, and the gatekeeper, seemingly given to over-employing her tongue whenever allowed the opportunity, was giving full vent to it when they came up to her.

'Make haste! Make haste!' she directed. 'Our holy Mother has already been escorted to where the litters wait below the narrow way. 'Tis a happy chance the storm has calmed, but have a care not to miss your footing on the slippery rock. Dispose yourself to afford the bride your tender care, Sister Adwen.' She paused to take a breath, then: 'Have you a notion as to where Sister Columb has concealed herself? She should be here, aiding this exodus, instead of taking ease to suit her own fitfulness...' The rest of her words were cut off, Sister Adwen having given no indication that she had heard them, as the three stragglers passed through the gates which were closed with a loud reverberation.

Now, the only sounds to be heard were those of shuffling

feet, the swish of skirts and the hissing and spluttering of torches held by those assigned the task. Three hearts beat fast with apprehension lest Sister Columb be found too soon, fearing the sudden, strident tone of the bell to warn of treachery, but for the present its tongue, unlike that of the gatekeeper, kept silent.

Once their feet were safely on the beach, Lowenna could see the prioress being carried on ahead as Adwen guided her to her own litter which consisted of a seat lashed midway between two long horizontal poles, with transverse short ones bound to each end to give it stability, and having sides and a back woven with canes.

Standing on the firm sand between the poles, she was wondering how she could sit down on a legless seat without soiling her white gown when four stalwart nuns, each with a leather sling over one shoulder hanging to the opposite hip, moved to stand at the ends of the poles. They gathered up the hems of their habits and tucked them into the cords circling their waists, thereby displaying unclothed, muscular legs, and threw their cloaks back over their shoulders, where they were folded upwards by a companion until they rested on the head and could be balanced or held in place with one hand. When this was completed they grasped the poles and lifted them, and Lowenna found herself caught by the edge of the seat and thrown back into the wickerwork, suspended in comparative comfort.

The bearers set off jerkily, avoiding rocks in their path as they neared the water, when they lifted the poles up on their shoulders. Other nuns, Lowenna saw, had staves to steady them, with some bearing torches and lanterns, and the procession was flanked by those carrying weapons for protection against beast or man. She glanced down at Sister Adwen by her side, her face wan and drawn, then at a figure that walked close behind her who must be Meralda. She took a firmer grip on the precious pouch, ensuring the strings were still wrapped around her wrist, then looked away to the sea when she heard the waves breaking boisterously on the shore, the surf appearing to draw back each time in frustration, thwarted in its purpose to surge forward to engulf all in its path. When she again looked for Meralda the figure behind Adwen was gone, and she felt alone and vulnerable viewing the dark waters, praying for a low tide and that those supporting her would not lose their footing and cast her beneath the waves.

The night was dry and had not yet acquired the chill of autumn, but clouds were forming to darken the sky, obscuring the faint light of the stars. The earlier raging of the sea having been quelled, there descended an oppressive atmosphere that hung heavily over the wayfarers now upon the other shore, where the procession was halted until those in the forefront had met with their guide, an old man astride an ass who was to lead them to the church. Then Lowenna's litter was lowered to waist height by her bearers, who rested the ends of the poles in their slings before releasing their cloaks and skirts and moving off steadily, soon to find a rhythm in their stride. She wished she was walking, too, finding it difficult to sit idle, and at the outset had been on the verge of suggesting it until she remembered they thought her to be Meralda, still suffering the effects of her severe beating.

And what of Meralda she wondered? Out of harm's way and safely in the arms of her lover as planned, she thought wistfully.

*

Once she was standing on the beach below the crag, Meralda bent down as if to gather up her skirts, hoping that others nearby would possibly be too busy making their own preparations to ford the narrow, swirling channel to notice her. She stayed leaning over until the indistinct white forms were all before her and none left behind, then dropped her cloak, swept it up beneath the purple skirt and ran to a high and bulky rock, putting it between her and the moving lights. She pressed against it, hardly daring to breathe in the excitement of freedom.

For a time she exulted in the smell and sound of the sea, the feel of sand under her bare feet and the friendly roughness of the rock against her hands before peering round it and seeing, to her relief, all the lights upon the opposite shore and fading into the distance. She was still somewhat fearful of Sister Columb being discovered too soon and the bell rung out to recall the travellers, knowing that the three of them would be adjudged guilty and have direful retribution cast on them. She shivered at the prospect, but removed the cloak from beneath her skirt, glad to wrap it round herself again, even though it had previously covered 'that hellhag'.

Where was Atlan? He should have been waiting. She became anxious and a mite annoyed, and wondered, fleetingly, how Lowenna was faring. It was then she heard the bell begin to toll, not slowly as was usual but rapidly, filling the air with an unmistakable urgency…

*

Lowenna had been envisaging the scene that would take place as she was being wedded to her beloved Vivian, as she now thought of him. When the time came for him to see her face, what would be his reaction? Amazement, certainly – but then? They would already have been joined as one, so what would he do? Accuse and strike her – turn his back on her forever? As she considered, she knew the one certain thing would be his refusal of a substitute, and also that he would be overcome by shock and outrage – as would everyone present. She shuddered and closed her eyes just as the resonance of a

175

bell became audible – and now rigidly attentive, she opened them wide, to find the expected dismay on the face of Sister Adwen beside her.

Ahead of them the prioress had been dozing, head drooped forward, lulled into sleep by the swaying of the litter. When the first faint clanging of the bell was heard she would possibly have continued in her dreams unhearing, had not the others shown alarm at the ominous sound, bringing the procession to an immediate stop. Had they still been within the familiar walls of the priory where they would have known the next move to make, there would have been no consternation, but in this unknown and hostile territory they were confounded. The guide, sensing their bewilderment, halted the ass and waited, a sound of murmuring arising as the flustered nuns, their vows temporarily suspended, turned to each other for guidance.

The prioress, unwillingly roused by this breach of discipline and so unable to ignore the bell – which she might have wished – took control of their dilemma.

'Silence!' she ordered, her voice unwavering, evincing her extreme anger, shocked and scandalised by the disobedience of her flock. 'Has Satan – having found himself baulked of his prey, the prey that travels in our midst – entered into the mouths of the rest of you? Spit him out and clamp your jaws shut! There will be punishment for all when we return, which will not be yet despite the summons hanging on the air, even as I speak. There is no need for you to fear pirates as that warning has a regular ring, one with which you should be familiar, unlike the quick strokes we now hear. I cannot tell what mishap has arisen but there is nought I can do to mend it from here, and any delay would incommode the archdeacon. If Sister Columb has found herself unable to devise a remedy then I must enquire into her fitness for the position of authority she holds. Now – take heed. We have far to travel and, as you have already stolen an unwarranted rest, you may bend your necks in prayer that you do not seek to prove God's patience – or mine – any further! Prepare to move onward!'

Resuming their journey by following the rutted track to the east behind their guide, the flustered nuns, disconcerted and abashed, hastened their steps, gradually distancing themselves from the insistent summons of the priory bell.

Lowenna, greatly relieved, leaned down and touched Sister Adwen's arm, squeezing it gently when the pretty, serious face was lifted to hers, but found little response in it. She saw the contention raging within that outward calm by the raised colour of the cheeks showing in the dim morning light, and longed to tell her that Meralda no longer posed a physical threat, then felt she already knew and that her conflict was being determined by her conscience. The inevitable had merely been postponed, and she must be contemplating the untenable plight she had been drawn into, to stand accused when Sister Columb had her say.

Lowenna felt a sudden rush of pity, for herself as well. They had both come under the influence of the artful persuasion of both Meralda and Atlan, and would be confronted by the resultant grievous consequences. She no longer cared about herself, only about making reparation to Vivian by returning the jewel, as Martin had said they were in honour bound to do.

She watched the sky growing lighter in the east, the daystar clearly visible. Her sister must be far away to the south by now, loved and loving and preparing for her own wedding.

*

When the bell began its clamour, Meralda wondered if she would ever leave the tiny island. It was now light enough to see where the rocky path led up to the priory, and at any moment she was expecting a vengeful Sister Columb to bear

177

down on her and carry her back to her prison. Her eye was caught by a flurry of white on the path, and the next instant her intended shriek was stifled by a hand across her mouth as she was held from behind and twisted around – to find herself clasped in Atlan's tight embrace, held so closely that she felt they could never again be parted. She tried to speak, but he kissed her lips with unceasing passion until Mordon loomed over them, and she was lifted up and cradled in loving arms, leaning against him, unmindful of the pressure and pain of her back.

Her hands explored her beloved's hair, his face, his warm breast. She breathed in the smell of him that was so special to her, holding him so that bosom touched bosom and heart beat against heart, only conscious of the ecstasy flooding through her veins and knowing that he was experiencing similar vivid feelings of delight. As Mordon splashed through the stretch of water, droplets of cold spray thrown upwards fell on the bare flesh of her legs and she knew a huge exhilaration, as if the sea was claiming the three of them, to be uplifted in a limitless ocean of joyousness.

Then they were on the road to the south making towards Carrag Uthek, far removed from the priory and that single bell which finally ceased its singular clamouring as others, with different tones, began to ring out to celebrate Saint Martin. Mordon galloped swiftly until Atlan made him slacken pace, and Meralda found herself able to speak without the words being stolen from her mouth by the wind.

'Oh, my love,' she said. 'I had a terrible fear while I looked so long for you. We have wasted much of this precious day – why were you not awaiting me?'

He bent to kiss her again. 'You may justly condemn me for that,' he answered. 'I lay in the boat for rest but could find none as the waters tossed it about 'til it was nigh overwhelmed and I feared for the strength of the timbers, but when the violence was stilled I slept, too long and too late and to my shame. 'Tis said that sleep is but a small, fleeting death, and I swear, nothing other than death could have kept me from you for longer than needs be – mayhap not even death itself!'

Meralda rubbed her face blissfully against his bare arm. 'Hide your remorse now we are together. By chance, I also was hindered, having to fight for freedom, and had the awful expectation of being caught as they were hunting for me.'

'Was that the reason for the bell? I had a certainty it concerned you, and urged Mordon to almost fly over the waters that were keeping us apart!'

The sun had crept up to their left, ignored by the lovers' eyes that only regarded each other. It was beginning to show as an angry red, an inverse reflection of the glorious sunset of the previous evening, and as Mordon skirted the base of Carrag Uthek, the Fire Rock appeared to glow of itself in the fiery light.

The horse came to the forest leading to Kellimargh, the Sacred Grove of the Horse, and having crossed a stream he halted in dense undergrowth. The lovers slid from his back, oblivious of the church bells ringing out joyously over Lyonesse and also all other previous concerns – they were fast losing their former importance. Soon they lay enfolded as one in the lush, sweet-smelling grass beneath the branches.

*

The sky was heavy and overcast, bathing in a crimson light those who had been awaiting the archdeacon as he stepped from the ferryboat. In the forefront was Lord Vivian who, as governor, would be the first to greet him, and he was flanked by Martin, as the representative of the church of Saint Perran, and Richard, as the father of the bride he was to join in wedlock. Two menservants attended on Vivian, and Old Jowan on Richard, and were accompanied by men-at-arms.

179

The storm had cast a doubt on whether the archdeacon would be able to complete his journey and his obligations, the violence of the seas keeping the ferry ashore on Cornish land. Then it seemed as if the hand of God was upon the waters, quelling them on the instant to enable the party to cross the choppy, narrow channel.

After the formal reception, during which only Martin and the archdeacon, with his accompanying clerics, had appeared at ease, they began the journey to the church. Vivian and Richard were restless, hardly conversing, fidgeting with whatever came under their hands, obviously so anxious to be about matters meriting a greater urgency that concentration was lost for present events.

Richard's disquiet lay upon the arrival of his daughters. His liability, though not his care and concern for his eldest swan, would end once she became the Lady of Lyonesse, but his duty to Lowenna lay heavily upon him. He had to be sure that those he loved dearly, despite any fall from grace, were safely away before nightfall, and already he regretted the wedding was taking place on this last day.

Martin had reported at sunset, having returned Lowenna to the priory, that she had intimated he need have no fear of the bride's non-arrival or that she would refuse to assent to the ceremony, and would neither dispraise nor reproach either him or Vivian at the altar. He had said she was cheerful and appeared to have a certainty regarding it. Richard had offered up thanks but stayed assailed by doubts.

Vivian's anxiety was in the waiting for the nuptial bond and how he could contain his fervour until the knot was tied, resenting every moment as it dragged away, resenting, too, the necessity for polite discourse when his impatience would have had him riding at full gallop to cool the ferment of his emotions, but none could have guessed this from his outwardly correct demeanour.

They at last arrived at the church and Vivian and Richard

were the first to go to Mass, afterwards going to the monastic dwelling where Martin was resident for refreshment and rest. Vivian could not avail himself of the hospitality, unable to eat or relax, so made an excuse to go outside, ostensibly to see that his men were being cared for. He made his way past stalls selling food and wine, clothes, curiosities, pots and sweet-meats, trying to avoid the wandering sellers with their baskets, barking dogs at their heels. He found his men already enjoying themselves with meat and drink, and after attempting a perfunctory inspection he walked a little distance away, standing apart from the noisy crowd gathering for the feast, and kept his eyes firmly fixed on the road from the north.

*

It seemed to Meralda that time had passed all too fleetingly before Atlan, his passion appeased, kissed her once more with tenderness and led her to the stream where they cleansed themselves. She voiced her concern when, casting her eyes lovingly over him, she saw the bruises on his face and arms, touching them gently.

'How came you by these?' she asked.

'Acquired honourably for your dear sake,' he said, smiling and kissing her hand. Then it was his turn to see the soreness around her wrists and feel anger. 'I put the same question to you,' he said, sharply.

'And I return your same answer, my love,' she replied, glad she had prevented him seeing her scarred back. ''Tis of no consequence, 'tis past and forgot.'

He accepted her soft words as they dressed themselves, and put the cloak around her, lifting her up face to face with him. 'Come, my adored bride – we have yet to be formally wed,' he murmured into her by now unwilling ear.

'That event appears to have lost the urgency it once had,'

she said, against his cheek. 'I feel I have again become an inseparable part of you without the benefit of a ceremony. Had I but listened in the first instance, availing myself of your better judgement and been less concerned with fearing guilt or gratifying my conscience, we could have avoided much of the annoyance we have put upon others.'

He set her down, not answering, as if not agreeing with her, and a pinprick of pique stung her as she thought of Lowenna and the reluctance she felt in having her join them. She said: 'As I now recall that once we were wed in Atlantis, may we not forgo this day's ritual and steal away to live out our lives alone in some secret place?'

Atlan was almost tempted into consenting but knew their presence would already have been observed by the watchers in the trees, and doubted they would be free to leave until he had met his obligation by bringing Lowenna and the jewel and Tardhamor had completed his side of their bargain. There could be no likelihood of the high priest allowing them to depart until those twin treasures were held safely in his hand. He was sure of Lowenna's rejection by Vivian in his desire for Meralda, and the confusion that would arise when she was found to be missing would provide her sister with the opportunity to make her escape on Mordon, but he had to gauge the time aright, not wanting her to be brought too soon. He had given no thought as to what the outcome would be for her, not knowing what espousal to his god might entail as no similar rite had taken place within his memory.

As soon as he and Meralda were wed, Atlan planned to encourage her to drink most of the mead from the loving cup, to induce light-headedness and remain in a stupor until Lowenna arrived. It was too early to send Mordon as the procession could not yet have reached the church, but he had already prepared the stallion for his errand, using no words, only thoughts. It was as the Atlanteans had always done, turning to good account their respect for, and rapport

182

with, horses, though in Mordon he had found a special awareness.

He looked again at Meralda's beautiful, pleading face and resolutely turned from temptation. His entire life had been spent in devotion to his god and, having made his pledge, knew he was committed to discharging it. Reluctantly, he shook his head. 'As this was your dearest wish 'twould be a pity not to fulfil it now, besides, we are expected and there is to be much revelry and feasting. 'Twill be something to keep in our memories for always.'

Meralda gave him a sideways glance. 'Could your refusal have aught to do with my sister?' she asked, hesitantly.

He controlled a guilty start – had she read his mind? 'What makes you ask?'

'She seemed to think Mordon would bring her here to us as part of your plan. I was mazed – and doubtful that I would welcome another to share out future bliss! Oh, and she required me to persuade you to take us three to the mainland in your boat as she feels danger threatens us here. What do you say to undo her fears?'

Atlan quickly marshalled his thoughts. 'I had to offer some purpose for her to lend her aid to us and so, ay, I spoke of a way to escape from the wrath of your family, but is it credible she will be desirous to leave Vivian's side – or be let leave? Though, should I be proven wrong, I have arranged for her to be fetched and cared for far from where we shall be.' He stroked the crease on her brow. 'As for a threat of disaster, Poseidon has too great a loyalty to the people who revere him to let any ill befall. My love, do not fuss, only let me taste the sweetness of your lips again.'

She yielded to his argument, and they walked, bare feet light with happiness, through the thinning trees until they came to the edge of the clearing, hearing laughter and music and the bustle of a crowd bent on pleasure. Then, leaving Mordon behind, they stepped into the glade.

Meralda held close to him, fingers entwined in his, beginning to feel restricted and hot on this sultry, unusually warm November day, so she let her hampering cloak fall to the ground. She gazed around the glade, seeing couples disporting themselves, eating, drinking, dancing and loving, some clothed, most unclothed, and indulging in practices she had never even guessed at. Taken by surprise, she felt aversion, scandalised at witnessing what she had been taught was decadence – especially when she saw not only the fisher folk but notables and friends of her family, even from distant Breonseyth. Some were red in the face and far gone in the head from over-indulging in mead and wine, the many jars clearly evident.

She turned to Atlan, looking up into his face, perplexed. 'Was it ever like this in Atlantis?' she enquired.

He shook his head. 'Not in the beginning when all was ordered – and not when we were there.' He was disconcerted by the display of debauchery from which he had always been inclined to hold himself aloof, the impact being the greater as he imagined Meralda's thoughts, viewing the scene through her innocent eyes. 'I was told it happened later, when the people were encouraged to give love freely to one another. Near the end there were almost continuous gatherings such as this, which so angered Zeus, the king of the gods, that he decided our people deserved punishment.'

Meralda shuddered. 'I am minded of a tale I heard about two cities called Sodom and Gomorrah...' she began, before glancing back over her shoulder to see the cloak she had discarded, the cross distinct upon it, fallen on with delight by a naked couple who commenced to desecrate it with erotic activity. Briefly, she felt outrage but, on recapturing the memory of her previous suffering, fervently wished that Sister Columb herself were here to observe the purpose for which her cloak was being used, and her momentary qualm was summarily dismissed. Rejected, too, to appease the insistent inner voice of her conscience, was what she now thought to be the false piety with which she had concurred all her life.

Atlan led her to where a group lounged on the grass around platters of meat and sweetmeats, lifting one up to her, smiling. 'These are for our festive day, the honey cakes I told you of, remember? Eat, you must be as famished as I am.' He was anxious to avoid a meeting with Tardhamor for as long as possible, to spin out the time before he should send Mordon on his way, but nothing escaped the alert eyes of the high priest for long. Atlan suddenly found him towering above them.

'At last!' Tardhamor quavered, as Meralda instinctively shrank back from the formidable, faceless figure. 'At last you are here, and I am jealous of my lowly priest that you will wed under the power bestowed upon me by our protector, Poseidon, who eagerly awaits his own lovely bride…' he said, with a meaningful look at Atlan. Then to Meralda: 'Are you Aphrodite, goddess of beauty, born of sea-foam and changed to mortal maid? Come with me – you must be prepared.' He bent down to assist her to rise but Atlan, unwilling for him to touch her, raised her himself. Tardhamor stiffened, a snort blowing out the cloth over his face, and he strode away.

White-robed priestesses led Meralda into the shelter of a shrubbery, where the purple gown and shift were removed and she was anointed with a sweet-smelling ointment. Amid murmurs of concern at the sight of her injuries, she was attired in a white robe and garlands of flowers put around her neck, but firmly resisted any attempt to loosen the hair pinned on top of her head, saying she would let it fall as she was wed. She was then taken to where Atlan, having been similarly clothed and garlanded waited, appearing in his fine physique and comeliness, to mirror the statue of his god. He was still hesitating as to when to send Mordon away then, feeling a breeze on his face, and seeing the clouds which had

185

hung low since dawn thinning enough for the sun to shine through, he was able to reckon the day as nearing the middle, and decided to delay signalling the horse to leave just yet.

The bridal couple were placed facing the loving cup set upon the altar, and the ritual of parading and chanting designed to whip up a fervour of excitement began. The high priest was escorted to a seat and the cloth over his head removed, revealing what was rarely shown to lesser beings – if they dared to look – that this was not an old man, though the unkempt hair and straggly beard were grey, growing from a narrow head, the sharp, long face centred by a thin, beaked nose. Heavy-lidded eyes held the wildness of a fanatic believing in his own omnipotence, as an acolyte put a circular silver torque round his neck, a medallion in the form of two dolphins intertwined set within the lower part to lie upon the chest. A silver, branched head-dress, wrought by the shapes of seashells, was placed on his head and a silver trident with a long shaft put in his hand amid rapturous cries from the crowd.

Tardhamor had submitted to these ministrations with some impatience, eager to be done with this part of the proceedings, rising at once to escort the lovers to the holed stone to stand on either side. 'Kneel when I command you and place a hand through the hole to clasp each other's 'til I bid you release them. You will then be joined as one, by virtue of the authority invested in me by our mighty god.' He went directly to the statues and began to chant prayers in unison with the priests.

The rim of the stone came just below Meralda's shoulder and the lower part of Atlan's chest, enabling them to stay within sight of each other and Atlan, feeling his heart would burst with emotion, was compelled to make some loving gesture. He lifted his talisman, the cross-within-a-circle, over his head and reached across to place it over hers. 'My wedding gift to you, my love, ' he murmured.

186

She caught her breath, enraptured with the bliss of the moment, swiftly pulling out the pins holding the twisted knot of shimmering hair to flood over her shoulders. Then it was her turn to stretch out over the top of the marriage stone, taking Atlan's face between her hands. 'And this is my wedding gift to you, my dearest husband,' she breathed, adding: 'You be Poseidon and I will be Cleito!'

He glanced down – to see the Vivian Jewel hanging amid his garlands…

# 11

*Changelings*

The processional party was in dire need of rest and refreshment by the time it reached the environs of the church, to find there was to be short period for the former but none for the latter, food being held in reserve until after Mass. The nuns thankfully relinquished the various things they carried and made themselves comfortable by excursions into the bushes, only then able to take the weight from their weary limbs by sitting on the grass, the prioress and bride reversing the process by exercising their legs.

Lowenna saw the crowd, gathered to celebrate Saint Martin, thronging the meadows around the church with decorated carts and a selection of tethered and caged livestock. As with all festive occasions, there were goods being offered by those who had come to sell for those who had come to buy, with food and drink and all manner of entertainments bringing gaiety to the scene. Her eyes searched, with apprehension, for the sight of a familiar face, Martin, her father, or Vivian, but to her relief they were nowhere to be found – she feared an unwelcome greeting. Sister Adwen was sitting alone, looking in her direction with troubled eyes, so she gave her an encouraging smile, knowing it would be unseen under the veil but in an effort to raise her own flagging spirits.

After a while the nuns began to form into a group behind

the prioress, standing conspicuous in her ornamental mantle, and if anyone had noted the absence of Lowenna then none had found the courage to approach the lady with the information – she was far too occupied with assembling her retinue to allow of any interruption anyway. Already she had been put into an ill-humour by what she felt was a considered slight in the way she was greeted by a secondary priest, when she thought that duty should have been performed by the priest-in-charge or, better still, a senior member of the archdeacon's party, and was ready to make a formal complaint whenever the opportunity should arise.

The archdeacon was being obliged to conduct several celebrations of Mass, and some had already received the bread and wine served them by the priests in the open air – or in the church, for especial communicants, the limited proportions of the building making it impossible to accommodate everyone together. It was now the turn of the nuns from the priory to begin their progress towards the open doors, and Sister Adwen came to usher the bride to join them.

Until then, shorter in stature than her mother or Meralda, Lowenna had been able to lift the gown clear of her feet with one hand, but knowing she would soon need two hands in order to raise the hem and the long sleeves as she knelt, she had to free her other hand of the pouch kept tightly in her palm both for its safety and close association with Vivian, whose own hand had held it. Now was the time to ask Sister Adwen to help her put the chain over her head and arrange the veil above it.

As they approached the entrance she unwound the strings from her wrist to slip her hand inside, and on withdrawing it stared in cold disbelief at what she held. For a moment she thought the jewel had been transmuted by some evil spell, before she recognised the broken chain from Sister Columb's crucifix and the knucklebone she herself had

189

given Meralda to bite on when her poultice was removed. She was so astounded that she found it difficult to accept the evidence of her eyes. Meralda! For what reason had she contrived this cruel deception?

Then she remembered how avidly she had regarded the jewel, assuming its possession, and the reluctance with which she had been parted from it. How she must have coveted it to do this – to effect the transference in front of her unknowing eyes with such cunning secrecy! Tears of resentment welled up and nearly spilled over. This was the one thing she felt might have eased the distress suffered by Vivian when he discovered Meralda's absence – to have his heirloom restored to him. Then, with a faint smile of self-derision she admitted her stupidity, realising the jewel would have done nothing to assuage his sorrow – nothing other than Meralda herself would content him. Blindly she dropped the spurious items back into the pouch, twisted its strings around her wrist, and let it remain hanging there as they moved inside.

\*

Tardhamor completed the marriage ritual, intoning his prayers in front of the statues before turning towards the couple standing at the stone. 'Kneel,' he directed. 'Be ready to clasp your hands within the wedding ring when I tell you so to do.'

The breeze had sent the clouds scudding across the sky, allowing the sun to illumine the scene within the glade, and for the sun to shine on a wedding was considered to be a blessing. Meralda silently thanked fate for it as Atlan tried to marshal his confused thoughts, having been rendered dumb-founded by the appearance of the jewel. He endeavoured to conceal it amongst his garlands, but as he bent to kneel it fell away from his hand, the sun causing brilliant flashes to reflect from the gold encircling the pendant pearl, but as there was no indication that the brilliance had been seen he quickly tried again to cover it with the flowers.

Meralda had lifted the talisman to her lips, her other hand poised to enter the aperture awaiting the next instruction. When it came, it came with the brutal shock of the totally unexpected as Tardhamor abruptly waved his trident, crying: 'Seize them!' and they were dragged away from the wedding ring.

The high priest strode up to Atlan, his eyes fixed on the gleaming jewel, seemingly mesmerised as he reached out to stroke it. 'Wondrous,' he breathed. 'A marvellous treasure indeed – a worthy possession for Poseidon.' His tone changed, malevolence distorting his face in his fury. 'How dared you risk defiling it by letting it touch your despicable body!'

In one swift movement he clutched the jewel and snatched it up and over Atlan's head, holding it aloft by the golden chain as it swung, shining in the sunlight. 'See,' he shouted to the crowd, 'this priceless pearl that rightfully belongs to our god, but which was wilfully stolen from him by some Lord of Lyonesse long ago. It has once again been stolen by this wretch, who shamelessly hoped to keep it for himself!'

He lowered his voice to a hoarse, menacing pitch as he directed it at Atlan, confronting him with studied insolence. 'You thought to flee with this treasure! Then where is she who was to bring it here? Did you think to deprive Poseidon of her also? Silence!' he shouted, not wishing to hear him, as Atlan, outraged by these accusations, endeavoured to refute them while struggling with his captors. 'Stop his mouth and tie him to the holding stone whilst I ponder on his fate.'

He watched with satisfaction as Atlan was gagged with a cloth, his garlands and robe torn from him and his wrists and ankles bound. Having seen him tied to the holding post his attention was diverted to Meralda, struggling to free herself while demanding to know the reason for this assault, saying she was the one who had bestowed the jewel upon Atlan – it had been hers to give!

The high priest ignored her pleas and stood regarding her, appraising her, as he had appraised the bull-calves brought by Atlan. 'Why await the other now?' he murmured to himself, then spoke loudly to the crowd, indicating Meralda.

'This is the promised bride for Poseidon – promised to him alone and not that worthless cur yonder who wanted her, like the jewel, solely for himself, so we will not be robbed of a ceremony this day and shall see the bride united with our god.'

He motioned to a priest to remove his headdress while he put the chain over his head, and then it was replaced. The shining purity of the pearl was emphasised as it hung atop the dingy folds of his robe below the entwined dolphins on the torque, then he walked to Meralda, firmly held by the priests, and tore her garlands in pieces. Next, he placed his bony fingers in the neck of her robe and rent it from her, so that she stood naked before the assembly, shamed, bewildered and crying in terror.

Tardhamor paused, studying her taut, slim body before starting to caress it intimately from the lovely, stricken face down to the dimpled knees, enjoying with excessive satisfaction her discomfiture and his own lusting, delaying as long as possible the culmination of this pagan ritual to enable it to be savoured by everyone present in full measure. Held by her arms, she twisted from side to side in a vain attempt to evade those evil prying hands and eyes, the silver cross-within-a-circle thrown behind her and entangled in the pale golden hair sent swinging away from her scarred back. Atlan, to the side and rear of her, was made a horrified witness to the ordeal she had previously suffered as well as the one she was now enduring. His eyes were stretched wide, agonising in his helplessness as he frantically attempted to remove the cloth from his mouth by rubbing it against the rough stone.

The high priest was at last ready to complete his ritual, and pointed to the altar with the trident. 'Lay her there,' he ordered, then walked to the statues and threw open his arms. 'O mighty ruler of Atlantis! God of the seas, of horses, of storms and earthquakes! Hear me!' His voice was thick in the expectant silence that pervaded the glade, a priest's hand effectively rendering Meralda's cries inaudible.

'Atlan, this vile and unworthy churl who wished to challenge your supremacy, at first chose this virgin as a bride for you then desired her for himself, thinking to find you another, lesser maiden. 'Twould seem that in this way he put himself in precedence over you, which cannot be tolerated and for which he will be justly punished. He meant, too, to keep your great pearl, the treasure once lost to you but now restored, which I will keep safe.' He lifted it to the statue then dropped it down on his chest again. 'The time is nigh for you to be joined with the bride who awaits you – aided by your humble priest, O powerful god. Will you then reward your people by calming the seas? To give them ease to harvest all that swims and grows beneath your waters? Will you let them reclaim the land you have taken in your anger? We ask nothing more than that you show us your mercy. We harken for the sound of your voice and your accord.'

He adopted a posture of listening intently, as did all those present that were not already fallen into an intoxicated stupor, hearing distinctly from the far-off seashore the sound of surf beating against the rocks. The high priest suddenly flung himself around, brandishing the trident. 'Your protector has spoken!' his cry was triumphant. 'He accepts the proffered bride, desiring this humble servant to be his proxy. He will do all that we ask – and more – having agreed our compact, so let the prescribed and solemn rite begin!'

Murmurs of excited anticipation swelled amongst the

193

crowd as priests ran to hollowed-out sections of tree trunks covered with stretched skins, preparing to strike them with what could have been human thighbones. Others, holding two pieces of metal, clashed them together in rhythm and joined with those wielding the bones to produce a weird, discordant, metallic and drummed beat, following the high priest as he began to pace around the glade. The white-robed figures at first paraded slowly in their circle but gradually gained momentum, the beat starting to be echoed by the throats of the pagan worshippers emulating the tempo. As the intoxicated fervour turned to frenzy the noise became uproar, the swirling figures lurching out of control until Tardhamor gave a loud shout: 'Enow!'

Everyone came to a standstill, some falling down, all dazed and breathless yet in a fever of ecstasy. Briefly, there was complete silence until Tardhamor moved with resolve once more and the drumming and clashing began anew, retarded and less strident but with an added, sinister urgency. Red-faced, the sweat running down into his matted beard and breathing harshly, he went deliberately toward the red-stained altar where Meralda was held spread-eagled. Priests on either side pinioned her wrists, her arms stretched side-ways, while another at her head stopped her cries. Two others held her legs over the end of the altar, the rough stone cutting into her thighs, crouching on either side as they held her ankles.

A distant memory came to Atlan, the reluctant observer of a rite once practised in Atlantis as it slumped into decadence, in which all the priests took a part, shocking him into making an extra effort to free his mouth, cheeks scratched and bleeding from the rough granite. No one heeded him, all eyes being on the victim and Tardhamor as he approached her.

An acolyte removed his headdress as another took the trident from his hand and the belt from his waist and, slavering, he gazed down at the helpless maid, feasting his eyes on her nude beauty. Hands were taken from her mouth so her screams could be heard the better, as he stepped on to a stone slab at the foot of the altar and stood looming over her with a Satanic grin, then flung open his malodorous robe to display his dirty, scrawny body and proud, prominent flesh as the drumming reached a crescendo – but not loud enough to drown her screams of terror – and prepared to fall upon her.

It was then that Atlan succeeded in freeing his mouth. 'Leave her be!' he shouted. 'She cannot be given to Poseidon – she is no longer a virgin!'

His cry was compelling enough to bring sounds of dismay from the assembly and Tardhamor to a shuddering halt. Barely able to check himself he remained teetering above her, beginning to shake with a terrible agitation as he looked across to the pillar where Atlan was tied. The whistled signal that came from the captive's lips was drowned from human ears by the dreadful roar coming from the throat of the high priest, like an imagined, awesome cry of one of the damned in hell.

For a short space he seemed demented, bereft of reason until, having covered his disarray with his robe he gained control over his demoniacal rage. He seized the sacrificial trident and held it high with both hands poised over Meralda's cringing abdomen, its sharpened points reflecting the rays of the sun in their turn.

'Great Poseidon,' he cried. 'We are abject in asking your pardon for causing you to suffer this perfidy in which we were misled. You know upon whom the blame must be cast – and your revenge will begin with the sacrifice of this useless creature who is unable to provide you with her virginal blood.' He nodded to a priest. 'Hold the cup close for the life-blood that shall not escape – let no drop be spilled!'

He was about to plunge the trident down when two things

occurred. A tremor, stronger than the one felt some weeks earlier, rumbled deep in the earth and shook all that lay above. It ceased soon after it had begun, but was severe enough to throw Tardhamor off balance and divert him from his intention.

Mordon, alerted by Atlan's signal and untroubled by the tremor, was galloping like a deliverer of vengeance across the glade, scattering all in his path, trampling under his hooves those who were neither capable nor swift enough to escape them. The message Atlan had conveyed to him was clear, and there was no hesitation as he approached Tardhamor with nostrils flaring and teeth bared, snorting wildly as he butted his head into the high priest's already unsteady body and knocked him out of reach of Meralda. The stallion stood on his hind legs ready to attack and subdue any challenge, his plunging forefeet pawing and striking out at the surrounding priests seeking cover, the epitome of Atlan – his alter ego!

'Meralda – ride him – hold fast to the halter!' Atlan was urging, aware that she might resist going without him. 'Hasten – for my sake – to save me from guilt of your further hurt! Do not fear for me – Mordon will take you to safety, my love, 'til we come together once more in some other place – some other time...'

Uncertain and afraid, she stood upright on the altar as Mordon thrust his neck against her, clutching frantically at his mane as she managed to overlie along his broad back. He swerved around the granite block and began to race away as she tried to catch a sight of Atlan, but had to flatten herself as they went beneath the branches, heading out of the grove. As they moved fast through the forest she was sobbing with the torment she was enduring, telling herself that it had not been of her choosing to abandon her lover and almost wishing the trident had completed its grisly task. It would have freed her from the anguish she was suffering in having to leave Atlan to certain, terrible torture and death.

And for what reason had she been allowed to keep her life? She could still hear his words in her ears, '…'til we come together once more in some other place – some other time…' and determined that her immediate purpose must be to save him, so the realisation of those words could be effected in the here and now. She must do her best to free him from that threatening and fearful Forbidden Place she had once believed to be the most wonderful place in their world.

As they travelled swiftly onward she guessed what their destination must be, Mordon moving with obvious intent as if guided by Atlan who knew the one place where she might find safety – but at what price her safety? She closed her eyes tight, trying to block out what might lie ahead. What could she hope for? How could she manage to save Atlan? And how would she be received by her father?

*

Richard had rested in Martin's room, then come out to seek Vivian at the time of the expected arrival of the priory Sisters to try to persuade him to return inside. He felt just as needful to have the proof of his sight that Meralda was really come, yet alive to the superstition that the groom should only lay eyes on his bride when they were within the church to ensure happiness during their lifetimes. He found him standing idle among the merrymakers, watching the road.

'Come friend, give me your company to partake of a draught to calm the worries that beset us. See how my hand shakes with disquiet. I would rather attempt to pacify a vicious wolf than endure the perplexity of bringing a daughter to a successful espousal. On every occasion when I have pined for my beloved Ysella it was never greater than now, when I am desirous of her presence more than can be guessed at. It has been forced upon me that a man is a fool if he thinks it an easy task to rear daughters – only a woman of wisdom can do it without falling foul of the tricks they are wont to play upon a credulous, unperceptive father...to be sure, I speak only in a general manner about daughters,' he ended hurriedly.

He need not have been concerned that Vivian might pick up his artless words. His friend had heard nothing after the mention of Ysella's name, imagining her standing beside him wearing the wedding gown he had never forgotten, so great had been his yearning on that poignant day long ago. Why, he had even encouraged Richard to imbibe so much wine that he had eventually lain insensible and in disgrace, simply to delay the unthinkable, but inevitable, deflowering of the bride. He had loved Richard as a brother – as he did now – but with Ysella he still suffered the pangs of rejection and jealousy. This day, however, this day would see the culmination of all his hopes and longings, when he would finally bring his nostalgic dream – now invested in flesh and blood – into his arms and into his bed! He unwillingly allowed himself to be persuaded to return inside, ashamed of his secret thoughts, trusting they were not written on his face for all to read, and glad he would not have much longer to contain his fretful mood.

Richard had told Jowan to watch the road, with an order not to venture near another jar of wine until after the union, and at last he burst into the room where they waited, his grin revealing his almost toothless gums. 'M'Lord – Master, they are now come! Meralda is in the midst of them, 'minding me of great, white birds of prey surrounding a defiant swan, sure of its own strength!'

Richard's relief was such that he was induced to attempt a play upon words to cheer his friend. 'D'ye hear, Vivian?' He slapped him on the back. 'I'faith, I believe Old Jowan jests! He says the Sisters are like birds of prey, and that, of a certainty, is how they spend their days – praying – d'ye see?

198

What could be more pertinent? Nay, old friend...' – he held Vivian by the arm as he rose to leave – '...we must give them time to compose themselves – and they have yet to attend Mass. I doubt we will be called 'til after the middle of the day, giving you a chance to once again scrape those portions of your face that warrant it – so as not to put a soreness on your bride's delicate skin!'

After what seemed an interminable wait, a cleric came to call them. Vivian, fearing to confront reality after all his years of living in the past, appeared unwilling to move and Richard felt obliged to encourage him. 'Come, what ails you? I know 'tis a common infirmity of those to be espoused to suffer a weakness of the knees, but 'tis not the first time you have stood entreating of God's mercy to bless your union. What we have both been contemplating with impatience is but a short step away, so let us progress with thankfulness.'

The cleric led them out to a side door of the church, Vivian entering first followed by the two servants attendant on him, then Richard and Old Jowan. They peered through a gloom that the many candles struggled to dispel, conscious of the smells of incense, tallow and sweat, inextricably mixed.

Richard's eyes were first taken by the concentration of candles illuminating a wooden cross, of a size once used for crucifixion, set against the east wall behind an altar covered by a purple cloth. They next fell upon the archdeacon, changed from his customary purple into a white vestment, Martin and the priest-in-charge at his right hand, the others on his left. He was filled with an immense pride as his gaze lingered on his son, before passing to the body of the church for a sight of his daughters. The supplicants, having received the bread and wine, remained on their knees, the nuns bent over with only their backs in evidence. Richard, smiling behind a hand, was mindful of Jowan's expressive phrase that 'they looked like white birds of prey' and the meaning he had put upon the last word. How apt at this moment, he thought, as he tried to detect his swans. There was Meralda being helped to her feet, but where was Lowenna? It could only be that she had been put into a nun's habit to conform to the others, and as they all appeared the same he would have to wait until she declared herself.

Vivian had seen nothing but the figure with the veiled head. A nun was assisting her to rise and divest her of her cloak, passing it to others who drew away, leaving her set apart, standing straight and seeming tall, her height enhanced by the chaplet on her head. He felt his heart leap as he gazed upon his bride, identical in his mind to that other, the one who had haunted his sleeping and waking life ever since she had imprinted her image on the inside of his eyelids in that same white gown, the instant when he knew she was lost to him, about to become Richard's wife and leave him yet a callow youth. He had suffered a miserable sense of becoming excluded, an outsider, and was why he had begun to shun their company and agreed to marry Kweras in a hopeless endeavour to emulate their happiness – and what a sad failure he had made of his marriage! From being a warm and pleasant maiden who professed to love him, over the years his wife had grown distant and sullen, until the only words she uttered in his presence were scathing and bitter, her face become a mask of reproach as she searched for love elsewhere.

During these last weeks, when he realised the pent-up love which had lain dormant for so long had burst free of his control, he had dimly begun to see where the blame could lie, and only now was he prepared to accept the fact that it had been his fault alone. He, Vivian, had ruined Kweras' life, instead of the reverse as he had been so ready to assert in the past, and at this moment, in this place and before God he begged her forgiveness with all his heart, and gradually became aware of a quietude and peace filling his being such as he had not known since his early years.

From the midst of this gentle wrapping of absolution he heard the archdeacon ask him to come forward, and as he complied it became Richard's turn.

'Richard of Trevelyan, bring forth your daughter Meralda to be given this day in wedlock to Vivian, Lord of Lyonesse.'

Richard had been pleased to note the air of composure that had descended on his friend and moved to the bride, holding his bent arm out to her to put her hand upon. Together they went to stand by Vivian, and Richard stepped back, leaving them side by side as Martin, from his position in front of the bride, gave a smile to cheer her, assuming by the trembling of her gown that she was suffering a natural timidity. The archdeacon began the ceremony which progressed without incident until nearly completed, with the nuptial pair voicing their vows, one firmly and the other in faltering, whispered tones.

It ended when an earth tremor rocked them, the same that thwarted Tardhamor, causing the bride to fling out a hand to regain her balance, and as Vivian caught her by the waist, Martin clutched the fluttering hand. A wave of consternation swept through the assembly waiting for further disturbance, but when nothing more occurred Richard assured them there had been rock falls before without hurt to any soul and requested the archdeacon to finish his service – anxious for them to be away to the mainland. Despite his show of bravado he felt an underlying menace.

The archdeacon nodded in assent and began to intone from the point where he had encountered the interruption, and it was Martin's startled cry that caused him to stop yet again. 'Lowenna…' The young priest's utterance was anguished as he stared down at the hand held in his, her ring with the black stone, that she had forgotten to conceal, obvious upon it. Unable to believe it, he pulled the veil and flowers from her head, freeing the black hair that fell about her shoulders, her despairing countenance exposed for all to see. She shrank away from his look of condemnation, a mixture of amazement anger and sorrow, while other faces reflected these emotions, their mouths agape.

It was as if time itself stood still for a moment and then moved on at a faster pace, bringing confusion. The congregation started to wander about, a babble of voices raised with question upon unanswered question filling the air. Martin was trying to explain to the archdeacon while Richard was loudly berating Lowenna, Vivian standing benumbed and regarding her with manifest incredulity, having withdrawn his hand from her waist.

'Where is Meralda? Why is your sister not here?' Richard was demanding with a fierceness that threatened to choke him. 'Have you done away with her because you crave the bed of her betrothed? I knew I was not mistaken in your desire for him – I had long suspected it! I charge you!'

Lowenna had sunk to her knees, afraid of his anger, feeling lost and utterly alone with every hand turned against her. 'I have not…I was told to…she can be found in the Town – in Breonseyth,' she faltered, terror filling her.

'In the Town?' bellowed Richard, his voice overpowering all the others. 'And why, in the name of all that is holy, is she attendant there when she should be here? And why are you clothed in my Ysella's gown when it should be adorning Meralda? What reason can you offer for this base deception? Speak – or have you swallowed your canting tongue?' He gripped her shoulders in his rage and helplessness, shaking her so that she was almost thrown from her knees to the ground until he felt himself checked.

'Let her have her say.' Vivian lifted her to her feet and supported her from falling, his face set hard, his words spoken in a low tone. 'We need your response, Lowenna. What has happened to Meralda and why have you befooled us so?'

She tried to control the sobs stifling her, occasioned by the fright in being discovered and finding that the actuality of this scene was far worse than she had ever envisaged. Too shamed to look at her father or, indeed, anyone, she pulled herself away from Vivian and addressed her defence to the paving in front of his feet as she released the pouch from her wrist.

'M-my Lord,' she stammered. 'I crave your forgiveness. I had hoped to bring your jewel to make amends for our misdoing but find it remains with Meralda. I durst not tell you before of her contrariness and refusal to wed you, while yet in the hope, ay, and belief that God would turn her from her waywardness. I can hardly abear to have to confess that she loves another – to the point of madness – and they are gone away to be wed this day...'

'And you aided her?' Richard, in an effort to keep his ire curbed had listened quietly until the last sentence, then snatched the pouch from her and emptied its contents into his hand. Exasperation overcame his restraint yet again.

'Whence came this dross?' and with no reply forthcoming: 'You say they are in the Town, thinking to keep the jewel and escape my wrath! Is that not so?' he shouted, and was rewarded with an almost imperceptible nod from the stricken maid before deciding to turn his anger on the alarmed prioress.

'How d'ye account for this sorry course of events, m'Lady?' he asked, aggressively. 'My daughters were left in your care to bring Meralda to her senses and you let her disappear from under your hand like a flea in the straw! I ask it again, how d'ye answer this?'

She drew herself up indignantly. 'I counter your charge by asking how you durst send those two children of Beelzebub – that you claim you fathered! – loose amongst our unsuspecting Sisters? Bringing about the corruption of at least one that I am aware of...' she cast a furious look at Sister Adwen, who had stayed standing motionless behind

203

Lowenna, her hands together and eyes lowered, '...by seducing her from the path of obedience and righteousness. As for the disappearance of Meralda – well, it could be that the Devil has claimed his own!'

Richard, apoplectic and red of face, seemed ready to burst with fury, but the archdeacon, though extremely perplexed, was determined not to allow the continuance of what was rapidly descending into a common brawl.

'This is a house of God!' he declared, bringing his authority forcefully to bear on the situation, 'and not to be desecrated by such sentiments revealed by spiteful quarrelling! I order everyone to depart these walls whilst I, aided by the priests and the grace of God, cleanse them again! Now, get you all hence!'

Suitably admonished and subdued, the company hurriedly made its way into the open air under the heavy, overcast sky, the brief period of sunshine having been replaced by clouds that hardly moved, the stillness that comes before a storm being so apparent as to be almost palpable. The protagonists formed themselves into two groups as they left the church, the prioress with her flock turning to one side while Richard and Vivian went to the other. Richard had already begun to advise their men-at-arms of a change of plan, that they were to travel to Breonseyth in search of Meralda, and Lowenna and Sister Adwen were left between the two, isolated and ignored – but not for long.

The prioress descended on her black sheep like an avenging angel ready to exact retribution, her body shaking with wrath at having to cope with this disagreeable situation. Instead of keeping her dignity and waiting until she regained the seclusion of her fastness, she shrilly blamed the unfortunate Adwen, who made no attempt to back away from the hands that tore the nun's veil from her head and pulled the wimple down around her neck, revealing bare, white shaven skin. The action aped the affront put on Lowenna, and was performed thus to occasion the utmost public humiliation and disgrace for the recipient.

'You were plainly a party to this trickery and are no longer fit to serve God,' she was saying, acidly. 'We must decide what is to become of you. Your punishment and penance will begin once you have been handed over to Sister Columb to assess your infamous conduct.' With that said, she turned her back to the blushing, shamed little figure, and went to the waiting group of assenting and conforming Sisters.

'We must break our fast and seek out our chattels and the guide, then leave with the offender without further respite. Lead us to the board!' This last command was aimed at the same unfortunate cleric sent to greet her, thereby earning her displeasure, and whom she now found hovering nervously at her elbow. He led them away in the direction of the refectory with all speed.

Vivian stood by as in a trance, blankly watching the scene just enacted, his thoughts chaotic, his mind grappling with the bitter facts. At last, he levelled his stare at Richard, who had also been an interested spectator of the holy mother's outburst, as he was hoping to learn more about Meralda.

'Richard, was it truth that Lowenna spoke? That Meralda has fled away to wed another, and you were knowing of this betimes without disclosing it to me?'

Richard was anxious to smooth over his part in the deception. ''Tis but a few days since I first learned of her perfidy and did what I deemed best to turn her back to the ways of virtue. The priory offered an excellent chastening place in which she could be kept safe and duly reminded of her dutiful obedience, though seemingly to no avail. Haply, she cannot be wed without my word upon't – but we waste the day – come, let us ride to seek out her abductor. We must hasten to claim her back and then take oar to the mainland, where you can be wed at some other place – when she comes to her senses!'

He resumed his efforts to hurry the men into readiness to leave just as the archdeacon and his clerics, accompanied by the priests and Martin, emerged from the church demanding that some light be shed on the situation. 'Forgive our hastiness in giving you no answers as yet,' Richard begged, 'but we have far to ride in a short space. I will tender our reasons and regrets with penitence when we return.' He then began to move away while regarding Vivian with misgiving, as he seemed reluctant to bestir himself and join them. The archdeacon, appearing to feel he had been misused in some obscure manner, did not intend to allow them to depart so easily and Richard found himself forced to hold back to impart more information for courtesy and for Martin's sake.

Cast out and rejected by both sides, the two luckless persons at the centre of the dissension were by now mainly disregarded by the crowd that had resumed the enjoyment of the feast day, returning to its idle pleasures once the entertainment provided by the espousal party was apparently at an end. Lowenna moved to Adwen's side.

'Do not fear,' she whispered, putting comforting arms around her. 'I cannot abear for you to suffer such an unjust punishment. There is something I had hoped not to have to do, but finding you so ill-used has made it easier for me to accept. A white horse is coming to carry me away from here and I mean to take you with me. It will deliver us far from here – where we can plan what measures to avail ourselves of for the future. Mayhap we could even gain the mainland shore…' Then to her great relief she saw Mordon appear against the skyline. 'Look – there is the horse – he is coming now.'

# 12

## *The Ferry*

The men-at-arms were preparing their horses and equip-
ment while Richard remained in converse with the clergy,
and Vivian walked slowly to where Lowenna clasped the little
nun close in her compassion. She had hidden the bare head
from curious and condemning eyes by replacing the wimple
that framed the rounded, dimpled face, then covered the
white linen with the hood of the cloak. Vivian stood
regarding them, his feelings unreadable from his fixed
expression, before beckoning the servant carrying his cloak.
Taking it he shook it out, and with little grace put it around
Lowenna's shoulders as she shrank from him, thinking he
only desired to hide the bridal gown from his sight. She
watched him retreat from her, so full of regret and longing
she thought her heart must break.

Determined to stay composed and not shame herself or
her family further, she looked again at Mordon galloping
down the rutted track and sensed that all was not as it should
be. There was something or someone on the stallion's back,
but who could it be? Not Atlan, or anyone riding in an
accustomed manner. She continued to watch with increasing
astonishment as the horse neared, a feeling of dread growing
within her as Mordon came neither towards her nor the
church door, but instead drew up by Richard who, facing the
archdeacon, remained unaware of the arrival until the

cessation of thudding hooves behind him claimed his scrutiny and he turned.

For one incredible moment he found himself gazing on the naked form of Meralda stretched along the horse, her long hair partly covering her. Her mouth was half open but silent, her misted eyes seeking his in the seeming hope of forgiveness and help, before she relaxed her hold and began to slide down to fall forward onto her knees. Her tresses parted to reveal the scars standing out in stark relief on the white skin, and a sibilant sound could be heard as people near by caught their breath.

Meralda, untroubled by her condition, humbled herself at Richard's feet, clutching his legs. 'Father, do not turn from me. I may have sinned in your eyes but have done nought for which I feel shame. Nay, hearken to me,' she entreated, as he attempted to free himself from her grasp. 'I am desperate for your aid! Atlan, my love, is in grave danger and held, because of me, in the Sacred Grove of the Forbidden Place. The high priest wears the Vivian Jewel he stole – he is vengeful and plans my dearest one harm, and my life will be forfeit should he not be stopped. If you have any love left for me I beg you to ride hard – you may yet save him!'

Richard found himself struggling to choose from the jumble of words threatening to overwhelm his mouth. He was still mute as Martin pushed forward, concern overcoming his natural aversion to physical contact with the Devil he now believed to be inhabiting the body of his sister, directing her actions in order to entice and claim her soul. Making the sign of the cross, he swept his priest's cloak around her to hide her nakedness, fastening it at the neck. 'This was dedicated to Saint Martin – let it cover and protect you from further evil, Meralda. I beg you confess what manner of monster inflicted those wounds upon you?'

Meralda favoured him with a twisted grimace. 'I'faith, an obtainment from m'lady of the priory, no less.' She returned

208

her gaze to Richard. 'Father, are you remaining deaf to my plea?'

Before he could answer, the archdeacon, an interested observer who was becoming bemused by the events that had marked his day, broke in with his own questioning. 'Am I to infer, Richard of Trevelyan, that your errant daughter has come in this unseemly fashion with strange words upon her lips? What manner of outlawed region is the "forbidden place" and a grove favoured with the title "sacred"?'

Martin hurriedly intervened to relieve his father of his natural disinclination to discuss Meralda's fall into iniquity. 'Allow me to tell you there is a grove at Kellimargh once sacred to the pagan god of the sea, Poseidon, worshipped because a goodly number of our people have always been fishers. When we embraced the Christian way of life the site was declared unholy and barred to all us true believers, thus becoming known as the Forbidden Place.'

The archdeacon showed alarm. 'An edict that has been ignored, 'twould appear! And what manner of person is this "high priest" you spoke of? Can pagan rites yet be practised on Lyonesse? If so, 'tis an abomination that must be effaced from the land! How far must we travel to rout them?'

'Carrag Uthek rises yonder, itself once a pagan place of human sacrifice to the sun god,' answered Martin, pointing. 'Kellimargh lies on t'other side, at its foot.' The archdeacon went at once to Vivian. 'As governor, you are surely beholden to your innocent fellows to remove the source of unrighteousness from their midst. Rally your men, and together we will go hence to fight and defeat the wily Serpent!'

Although the onus for action had thus been thrust upon him, Vivian was still preoccupied with accepting that his own hopes and dreams had been shattered beyond repair. His thoughts were turned inwards and, unhearing, he appeared to hesitate, being saved from embarrassment when the matter was resolved for him by Richard, whose anger had

209

reached a point where he could contain it no longer. It was fuelled by his guilt at letting what he now was sure must be the origin of the evil on Lyonesse to escape him – more – at allowing his laxity and blindness to tear his friends and family and his people apart and put their lives in danger, desperately aware there might still be time to redeem his error and knowing it to be his sole responsibility.

He bowed to the archdeacon. 'M'Lord Vivian is required to be taken up by another task, so 'tis my duty and desire to lead you into conflict. Let every able man be armed and ready to ride!' he commanded, and without waiting for possible dissent from those who might mention the pressing need to depart for the mainland, went to his horse. 'We leave at once to destroy the pagans!'

'Father...stay!' screamed Meralda. 'You must spare Atlan! I will ride with you...' She gripped Mordon's halter, but her brother pulled her hands away.

Richard, looking around, espied Vivian shaking his head as if ridding himself of a nightmare, already mounted and bearing down on him with displeasure written on his troubled features. 'Nay, old friend,' he said, urgently. 'Forgive my seeming to usurp your authority, but you can provide a service that I can trust to none other. I entreat you to forgo your revenge, which I will undertake for you, and convey my two artful maidens to the mainland lest they make more mischief for us all. Deliver them to those who expect us.' He lowered his voice. 'I place reliance upon you to give my dependants the care they will need should I not return. I feel it imperative to lead the affray as 'twas I who failed to find the infamy in what was the obvious place, had I the wit to pursue it, so obvious that I did not believe it could be.'

Vivian stared down at him. 'And what if I am branded coward should I not lead our men and fight?'

'If any man durst utter that opinion in my hearing, I will relish running him through, my friend! Let it not be forgot that I am the older, so you must do as I bid!' A smile lit Richard's face, and he was relieved to find it matched by the softening of Vivian's own. 'I will also attempt to recover your jewel. Then, 'tis agreed?'

Vivian nodded, reluctantly. 'Ay. I will take them by the ferry and go to Trevivian first before continuing on to the hillfort to reunite with your people, so will look to meet with you at one place or t'other before nightfall – Brother!' They clasped forearms to affirm it as Richard said: 'I ask pardon regarding Meralda's duplicity but thought, were I to overcome her disobedience, you would be saved pain.' He knew by the returning pressure that he had been forgiven, and this was to be their parting.

He went hurriedly to where Meralda was attempting to wrest Mordon's halter from Martin's grasp, the horse tossing its head and stamping its hooves uneasily, anxious to be gone. Richard deftly twisted her hands away, and cocooned her in Martin's cloak so that her arms were pinioned within it, then picked up his protesting daughter and flung her over the saddle in front of Vivian like a sack of his own grain, averting his face from the source of his anguish before going to his son.

'Martin, favour me with your horse for Lowenna. This white stallion is not saddled and you are well able to ride without one.' He led Martin's mount to where Lowenna crouched, her arms protecting the small nun. 'M'Lord will escort you to the mainland with Meralda,' her father said, grimly. 'I shall settle your future betterment when I rejoin you.' He bent to raise her but she resisted, refusing to be parted from Adwen, speaking defiantly. 'I cannot leave her here to suffer a punishment for which I am equally guilty. Either she comes with me or I stay!'

Richard was about to tear them roughly apart, furious that she should put a condition on his ruling, when he chanced to look directly into the nun's grey eyes, noticing they were flecked with green. They seemed strangely calm, not fearful, but as if accepting whatever God willed. He felt a bonding with his own and a desire to be held longer by that tranquil gaze, at the same time surprised to be even considering having an unwanted encumbrance thrust upon them, and the next moment was reflecting how much he regretted that this childlike nun's bald pate had been made the object of such ridicule. 'As you will,' he said meekly, forcing his eyes away.

He helped Lowenna into the saddle before taking Adwen about the waist to gently swing her up to sit in front of his daughter, who put her arms on each side and took the reins. 'Father, have a care for yourself and Martin, and grant me your forgiveness,' she called, beginning to follow Vivian.

He gave no answer, merely waved in farewell, staring after them, then mounted and placed himself beside Old Jowan in the forefront of the fighting men. They were joined by Martin on Mordon who, unresisting, had allowed him the privilege, and followed by the archdeacon and his clerics uttering threats of eternal damnation as they galloped towards Carrag Uthek.

Vivian and his three charges went the opposite way, making for the ferry on the eastern point. A fickle wind veered around, blowing in different directions, so their progress was neither helped nor hindered, a warm wind that brought no refreshing air in its wake. On reaching the part of the coast nearest that of the mainland, they looked down from the top of the cliff into a coomb to see the flat-bottomed ferryboat, similar to a scow, made fast on the beach below. Across the narrow channel on the opposite shore, cliffs rose above a similar beach and coomb.

The wind-blown scrub around them showed no overt signs of life, so without dismounting and keeping a firm hold on Meralda who had not once ceased bewailing her forced removal, distancing her even further from Atlan, he hailed the cluster of huts grouped together that housed the ferrymen. Eventually he was rewarded by the appearance of a few bleary-eyed individuals who lurched into the open. 'Ho, there,' he called again. 'Make ready the ferry!'

Two men, one in his middle years, tall, well-built and brawny, the other shorter and younger, rather misshapen but no less muscular, stood scratching their louse-ridden heads, studying the tumbling waves before the tall one spoke. ''Tis feast day and tide's wrong withal. Return at dawn, if it should please you.'

'It does not!' cried Vivian, anxious to get away. 'I see sand on t'other side where the ferry beaches. I demand you take us over on the instant, you idle layabouts, or you will have me to answer to! You well know who I am, having been here almost daily of late, and the last time you laid eyes on me was this very morn when you ferried the archdeacon. Let me remind you that I am the governor of this island!'

There was no further demur from the men, who called for two others to aid them. The horses at once began filing down the narrow way between the rock faces, then across the wet sand to the ferryboat. One of its angled ends was pulled up on the sloping beach, so that the broad wale running round the upper edge of the boat rested on the sand, providing access for animal and man to step into the body of the craft. The ferrymen blindfolded the horses and led them aboard, tying the reins to ropes threaded through holes beneath the wale, and only when that was done did Vivian lift the closely wrapped Meralda into the boat and stand her feet on the deck.

Lowenna came next, helping Adwen aboard, and, having concern for her mother's gown, lifted up the hems of her skirts and pleated them round her waist, twisting the last piece into a strip to wind it around to keep the pleats in place, then tucked the loose end into the top. Next, she tied the trailing ends of the long sleeves together and slipped them over her head to the back of her neck, and all of this was accomplished under Vivian's cloak, which she still wore, before going to help him try to pacify her distraught sister, who was flinging herself away from him with such determination that she more than once nearly tipped over the side. He finally subdued her, pitting his greater strength against her frantic efforts to remain on Lyonesse soil.

After the men had edged the boat from the shore, the first two waded in and climbed aboard, putting the long, narrow-bladed oars between the thole-pins and, standing, began to manoeuvre out into the surf. The tide was set with a fairly strong race and the waters, though choppy, gave no hint of trouble, but as soon as the boat had moved from the shelter of the cove, the normal flow was suddenly and inexplicably reversed. At the same time, with no warning of its approach, a brilliant streak of lightening snaked overhead towards the mainland, accompanied by a deafening clap of thunder. The sea swirled violently, as in a whirlpool, the wooden oars shearing like stalks of wheat under a scythe, and with nothing to hold it steady and no means of controlling speed or direction, the ferryboat moved fast through the narrow channel, turning and twisting amid the treacherous rocks lying beneath the high cliffs on either side. When it came to those at the furthest end of the mainland it was swept around them, miraculously avoiding all hazards, as the people aboard were flung from side to side. Vivian was holding on to Meralda, and Lowenna and Adwen were holding each other before everyone fell, to be rolled upon the deck perilously close to the hooves of the terrified horses as they struggled to keep their footing.

Adwen at last managed to grasp a rope and drag herself to her knees. She abandoned forever her vow of silence as she prayed in a forceful, lusty voice for their deliverance from the mighty seas that threatened to engulf the frail craft. 'Good Lord, deliver us from lightening and tempest, we beseech thee,' she begged. 'O God, the Father of Heaven, have mercy upon us miserable sinners. If you need to take any to make atonement, then let it be me that you take!'

A wild laugh, rising above the tumult of the roaring waters, came from Meralda. She had been freed from Vivian's constraint as he was torn away from her, and pulled herself upright by gripping ropes and the wale, finding strength in her fury, resembling a sea-creature in her wild abandon, showing no fear and exulting in their peril as she held herself against the wale in a proud posture, like a beautiful, carved figurehead fixed in the forefront of a mighty ship.

'You err, nun!' she cried loudly, amid the uproar. ''Tis our god, Poseidon, who rages at the sin occasioned by my cruel abduction from Lyonesse. Should *he* want a sacrifice then let him take you – all of you – and Atlan and I can be together again. Atlan…Atlan…'

The wind stole away the rest of her imploring voice, as the ferryboat was swept around a last point and flung against a rocky outcrop with an alarming, fearful sound of splintering wood, one of its angled ends striking the rocks so violently that a large section was shattered by the impact. Fortunately, the jagged timbers of the hull became firmly wedged in a cleft between the rocks and held clear of the water, the deck and opposite end inclining towards the surface of the sea. Having been brought to such a sudden, jarring halt, those aboard had the breath knocked from them and lay inert while awaiting any further immediate adversity that might be inflicted upon them. Gradually, they became aware that the sea was gently undulating without its previous agitation, and the only sounds to be heard were the lapping of the waves and the neighing and stamping of the frightened horses.

One of the ferrymen, having judged their situation, gave a joyful shout. 'Look yonder! We lie but a short length from land! Water seems shallow enow to wade ashore with ease. Praise be to God!' He climbed over the lowest end of the wrecked ferry and let himself down on the sand between the small rocks dotting the way to the beach, the sea just above his knees.

Everyone muttered thanks to the Almighty except one. Meralda, her passion subdued by this return to calm remained unmoving, as Vivian wrapped the cloak around her again to hide the nudity for which she had no care. Lowenna, having helped Adwen regain her feet, watched him from the corner of her eye. 'Can he not see she will never submit to his love, whatever he does?' she asked herself, bitterly. 'Even now his foremost thoughts are for her, though she spurns his every attempt to gain her esteem.'

'Leave the horses 'til last,' Vivian ordered the ferrymen, 'and first let us carry these maids to dry land.' So saying, he lifted Meralda over the side and into the arms of the brawny ferryman who stood in the water. The other man picked up little Adwen as if she had been a doll, put her over his shoulder and eased himself off the end of the wreck, gingerly wading through the intervening shallows behind his fellow.

Only then did Vivian step into the sea, motioning for Lowenna to approach. He reached up and pulled her to him, lifted and held her in his arms while guardedly making for the beach, ensuring that each foot was firmly placed so as not to stumble. Held close to him and feeling the warmth issuing through the leather jerkin pressed against her breast, Lowenna was almost afraid to breathe, and shyly turned her face towards the shore. She could see small boats beached high, their owners beginning to converge from the few dwellings above the cove, hurrying to the wreck in the hope of finding some worthwhile reward for their curiosity.

Vivian, still impassive, stood Lowenna on the beach and called for the ferrymen to help with the horses who, from a cursory inspection, had not appeared to suffer injury, and the three waded back and climbed aboard. The ferrymen untethered the mare, removed its blindfold and encouraged it to walk down the sloping deck into the water, and by both of them hanging on to the reins they reached the shore safely.

Without awaiting the men's return, Vivian tried to calm the other horse, stroking its muzzle and speaking soothingly. He untied the reins and held the animal in check as it fought to find a level footing, and once in the water he took off the blindfold and swung himself onto its back as it sprang forward to splash its way to where the waves lapped the sand. Here, they were confronted by a noisy band of the local fishers rushing down to the wreck intent on salvage, shouting to others to follow. The horse, already highly nervous, reared away from them so violently that Vivian was thrown off with great force, but the fishers continued to run past as the horse careered on its way up the beach, kicking up sand and endangering all in its path, holding everyone's attention either by avoiding it or trying to stop its desperate flight.

Lowenna moved her eyes back from the runaway horse to scan the shoreline for Vivian's whereabouts – and saw him lying face down in the surf, waves breaking over his head. With a cry of alarm she ran to where he lay, reaching him as he was endeavouring to lift his head from the water but each time dropping it down again. A moment later Adwen joined her, and together they pulled him onto the dry sand where he lay coughing up water, blood seeping from a wound where his head had struck a rock. Adwen tore strips of linen from her underskirt, wetting them and passing them to Lowenna, and with one she cleansed his face, then gently lifted his head onto her lap and attempted to staunch the blood. After applying pressure the flow was stemmed, the cloth but lightly stained, and they found the wound to be no more than a broad gash fast swelling above his right temple.

In a while he began to roll his head, then opened his eyes and looked directly at Lowenna. Evasively, she turned away until she felt his hand reach out to grip her own, when, wondering, she brought her gaze back to meet his as he spoke, his voice faint and halting. 'Both your countenance and the sky above spin round so fast that I have no hope of catching up with either. Or can it be this lowly body that contains myself that moves? I am afeared of one or t'other being flung out afar and dashed into pieces – but mayhap that has already come about. Hold me still.'

'You are safe, m'Lord,' she answered, her hand on his, 'and, it appears not badly hurt but somewhat dazed. You must rest awhile.'

'My head pains me,' he touched the wound, seeing blood on his fingers, 'but the sky is fixed again and I see you are Lowenna. What came about to bring me to this unhappy pass?' His stare was questioning but he made no move to recoil from her, continuing to clutch her hand as if needing to hold on to something familiar while gathering his scattered wits. 'Have I bled much upon your garment?'

''Tis your own cloak I wear and that you lie upon, m'Lord, and the bleeding has all but ceased. You were thrown from your horse into the sea – we feared you might be drowned.'

'It seems I was not – as the soreness of my limbs inform me. Who gave me rescue?' He carefully raised himself into a sitting position and peered around, seeing only Lowenna and Adwen by him, the ferrymen attending to the horses. ''Twould seem I must proffer my thanks to you two for the gift of my life,' he said, 'which I will fain do at length at some appropriate time, but for now…On what shore do we lie?' he called, to attract the notice of a passing fisherman carrying pieces of the wreck. 'What place is this?'

''Tis the cove below Sennen.' The man hardly paused in hurrying on his way up from the beach.

'Then 'tis here I will erect a chapel as a thank-offering – to be abiding evidence of our deliverance,' Vivian vowed, resuming his contemplation of the maiden whose black hair had brushed against his cheek as she helped him put his back to a rock, 'and because I might have died, my lips sealed forever, without having asked your pardon for my disregard of you. Lowenna, I will do my utmost to make amends – 'twas as if a spell had been put upon me, so entranced was I by Meralda.'

She listened to his words in growing wonder. 'I fear your hurt causes you to speak in an ill-considered manner, m'Lord,' she said, perplexed, but his mention of her forgotten sister prompted her to seek her whereabouts. Worried, she twisted around to find there was no need for concern, as Meralda had neither tried to flee nor cast herself back into the water, her desolate figure remaining where it had been sat, gazing out over the sea with blank eyes to Lyonesse.

Lowenna returned her attention to Vivian, taking a strip of cloth to bind his head to hide her confusion over his changed attitude. If his self-reproach had been voiced in truth and not derangement, there was the possibility of a change in her previously hopeless situation – should he now be able to look on her with kindness.

Vivian was feeling strong enough to bestir himself, managing to rise and make his way unsteadily to the ferrymen to enquire how they intended to dispose themselves. The two unkempt individuals had considered robbing and killing the other survivors, but second thoughts and a furtive parley had decided them that their reward might be greater by keeping them alive. They had maintained a watchful guard over the hapless four, knives at the ready should either the fishers or their wives be smitten with the same idea, the slatternly, fierce-looking women all grouped together, eyeing the party with avid curiosity while their men stood by.

The chief ferryman answered him, saying they would walk to the huts that served the Cornish side of the ferry, adding, with a nod towards the fisher folk, how his Lordship's two faithful servants had prevented any assault upon him or his charges. Vivian, as intended, was grateful, aware of how vulnerable they had been, giving them what reward he had about him, pledging more sometime later and promising to replace the ferryboat. With Lowenna and Adwen lifted into the saddle, he was aided to mount, with Meralda, still silent, put up before him. To the watching fisher folk he said: 'This is a portion of my land, and I shall be returning here to build a chapel for thanksgiving – and none of you shall go without bounty.'

They set off on the brief ride to Trevivian, but with only a short way travelled an acrid smell filled their nostrils and they saw smoke rising above the trees ahead. Vivian urged his horse faster until he topped a rise overlooking their route and could clearly see the source from which it arose, and though having already suspected it, he was yet alarmed to find a part of Trevivian ablaze, men and women frantically filling buckets and passing them from hand to hand in a continuous chain. Dismayed, he rode swiftly down, demanding to know of the first men he met how it had started. They shook their heads, either ignorant of the cause or too agitated to give him answer so, dismounting, he sought out his steward, while noting that it was only the buildings comprising his private residence that were burning.

'M'Lord,' coughed the steward, seeing the linen tied around his master's head, 'you have suffered hurt!' Then, as Vivian removed the cloth and cast it down with an impatient gesture, the man hurriedly went on: ''Twas but a single flash that struck the thatch to set it aflame. 'Twas thought hazardous to try to save aught within so all is being burned that had been made ready to welcome you and your Lady.'

Vivian studied the eager flames. 'We need a change of garments and the room which holds our clothing is spared as yet, so I will go in by the door at the side and save what I can.' He hastened towards it, and though wisps of smoke were evident it appeared to be well away from the insidious spread

220

from the seat of the fire, but as he made to step over the threshold, Lowenna ran to clutch his arm, halting his progress. He turned to her, a mite impatiently, just as the heavy lintel supported above the door fell with a crash upon the very spot where he would have stood but one step more. Shaken, he pulled Lowenna back, holding her close to quieten her trembling, and stood silent from the shock of yet another escape from the vengeful figure of Death which seemed to be stalking him.

''Tis apparent I am threatened and pursued by some mysterious force that has as yet proved unsuccessful in its deadly intent,' he murmured, breathing deeply, 'and once again it is you who has repulsed the Grim Reaper. Less than half a day gone I might have welcomed the blade of his scythe to cut me down and cursed you for your interference, but since...'

She lifted her face to look into his. 'M'Lord – I believe I know the source from whence it comes. Meralda's lover, Atlan, told me himself that he would seek out and kill you so you could nevermore pose a threat to him. That was the reason I agreed to the exchange of places with her – so they could be wed and he content to leave you unharmed. As he is held on Lyonesse he must have entreated Poseidon, his god of the seas and horses and storms, to carry out his wrong-doing for him, using each of those means to try to harm you. But greater is our own merciful God to whom I pray for your well-being – He has overcome this evil and kept you safe, not I!'

'Lowenna...' But further speech was denied Vivian, as he was pressed to help subdue the fire until it was brought safely under control. He replaced his clothing with some borrowed from his steward, but Lowenna refused a similar offer from his wife by saying her own awaited her at the hillfort, though she did avail herself of a clean cape. Meralda kept Martin's cloak tightly about her, declining any con-

221

versation, and no one suggested that Adwen should relinquish her habit.

The Trevivian residents, in gossip, were blaming the fact that their lord had not seen fit to introduce his new lady, on the crisis that had greeted their arrival, compelling him to dispense with formality, and though understanding that this was no moment for rejoicing, they did wonder at the subdued demeanour of the wedding party. This, too, was smaller than expected, more noticeable when everyone gathered for refreshment – everyone, it was noted, except one maiden who seemed insensible to anything around her. They assumed the black-haired beauty, seated at their lord's side to be the bride, and Vivian soon realised this but did nothing to correct the false assumption. He spoke low, into her ear.

'My dear Lowenna, I must confess I had no notion of the depth of your caring.' He put a hand on hers. 'I beg you not to think of me as having an inconstant nature but my eyes were blinded by the outward form of your sister, whom I believed to be the embodiment of your beloved mother whom I adored, as your father well knows. It rendered me unable to perceive the virtue of your inmost nature, to see that 'tis you who holds the very essence of Ysella, her gentleness and compassion. Those were the qualities I loved her for and so sought in a wife, while hoping for the blessing of mutual love, and I now know that Meralda could never have satisfied those needs.' He put the ring with the black stone to his lips.

Lowenna let her fingers remain in his, but her eyes stayed downcast. 'I urge you not to favour me with soft words, which you may later regret, out of gratitude for my having served you as any other would have done. Also, I trust m'Lord will give me pardon if I venture to remind him that I am not my mother – I am me, myself alone – and none other.'

The more he spoke with her, the more Vivian was admiring of her level-headedness, despite her lack of years. 'I have been made well aware that you are unmatched by any other – and that is how I regard you,' he said. 'As like to your father with his courage and wisdom as to your mother with her goodness.'

He had hardly noticed the rapid passing of time, but suddenly felt near to exhaustion, his head throbbing from the wound, and declining to stay dallying longer, determined that he must continue on to the hillfort and distance himself from any additional ill that might beset him at Trevivian. Also, the daylight would soon begin to fade and Lowenna had expressed a desire for familiar faces around her, wishing to prepare the families at the fort for the unwelcome news that their men had been left to seek out and rout the pagans – and some might not return.

So, having changed horses, they set out along the coast road making for Perranuthnoe, and as they went Vivian glanced over at the Mount of Saint Michael that topped the forest surrounding it. He told Lowenna how the saint was said to have appeared to some fishermen who were casting their lines from the grey rock, while silently praying for a similar miracle to help Lyonesse and those who remained on her soil. His thoughts drifted to when he had last seen Richard, riding beside his son astride the white horse and proudly wearing his priest's habit, leading them to the Forbidden Place. He wondered how they had fared in the encounter and imagined them already sailing over the water, soon to meet up with their dear ones, hoping yet that Martin might be amongst them.

He saw the sun was all but vanishing below the horizon in the west, and clouds had gathered like a thick, rumpled blanket, obscuring the heavens. As he watched, a strip of clear sky showed through, and he found himself gazing with apprehension at a thin silver crescent that, to his troubled mind, clearly resembled an ominous, curved sword hanging menacingly over Lyonesse.

# 13

## *The Fire Rock*

Directly Meralda had succeeded in escaping from the grove, Tardhamor made preliminary plans for the ultimate punishment of Atlan. While his prisoner underwent the various tortures devised, so designed that they would not end in premature death, his followers cleared a piece of land at the furthest boundary of Kellimargh, at the foot of Carrag Uthek. They felled saplings and young trees, gathering kindling and mature wood to build a pyre beneath a rocky prominence that protruded out from the side of the awesome Fire Rock. The apex of the spur formed the point where the stream, gushing from the spring above divided into two, diverging on each side to become the twin streams flowing down to the southern coast, thus forming the watery triangle enclosing Kellimargh, the Grove of the Horse.

Tardhamor had felt himself drawn to celebrate the original evil of those primitive, bygone days when the sun god was worshipped, as if past Satanic demons still lurked about the Fire Rock and its adjacent areas to encourage men to indulge in further heinous crimes. He would have preferred to climb the ancient path to the original site of sacrifice at the top, but it had been so long overgrown as to become lost above a certain height. Then, too, a fire at the top might have been visible even as far away as Cornwall, exciting curiosity and conjecture.

As it was, the infamous rock now had the semblance of glowing from within, the evening sun, a dull red orb sinking behind gathering clouds in the western sky, bathing it in its fiery light as the pyre was built ever higher. A framework, lying on the ground, had been fashioned with green saplings that would take a long time to burn, the struts fastened with wetted ropes. Atlan, lacerated and bleeding, had been dragged from the altar through the grove and tied to the frame with leather thongs in the same form as Christ on the cross, before it was supported upright against the spur and over the pyre, the pain-racked body hanging awkwardly, head drooped forward.

The high priest was directing the proceedings with calculated vindictiveness to occasion the utmost hurt to his victim. Slow roasting had been chosen from other alternatives, the heat of the fire controlled by the judicious use of water poured on the flames, and when he deemed the preparations to be complete he summoned everyone to begin the ceremony – even those assigned to watch for intruders had made their way there, determined not to be robbed of this unusual and unexpected entertainment. Some carried lighted torches to combat the time when dusk should fall, so as not to be left facing the unknown, fearful darkness in this place of unquiet spirits, and for the second time that day, Tardhamor and his priests began the ritual of parading and chanting designed to whip emotions into a frenzy.

He abruptly came to the end of his gyrating and reciting and tore the cloth from his head, the better to see the suffering, his face a twisted mask of wickedness, the Vivian Jewel swinging across his chest. He faced in the direction of the glade, to the temple and statues hidden behind the trees, prostrated himself then rose and began intoning his invocation.

'O wondrous One, hear me. God of the seas, of horses, of storms, of earthquakes, and god of Atlantis and Lyonesse, we bow before your all-embracing power. Show us your mercy as we make you this offering, this wretch who thought to put himself over you, usurping your great pearl and your bride by making her unchaste, a vile Christian maid who will, no doubt, have lured him to embrace her belief – so he himself will be made to die in a Christian posture!' He looked toward the sagging figure, wrists and shoulders taking the weight of the body. 'Traitor!' he shouted. 'You pay for your treachery with your life!'

Seizing a flaming torch he thrust it at the pyre, but before it could touch the kindling a single arrow flew through the air from the cover of the trees to find its mark in the breast of the high priest. He staggered back, dropping the torch as he grasped the haft of the arrow in a ghastly, vain attempt to pull it out. 'Avenge me…Poseido…' The shout ended in a gurgle in his throat as he fell backwards, still gripping the arrow with both hands, back arched, the spurting blood drenching the Vivian Jewel.

A stunned hush descended on the assembly – most too stupefied to realise what was happening before the avenging force fell upon them. Men flooded from the surrounding undergrowth and trees giving no quarter, slashing at anything in their path as Martin rode up on Mordon. While unprepared to take part in the carnage, he was anxious to do whatever he could to assist in the destruction of the pagan site, his attention being caught by the torch dropped by Tardhamor which had set alight the dry grass, smoke beginning to curl upwards from the flames spreading to the wood piled beneath a figure suspended above it.

He was taken aback by the sight, overwhelmed by its semblance to the agony endured by Jesus. In moments of daydreaming he had often imagined himself there, in Jerusalem on that fateful day, observing the scene of betrayal as a faithful follower of the One destined to be their Saviour. He saw himself, although unable to prevent the Crucifixion,

226

yet endeavouring to ease his suffering, showing his loyalty, ready to die for him. This ardent desire still lay close to the surface of his mind, and the longing he had to be of service found him incapable of abandoning this like figure, whether pagan or not.

He called urgently to others to help him lift the frame free of the fire growing in intensity, the flames leaping hungrily, devouring the dry kindling. When they dropped it down on the grass, Martin pulled out his knife to sever the thongs binding the bloodied, swollen limbs, but too weak to move, Atlan lay peering about him, his gaze coming to rest on Mordon, uneasily pawing the ground nearby. 'Mordon...,' he said faintly. His blood-filled eyes settled on the man beside him and knew it to be Martin. 'Meralda...? Is she safe?'

'Ay, and far away on the mainland.' An involuntary feeling of revulsion had filled Martin at the mention of her name, now sure this tortured man was Atlan – a pagan, the enemy of Christ and himself, the seducer of his sister and the originator, aided by the Devil, of his family's distress.

The archdeacon, well rounded and never a notable horseman, had arrived late, yet in time to observe the sinister tableau against the Fire Rock as the frame was lowered. Dismounting, he stood surveying the scene, satisfied with the slaughter being wreaked upon the screaming enemies of his Church and his God. 'Is this where they worship?' he demanded of Martin.

The young priest was diverted both from his anger and Atlan to answer: 'I believe there was a temple once – if so, it must lie yonder.'

'Then let us seek it out!' The archdeacon grasped his arm, hurrying them both off through the trees.

When they came to the glade the archdeacon stopped abruptly in surprise, appalled by the sight. 'This evil place must be wiped from the face of the earth, put to the torch!' he cried. 'Everything must be effaced!'

He ordered his clerics to commence the destruction, and some started an assault on the temple while others fetched ropes they carried to fell the statues, tying them around and preparing to concentrate their combined weight on each in turn. They were so busily engaged that no one heeded the agonised figure of Atlan crawling painfully in their wake to make his peace with his god face to face.

Richard had been helping to round up those able to flee, only pausing in this exercise to smite the head from Tardhamor's torso and recover the jewel, the pearl no longer white but red, caked in blood, dropping it into a pouch at his belt for safe keeping. He now followed the others, and as he came into the clearing he glanced up at the sky, wondering how much longer they could delay before riding to board the boats. He was surprised to find the day coming to its end, seeing a section of darkening blue amid a rift in the clouds, the violent activity having caused him to misjudge the passing of time. His dismayed eye was caught by the shape of a pale sickle moon, unknowing that Vivian was observing it at that very instant and, filled with alarm, he recalled the Seer's warning, aware that the sands allotted to his personal hour-glass were emptying into the lower bowl, his task not yet accomplished. Was he, then, too late? If so, what chance of escape remained for anyone left in jeopardy on the island?

He blew a loud blast on his hunting horn to recall those still pursuing their victims and recognised Martin near two statues, the archdeacon with him urging the men into action. 'Destroy these false idols…!'

The man of the cloth was encouraging what was proving to be a test of strength, but the next moment Richard saw him roughly pushed aside by a hunched and bloody, naked man. The archdeacon appeared disconcerted, sweeping his white robes aside from the blood-smeared hands of Atlan who had managed to reach his place of worship by a superhuman

228

effort of will, the cut leather strips that had bound him hanging from the wounds they had made in the flesh.

'They must not be touched!' this no longer handsome youth was hoarsely crying, fearful for the statues. 'They must be saved! Poseidon guards our lives...!'

The archdeacon turned on him. 'Pagan! Idolater! Devil-worshipper!' He contemptuously spat out the epithets. 'Better had you been left to roast – 'twould have been a foretaste of what you can expect to find in hell with the other heathens!'

Martin stepped forward to intervene, still carrying the knife used to cut the bonds, trying to calm the contention, but Atlan was incensed by the arrogance of the archdeacon's words and, although almost blinded, suddenly found Martin's hand within his vision and found, too, strength enough to seize the opportunity. He tore the knife from the young priest and, in the same movement, thrust it up to the hilt into the archdeacon's body. Martin, caught off guard, made a futile effort to prevent the attack but was merely able to grasp Atlan's wrist as he withdrew the knife. There was a brief struggle to gain possession of it until Atlan, weakened by torture, suddenly ceased to offer any further resistance, and in the split second before Martin realised this he found he had plunged the knife deep into Atlan's side...

Excitement and clamour filled the glade with the clerics running in horror to where their superior lay dead. Martin stood unmoving, Atlan's blood standing out in stark relief upon the white vestment. He stared at the hand holding the knife he had involuntarily withdrawn, at first in disbelief and then in the vain hope that it had done no harm. Atlan had fallen to his knees, arms outstretched in supplication. 'Poseidon – my father...curse and destroy these unbelievers...' he entreated. Then softly, so that Martin was just able to hear: '...and keep Meralda safe...for me...' His failing eyes sought, and found, those of the white horse who had followed him, briefly but surely conveying his last message, '…and…Mor..do…' He slumped forward and lay still.

Martin was forced to accept that his hand had taken a life. He had ever advocated peace, abhorring violence, although allowing for that necessity in defence of man and God. Now he was wondering whether, unconsciously, he had submitted to a baser instinct in a desire for vengeance on the murderer of the archdeacon and the ravisher of his sister.

Richard approached him, a witness of all that had occurred, aware of a sense of oppression and extreme tension in the air, a tension that seemed to stretch every nerve to breaking point. He took the knife from his son, striking his back with his fist in an endeavour to recall him from his distraction. 'You prevailed against this cur to some good purpose, Martin, exacting retribution for us all,' he said, with forced cheerfulness. 'I well know who this spawn of Satan must be, so you have saved me the trouble of sharpening my blade against his backbone. Come, my son, let us be gone in haste, this place reeks of ancient blood wantonly spilled in days gone by. See, our men are succeeding in avenging it.'

Jowan, who had also observed the event, came up to them and shouted to the men to apply themselves to their task with renewed energy. They first attacked the statue of Cleito, which showed a marked unwillingness to be displaced, and when finally it was toppled from its plinth, there came a shaking and rumbling in the earth, instantly matched by one in the sky as a flash of vivid lightening cracked above them. More hesitantly, they turned their efforts upon the towering statue of Poseidon, sweat pouring from them as they pulled on the ropes, and despite a similar reluctance and determination not to give way, it fell at last. This was marked by an even brighter flash of blue lightening, its thunder reverberating as it echoed in the heavens.

The heightened, superstitious imaginations of the men

likened it to the sound that would be produced should the ancient and neglected gods, watching from their home on Mount Olympus, beat with swords on their shields to express their fury. At the same time, the rumbling movements of the earth increased and were added to by the sounds of wind and tumult and the differing tones of the church bells as, hanging from supports disturbed by the agitation, they rang out their dire warnings by themselves. The men cowered back, frightened, and the shout went up to take flight – fast! 'The earth moves beneath out feet! Get to the horses!' Panic overtook them as they began to run blindly, in any direction.

Only Martin remained unheeding, and apparently un-caring. Jowan managed to catch the bridle of one scared horse and Richard held another while looking about for a third, before espying Mordon who had come up to nuzzle at Atlan's body. He pushed Martin to the stallion and persuaded him to take the halter as he helped him on to the broad back, then the three rode off rapidly, taking the road that led to the tongue of land that pointed towards the hillfort at Perranuthnoe on the mainland, the road that passed by the church of Saint Perran.

Richard despaired of the horses ever reaching there as the ground shook under their hooves, boulders rolled into their path and trees became uprooted causing them to swerve. Flashes of lightening, and what seemed to be balls of fire arcing in the sky lit their way, seeming like flaming brands from a giant's campfire that he was kicking into the air upon some angry whim. As they raced on through the countryside Morden led the way as if entranced, while Richard and Old Jowan had to urge their mounts to try to keep within his distance. They passed folk on horseback, in carts, and some fleeing on foot, all seeking to escape the terror and pandemonium but not knowing where to go. The bells were ringing out ever louder, bringing more panic by the sound of those insistent, strident, metal tongues.

When they neared the church Mordon was forced to slow his pace, his headlong flight stayed by the press of people, carts and animals along the road. By the time they reached the environs of the church, into which men, women and children were crowding in their fear, Martin was looking over his shoulder, calling for assistance to help restrain his horse, concerned lest it break through and carry him onward. When they came up to him Richard queried his reason for halting, as Jowan manoeuvred his horse to grasp Morden's halter, having to use all his weight to discourage the stallion's purposeful advance. Thus checked, Martin let himself down onto the unsteady earth while aiding the old man to keep a hold on the halter. 'Thanks be to God – and yourself,' he said to him.

Richard reached down, clutching his shoulder. 'What means this? There can be no delaying – we have only halved the distance and the road ahead appears to be less cluttered. And you, Jowan, why are you now on your feet? Have you both been taken by madness?'

Jowan bowed his balding head. 'Master, I cannot leave the land of my fathers – as I told you. I will stand and endure by the side of your son.'

Martin lifted his eyes to meet Richard's. 'You well know I had already made my decision to stay – and even more so now. I have sinned most grievously, and must confess and make my peace with my heavenly Father. 'Tis also my duty and desire to comfort these others who remain.'

'You will join with me – both! I order you to obey!' Richard shouted the words in his distress, throwing himself from his horse and tugging at their clothing.

Martin disengaged himself, his sympathy and under-standing of his father's anguish evident in his face. 'This is no time for dissent, my dearly loved father.' His voice was tender, though hurried and raised to be heard above the storm. 'Moreover, I am not afeared and, mayhap, curious and even eager to experience the joys of Paradise – should I find

232

forgiveness.' He held Richard close. 'You have another son to take my place, who may serve you better, and must explain to him and everyone else the reason for this tragedy so they will cast out their evil ways. This land will be overwhelmed to hide its wickedness, so ride swiftly – and forgive Lowenna – I will ever stay near her.'

Martin thrust Mordon's halter into his father's hand. 'Here – take this white horse – 'tis powerful and strong – and tarry no longer – there is no more time to lose!' They helped Richard mount the horse they were holding as it struggled to be free. 'Hurry, Father!' Martin urged. 'Saint Perran will lead you safely to the place that bears his name – and God be with you…'

They released the impatient Mordon who, finding himself unrestrained, plunged forward. Richard, too choked with the pain of severance to give answer, had his wet eyes torn from the men he loved as he was carried swiftly into the uncertain night without a backward glance. Unused to riding without a saddle, he found it needed all his concentration to remain on the speeding horse.

There had been no time to consider what he would do when he arrived at the end of the spit of land that sloped down to the sea – mayhap there would be a boat. What did it matter? He was leaving so many behind, and the sadness he would have to endure should his beloved son and Old Jowan not survive, almost brought him to the verge of abandoning care in respect of his own safety. Almost – until a pair of calm, soft, grey-green eyes impinged on his memory, bringing an urgent desire for their closer scrutiny. Reminded him too, of his continuing responsibility for those others he loved who would be eagerly awaiting his arrival.

Thus, amidst the fast growing havoc and ravaging of Lyonesse, Mordon, precipitate, heedless, and whether wittingly or unwittingly carrying Richard on his back, sped along the tongue of land aimed directly at his destination.

*

Lord Vivian and his companions had arrived at the hillfort
earlier, and as they approached the men on lookout alerted
those waiting to their coming and to the smallness of the
party, these being the first arrivals, they supposed, in advance
of the main body not far behind. The gate was open wide
with an assembly, chiefly of women and children gathered to
greet their kin, Tressa and Hicca close to Gweniver's buxom
figure. They all had joy on their faces, eager to resume the
stability of the life they had shared at Trevelyan, as until now
only the rare, periodic events of wedlock or death had
altered its structure, creating separation but never changing
routine. Such events had been foreseen and accepted, and
their happy anticipation this day rendered them unprepared
for the constrained manner of the arrivals.

Lowenna was the first to wearily move to greet them after
dismounting with Adwen, hugging the children, tears filling
her eyes as she wordlessly looked into those of Gweniver to
warn her not to show alarm. The old nurse was quick to sense
her mood, and a glance at Meralda standing forlorn where
Vivian had set her down, her face visibly tormented, advised
her to prepare for some unpleasantness and to shield the
children. They were, as usual, full of lively questioning,
seeming not to notice the lack of enthusiasm shown to their
welcome. Where were Father and Martin and the others?
Vivian, to save Lowenna distress, came to them and answered
kindly enough, announcing for everyone to hear that the
men had been delayed on Lyonesse but should soon arrive
after making the crossing.

Tressa looked up into his face. 'You were not expected
here this day with our sister, your bride,' she said pointedly,
though giving a bob of respect, 'but we are glad you saw fit to
pleasure us with your company since we were not let be at the
espousal – as has ever been the custom for members of

families.' Her resentment at her exclusion still rankled – and she was not going to let anyone forget her hurt!

Hicca's sharp eyes had noticed Adwen. 'I espy a nun,' he cried, as Adwen threw back the hood that covered the wimple hiding her shaven head.

'You are in error, boy,' she said, her friendly grin establishing an immediate intimacy. 'A nun without a veil is no nun at all. I come here as an ordinary, very commonplace person to make your acquaintance.'

As Hicca opened his mouth to reply, lightening rent the sky accompanied by the sound of distant thunder, and Vivian swung his head in the direction of Lyonesse, nerves on edge and apprehensive. The evening light darkened and the noise in the heavens increased, the earth beginning to shudder slightly as if fearful of what was to come, so Vivian picked up Meralda and carried her towards the fort, his pity for her plight undiminished by her perfidy. 'Let everyone take shelter,' he called over his shoulder, to those women who showed an inclination to tarry outside for a first sight of their menfolk. 'We are not done with this night yet!'

He felt Meralda shivering with a violent ague and saw her eyes wide open, stark, as if viewing with horror a waking nightmare, and a sixth sense told him that mayhap she was – gazing upon some ghastly vision invisible to any other. He sat her down beside the fire and sought a serving woman to attend her, but found that Adwen, having also seen her unknown terror, had come to take her icily cold hands in her own to try to instil some warmth in the limp, lifeless fingers. Then, with Hicca hard on his heels, the boy feeling important as the only Trevelyan male there, he climbed the steps to the walkway above to join three Lyonesse men on lookout who were hoping for signs of their kin, on foot or in boats beaching below the cliff.

Lowenna had heeded Vivian's concern for Meralda, but now without a mite of jealousy or envy, loving him the more for the care he was showing to the sister who was suffering such obvious inner pain. After sending Tressa to ask for bowls of hot water for freshening themselves, she took Gweniver aside and briefly acquainted her with a few of the more pertinent happenings that had befallen them, and when Tessa returned, again to keep her from overhearing, she asked her to find a serving woman to fetch winewhey – a beverage of wine and curdled milk – and victuals to sustain them in their weariness.

Gweniver was finding it hard to believe that Meralda, contrary to her gentle upbringing, had defied her father in refusing to be espoused and that they had both been imprisoned in the Priory on the Rock. 'And now, what of your own future?' she asked, and Lowenna smiled cautiously. 'That rests upon the favour of Lord Vivian,' she said, putting her lips to the ring on her finger. 'He knows of my love for him.'

This was too much for the old nurse, already upset by the turn of events, having done her best to teach her charges how to conduct themselves in a dutiful fashion, so she hurriedly led the way to search for Meralda, wishing to hear from her own mouth what she might have to say in defence of her actions, hopeful that Lowenna had distorted the facts.

She found her beside the fire, Adwen still chafing her hands, and was shocked by the sight of Ysella's eldest daughter, the daughter who had so resembled her mother, though displaying her own personality. She appeared now as a pitiful shell, empty of any substance or will of her own, and Gweniver, clucking round her like a hen with its chick, made to remove Martin's damp cloak. She gave a sharp cry of disbelief as she discovered her nakedness, quickly covering her again as Tressa and a woman brought the winewhey.

Tressa handed a bowl to Adwen and another to Lowenna, who, reaching to take it, let her cape fall open to reveal the wedding gown that, although draped up by the hems, was yet unmistakable. Tressa regarded it in amazement. 'What sorcery is this? Meralda is the Lady of Lyonesse and you wear her gown!'

Lowenna stroked the curly head. ''Twould take too long to tell and we are overmuch wearied. 'Tis enow to say that Meralda is not the Lady of Lyonesse and neither am I. You will have to await a fuller account when Father and Martin return. For now, I wish to rid my body of it – it sits ill upon me. You must know where my own garments lie, Tressa, so go and seek for something more suited to my needs in weight and warmth.'

'Ay,' agreed Gweniver, 'and clothing for Meralda. 'Tis a pity we kept nothing of hers here – 'twas all taken to Trevivian. I will come too, Tressa, to fetch garments for her to choose from.'

'Might there be aught for me?' asked Adwen. 'This habit yet holds the water it soaked up when we were near drowned. Also – I want to be recognised for what I am – not what I once was.'

The garments fetched, they moved to a screened-off alcove and Adwen and Lowenna disrobed, care being taken to shake out and smooth the diaphanous white gown and untie the sleeves. 'You protected it well,' complimented Gweniver, 'if it has indeed suffered as much adversity as you describe. It just holds a slight dampness and the smell of the sea.' She laid it carefully across the top of a wooden chest and turned to Meralda who had been half-carried along with them, as yet showing no interest in her surroundings or situation, silent and withdrawn, her features taut.

The old nurse uncovered her and prepared to put a shift over her head, but when she saw the injured back, sympathy overwhelmed her. 'Oh, my poor bird, my wounded swan! What misfortune has befallen you? Even the cross you wear about your neck has not protected you from harm. 'Tis no wonder your wits have deserted your skull!' She turned angrily on Lowenna, blaming her. 'How could you allow this to be done to your sister?'

The ground moved more restlessly, the fury of the storm growing in intensity, causing everyone disquiet, and Lowenna knew this was not the moment to divulge confidences. She held her peace and her tongue as Gweniver chose between the gowns, selecting a pale mauve of Lowenna's in a thick weave to bring warmth to Meralda's shivering body. The nurse began to try to clothe her, again speaking of the cross-within-a-circle at her neck. 'What bauble is this that I have never before set eyes upon?' she enquired, hoping for some answer and making as if to finger it.

Meralda, until then unresponsive and totally absorbed in her misery, quickly snatched it from her reach. She tore the mauve gown from her grasp and threw it down on the straw. 'What ails you to think to attire me in this rag?' she demanded imperiously of the startled nurse, standing up tall and straight once more, chin lifted, eyes darting wildly from side to side but without recognition. 'Is't not common knowledge that I am to be wed? See, my gown lies yonder, already scented with the fragrance of the sea to pleasure me. Be so good as to aid me in donning it, woman!'

They were so taken by surprise that no one moved until Lowenna touched an arm of the hurt, bewildered Gweniver. 'Do as she asks without demur,' she whispered. 'Her brain is addled with her suffering.'

While the nurse helped Meralda, Lowenna clad herself in her favourite purple and Adwen chose to be attired in a gown intended for Tressa when she was older, but of a size perfect for the erstwhile nun. None would have guessed that now, to see her in bright saffron yellow with a cloth of the same hue covering her head.

'I have missed colour most dreadfully,' she confessed, 'being but a young child when my mother gave me to the priory, where even the flowers are mostly white. I was later told she was nigh unto death that day, and I 'member she had clothed me in this very shade of brightness to give us both courage. 'Tis proper I should wear it now, having been thrust out of the Sisterhood,' she ended with a smile.

Meralda, her face expressionless, had been attired in the wedding gown that showed little sign of having been mistreated. She exhibited a sylphlike beauty, despite the obvious disparity in the lack of any manifest awareness of her true self and the condition of her long, pale gold hair that hung lank, matted and tangled. 'Come with me into the warmth, m'Lady,' urged Gweniver, being careful to show her the respect she seemed to expect, 'and let me comb and smooth your hair.'

They all went back into the communal room and hung the cloaks about the huge, cheerful fire to dry, doing their best to ignore the raging of the elements outside and not daring to think about the condition of their absent kin – feeling it was not the time to be tempted by the smells of cooking food, though it teased their nostrils.

Lowenna decided it was time to divulge to the women why their menfolk had been delayed, and tried to dispel their fearful speculations by exhorting them to prayer. Afterwards, as she sat deep in thought, the cloak with the cross upon the back now drying by the fire, that Martin had put around Meralda to give her the saint's protection, brought an urgent reminder of him. They had always been close, and she felt very close to him now. Where was he? And how was he faring in this storm-ridden night?

# 14

## *Culmination*

As soon as Richard had ridden away from the church, Martin and Jowan forced themselves into the press of people that filled it. All those able to do so had crammed inside, trying to escape from the terror induced by the storm, seeking comfort from God and the priests, the latter mostly engaged in saying their own prayers and begging to be saved. The two men, blood from the conflict staining Jowan's garments and Atlan's blood marking Martin's vestment, tried to appraise the situation by the light of the flickering candles before forcibly pushing their way to the altar, the large cross behind it fixed against the wall.

Martin faced the disorder, endeavouring to make his voice heard, but to little avail until he saw a bench, and with Jowan's assistance pulled it to the base of the cross and stood on it. Jowan held him steady, arms locked around his knees, bracing his shoulder against the cross to prevent them both being thrown down. Martin shouted above the contending stridency of the thunder, bells and human cries of despair, and at last held the attention of those nearest him, which gradually spread to others.

'Silence! Be silent! How can you expect God to hear you and you hear Him? You are gathered in His house and should hearken to His words – open your ears to them!' He pulled his Mass-book from a pocket, the missal he had laboriously copied out, and held it between his palms. Then, having commanded a qualified silence, he began to intone relevant phrases that came into his mind from its pages.

'We have sinned, O Lord, we have sinned, spare us sinners and save us…O Thou, who guidedst Noah on the waters of the Deluge, hear us! And calledst Jonah from the abyss, O deliver us…O Thou who stretchedst Thy hand to Peter drowning, O help us, O Christ…Stretch out Thy hand from above…O Christ, deliver us! Deliver us from all evil, past, present and to come…Behold the Lamb of God…Behold! He who taketh away the sins of the world…My peace I give to you, Alleluia! Peace I leave with you, Alleluia!'

As was the custom, the assembly joined in to chorus a second 'Alleluia' each time it was said, and with the last one Martin dropped his missal, its work ended. He had managed to stay upright with Jowan's help, his face transfigured with joy to see the dream he had dreamed so long ago confirming its prediction, fulfilled by his being able to uplift those who had shared in his prayer, and inwardly knowing that he had received absolution for his sin. Knew, too, that their earthly struggle was almost over.

He flung wide his arms, matching the transverse bar of the wooden cross as he leaned his back against it, and felt what proved to be the last, violent massive convulsion, aware of a great pounding, roaring noise of water rushing ever nearer, overpowering and drowning everything in its path. The bells were being silenced one by one until there remained only their own, jangling in a confused, frantic way as if appealing for help for them all – and Lyonesse.

Martin concluded his prayer with a mighty shout of triumph. 'Come, ye blessed of my Father, possess the kingdom! Alleluia! which was prepared for you from the beginning of the world! Alleluia!…Alle…lu…'

\*

Far away in the hillfort Lowenna was staring into the glowing depths of the fire, filled with a sudden concern for Martin. Vivian and Hicca had stayed with the lookout men above, resting against the parapet, the boy squeezed close beside his tall companion. There was no rain as yet but the air was beginning to dampen as he stood on tiptoes, stretching his neck to see over the top, unmindful of the raging storm.

'Why do we have to overtask our eyes to seek nought?' he asked. 'Any persons out there would have taken shelter long since.'

''Tis possible some may try to reach us, needing our aid,' answered Vivian, 'though doubtful we could provide it,' he added to himself.

'Why do we hear the bells ring out, though faint, from where Lyonesse lies?'

'They warn of approaching danger – which is why we came here, hoping to outrun it.'

'And what is making the whole world to thump and quake?'

'I cannot give answer to that, Hicca – I have never before known the like. Many thunderbolts must be falling to shake the earth in such an unbridled fashion.'

As he spoke, a greater agitation caused the hillfort to momentarily convulse like a living thing, but the walls withstood the shock and held steady. Hicca screeched, making as if to run, only to be held back by Vivian's hand. 'Let me go!' sobbed the child. 'I – I am affrighted!'

'And where would you run to?' enquired the other, displaying a composure he was far from feeling, talking fast to divert the lad's attention. 'See, these three men up here have kept to their posts and not fled whimpering like craven dogs – 'tis a bonehead's way to run in panic without thought. Dumb beasts of the fields and hearth have not been given the ability to reason such as you and I have been blessed with,

242

and thus we are enabled to keep our wits about us even when we are affrighted. Fear is necessary for all – it enlivens us when danger is nigh, but it also has the power to destroy should you be overcome by it. Legs become palsied, preventing escape from whatever threatens, but with courage and prayer you can succeed in surviving. So, in the first instance, Hicca, I earnestly commend you to beware of uncurbed fear and then to fear the despair of defeat by the forces of evil. Lastly, and most important of all, you must fear the wrath of God should you remain impenitent for wrongdoing.'

The earth had steadied after its violent shaking, and since there had been no further recurrence of the convulsion that had caused him such alarm, Hicca felt obliged to put on a show of bravado to cover his faint-heartedness. 'I am told God is up there,' he said, pointing at the sky, 'and throws down thunderbolts when He is angry. Should that be so, He must be very angry now, but I am mistrustful that He is there at all. If He is, why does He not show Himself? Or is't but a tale put about by you elders to make us behave as you think we should?' he gave Vivian a querying look. 'And if, perchance, 'twere true, in no way would He be able to see what we do both by day *and* night, would He? So mostly we should be able to do as we please.'

'You should give thanks to Him that your earthly father cannot hear your words – else your skin would surely regret them!' As Hicca made to pull away, Vivian prevented him. 'Nay, stay and hearken and give me answer. You know 'tis true that Jesus walked this earth with His apostles, who saw His miracles. He proved to them that He was God's Son, sent by Him as messenger and proxy, and wrote about all they had seen and heard so that everyone coming after could share in the good tidings. Why should they write falsely? And why should your brother devote his life to serving an imaginary master? It is because, deep within himself, he has a certainty

243

of God's existence and loves both Him and His Son with all his heart!'

'Does he love Them more than me? Or the family?' Hicca raised a tear-stained face, anxious for reassurance, and was given a comforting hug.

'I think he would tell you that his love for Them helps him to love you more.'

After a thoughtful pause, Hicca asked: 'Why has that nun, who is not a nun, that you brought here with you – Adwen – is't? Why has she left the priory, turning her back to God and spurning Him?'

'In nowise has she turned her back, Hicca, for by leaving the narrow life of a nun she will be able to find other ways of living for which she may be better matched, and thus be of greater service to Him whom she will never cease to honour.' Vivian was finding uneasiness intruding upon him once again as he gazed on the hostile energies surrounding them, filling the air with noise and streaking light.

One of the men on lookout approached, tapping his arm to gain his notice. 'M'Lord, are you not heedful that the sound of bells from over the water has quieted on a sudden? I can hear nought but the howling of the wind now the storm tends to abate. Does it mean there is nothing more over there to daunt our men?'

Vivian gripped the edge of the parapet, his knuckles white. 'I would say 'tis sure that Lyonesse can hold no other terrors for them,' he said gravely, muttering a prayer for their salvation before turning back to Hicca. 'Come, boy, let us go below.'

With a word to the men to stay alert, Vivian guided him down the steps to the lower floor, and had barely reached it when an excited cry caused him to look up to the walkway, the front section being within his vision. Peering through the smoky, dim light, he saw a lookout man beckon, swinging a lantern with urgency, and hastily climbed back, asking what was amiss. The fellow shouted but the gale snatched the words from his mouth, and Vivian had to bend close to hear them repeated.

'Look y-yonder…!' the man stammered, indicating the expanse of sea directly before them, his face ashen. 'A mighty wall of water bears down on us!'

As Vivian stared, two or three simultaneous flashes vividly illuminated the scene to provide the truth of the report. A huge wave, seeming to be only moderately lower than the top of the cliff itself was surging towards them, rearing up over the waiting sands like some greedy monster eager to engulf them. He caught his breath as another man excitedly gestured, calling wildly.

'I see something out there! It looks like…it could be a man on a white horse…carried on the crest of the wave…'

Vivian's gaze followed the gesture, but as the lightening faded he caught only a brief glimpse, too fleeting to identify it, though when he blinked he found he retained a picture on the inside of his eyelids of what seemed to be one waterborne creature carrying another, but was doubtful if he had been seeing aright.

The lookout man, never doubting, continued to comment. 'They are deserving of our pity – there can be no escape. They must be dashed to pieces against the face of the cliff!'

After a further moment of suspense in continuing darkness, they heard the inevitable tumultuous crash as the relentless waters hit, feeling the resultant tremor that shook the very foundations of the fort, and although it lay on the top of a hill and far back from the edge of the cliff, the watchers were drenched in sea spray. They stood in silence, praying for the unknown rider, before becoming aware of a commotion having started beneath their feet, caused by the capricious wind having blown the shouted words down to the ears of those who anxiously awaited news of the men they loved. At the mention of a white horse, Meralda had come back to life and reordered her deranged senses.

'Mordon…and Atlan…!' She had risen and moved fast to the closed gate, the guards intercepting her. 'Open it!' she was demanding, but they took no heed, indifferent to her frenzied struggles, while others ran to their aid and held her. 'Atlan! Atlan!' Meralda was screaming. 'Let me go to him! He is out there – he needs me!'

Vivian had hurried down the steps and tried to calm her. 'Tis no use – they will not let you pass – and anywise, to what purpose? If true, it could have been any one of a hundred men, and whoever 'twas he will have met his end by now. Come with me, Meralda,' he pleaded, an arm about her, and all her resistance melted away in a sudden, surprising acceptance as she allowed herself to be led back to the fire.

'She is cold as death,' he said to Lowenna, while he divested himself of his wet cloak, 'and is only clothed, for a reason with which I have not been acquainted, in this fragile gown that but lately adorned your own fair self.'

Lowenna shrugged. 'She would not be gainsaid – insisting she was going to be wed. 'Tis a whim on her part without a credible reason that I am wise to.' She went to fetch Martin's cloak, now dry, and put it once more around her sister. 'Martin believed his cloak would save you from evil while you wear it, Meralda,' she said, kissing her, 'and 'tis my earnest hope that it helps you find peace and contentment.'

Vivian was being besieged by fretting women separated from their men as they nervously discussed the snippets of hearsay heard from the walkway, all begging for answers to unanswerable questions. He did what he could to lift their spirits by demonstrating an optimism he hoped would temporarily soothe their worrying, and ended by saying: 'The storm is diminishing – we must retire to rest and renew our strength for the morrow. Let us all prepare for slumber.'

They set about dousing the lanterns, leaving some burning

in dark corners, and more logs were thrown on the fire. Only the occasional faint flash and rumble of thunder in the far distance remained to disturb them as they sought their sleeping places, Adwen next to Gweniver and the children. Lowenna, having thrown off her weariness, was assuming a new authority, accepting her role as the only member of the family here able to oversee their welfare. She tried to persuade Meralda to abandon her vigil by the fire, but was met with a stubborn resistance and so left her there.

Vivian's appreciative eyes had followed Lowenna's every movement and he came to her now, gently taking her hand and leading her to the opposite side of the fire from her sister. 'I cannot conceal how full of doubt I feel for those who should have rejoined us ere now,' he began. 'I am fearful that the prophesied calamity has, of a certainty, overtaken them. I only say this to prepare you for what would occasion you the deepest sorrow – and mine would hardly prove less.' His mouth brushed against her hair as her head fell against him.

'I am aware,' she whispered, 'and have expected it from the very beginning. There was always a sense of foredoom, and I never felt there could be an avoidance of what threatened Lyonesse. The menace was too well hid and the forces of evil too strong for her to escape – unless it had been by the desire and strength of all our people working as one – which failed to come about due to the idleness, arrogance and, yes, self-caring of most. They had the power to prevent it – as Father tried to tell them.' She resolutely pushed his image away. 'I am thankful that some of us reached safety – and we must hope for more to come.'

'And I give my thanks that we have found each other.' Vivian pressed his lips to her forehead, 'and have been spared to spend the rest of our lives together.'

She lifted her face to look into his, her happiness in this wonderful moment of feeling as one with him diminished only by her anxiety for those others dear to her.

'Father…Martin…Old Jowan…' Her voice betrayed the tears held beneath the surface. 'The man you saw on the white horse – might it have been any of them?'

He held her closer, sharing the pain of her uncertainty. 'Who can say? I was afforded but a moment's glimpse and even now wonder if 'twas nothing more than fancy bred from words spoken. I would not be reliant on't, my dear one.'

''Tis Martin who has been in the forefront of my thoughts this eventide,' Lowenna persisted. 'I feel an emptiness in my soul for him. Was it he riding the wave? Tell me it was so.'

Vivian pursed his lips. ''Tis truth that the last time my eyes were upon him he was sat on a white horse, but if 'twere he out there, there can be no hope left for him.' He made an impatient gesture. 'But these are idle thoughts – they may all have gained the boats and beached elsewhere.'

He caressed the ring on her hand. 'What is certain, though, is that this ring was ever destined to bind us together. We have to think of the morrow, our lives held forever in each other's company – if to live we will live, and if to die we will die, but as one. I will hold these words to be a family watchword for our future kin on which to fashion themselves.'

'What greater love and comfort could you offer?' Lowenna's heart was full. 'For myself, I have nought to give but my devotion…'

'Which you showed when you twice prevented my life being taken, and to mark the first, as I have already made promise, I will build a chapel in the cove at Sennen by which we will be remembered alway.'

'My sorrow is tempered by the happiness I feel now you have declared yourself…' Lowenna ceased speaking, sensing a movement in the darkness on the edge of her sight. 'Who waits there?' she challenged, alert.

Vivian was on his feet in an instant, hand unsheathing his dagger, as a tenuous voice was heard saying in answer: 'Do not fear – 'tis but your brother…'

'Martin!' Lowenna's musing had dwelt so much on him that his name leapt at once into her mind, but found hope replaced by disillusion as a small figure shuffled into the firelight. She covered her face to hide her hurt.

Hicca stood revealed, shamefaced and unprepared for this reaction, not realising how much his stealthy approach had startled them. Vivian recovered more quickly, resuming his seat and drawing Lowenna down beside him. He regarded Hicca quizzically, before holding out a hand to bring him to sit facing them.

The boy was near to tears himself, his cheeks bright red. 'I meant no harm,' he whispered. 'I could not rest and merely came for further speech with you.'

'You caused us alarm – but without intent – and so are forgiven. Now, I see something troubles you. Is it the same as you mentioned earlier? Can it be you deem it possible that God does watch you constantly – as you denied He could when last we spoke?' And when Hicca nodded, he said, 'I see. Tell me why it weighs so heavily upon you.'

Hicca searched for words, letting them burst forth when he found them. 'Gweniver says He is my heavenly Father and knows everything I do, and sometimes I do things I know I should not but I like doing them and I want to go on doing them, so I shut my eyes and pretend that everyone is in error and there is no God at all. Anywise, by hiding behind my lids I can prevent Him seeing me!' He drew a deep breath, blinking rapidly.

Vivian smiled, saying: 'As you admit, 'tis nought but pretence. What you desire to hide from is your own shame in doing what you know to be wrong. 'Twould be better, and easier on your conscience, were you to accept that you offend Him by doing these things and mend your ways. You would restrain yourself if you knew 'twas your earthly father watching you, are you not agreed? Ay, I see you are. I truly believe that only by obeying God's holy laws can we have order and peace in our lives and in our world. That was His purpose in making them known to us, so everyone could learn and act upon them.'

He felt Lowenna move and touched his fingers to his wound. 'My head pains me – I must give it rest. Now, think on these things, Hicca. There may come a day when you are alone and in need of aid. Whom else could you call upon when there is none but God left to ask? I would enjoin you to mirror your father, Richard, who talks to Him daily and has made a friend of Him.'

Lowenna had been listening and gaining comfort from the words, but then, glancing at Vivian's tired face, she made the sleepy-eyed boy get to his feet. 'Come, little brother, m'Lord is fordone and weariness hangs about us like a heavy drape. Come to where you may sleep without further thought and awaken to a new day.'

After she settled him she went to Meralda, and finding her awake asked if she had any need, but receiving no response she returned to Vivian to find him already stretched out asleep. She gently covered him with an overlay and kissed him lightly, loving this gentle man even more for the way in which he had exercised such patience and wisdom in clarifying Hicca's dilemma, when he himself had been near to exhaustion. Then, on her knees, she rendered her grateful thanks for being blessed with this wonderful, unexpected and shared love, before lying down at Vivian's side.

Although her apprehensive imaginings were held at bay by sleep, she still continued to be plagued by disturbing dreams of Martin, but he was different, no longer the brother she knew, having seemingly changed into a centaur, half man and half white horse, and was standing beside her in the shadows observing her lovingly. When she tried to touch him she discovered that to be impossible, as however hard she tried he always remained just beyond her reach.

*

It was not until first light that anyone began to stir, so wearied had they been in suffering both the awesome agitation generated by the storm and the heartache brought about by the lack of news. Even the men on lookout had been unable to prevent their eyelids closing, wholly worn out by the violent events of the night and vastly relieved by the cessation of the uproar. Thankful for the resultant quietude, they had let themselves relax their vigilance and they, like everyone else, had slept deeply – all except Meralda still sitting beside the dying fire.

When the first glimmer of the soft-hued dawn fell on the men lying on the walkway, arousing them before it reached those sheltered beneath, they guiltily pulled themselves from their slumber. Yawning and stretching they stood stiffly, stamping feet and beating arms with numbed hands to restore the flow of blood, while calling to those below to prepare for the day. Two of the men descended the steps, leaving their companion leaning with his back to the parapet as he rubbed the sleep from his eyes.

By now the rest had bestirred themselves and begun the daily tasks, throwing logs on the fire and blowing it into flame, heating water and milk and putting food in pans. Men sharpened knives, whetting them on stone, and those employed with outside matters and caring for the animals discussed their needs for the hours ahead. So far, no one dared conjecture what those might bring forth.

When the dawn light had improved enough, the guards on the gate called up to the man left on the walkway, asking if it was safe to unbar and go out to replace the bridges over the ditches. With a casual glance at the area facing inland, the man shouted that all was well. Afterwards, he strolled around to look out to sea where a faint mist hung suspended, before turning to rest his back against the parapet again. A few moments later, when the full import of what he had actually observed, but which had failed to register on his consciousness at last became clear to him, he swung around, staring, transfixed with horror.

'I am bewitched!' he yelled. 'Come to my aid and tear these scales from my eyes! What devilish trick is being played upon me? It must be induced by sorcery!'

As his two companions, with Vivian hard on their heels, quickly climbed the steps and approached him, he was still crying out. 'Tell me I am deceived, I beg you! Look! Look yonder! The cliffs of Lyonesse no longer stand proud from the sea! Mayhap they are hid by the mist, but…' He knew that could not be so, the mist being too thin for concealment, and finished his sentence with an agonised groan. 'Ooh…h, I vow I can see nothing beyond this coast – but water!'

A stunned silence fell over the fort, the man's shouted words audible throughout. Everyone stayed their hand from whatever they were doing, faces lifted up fearfully, as another lookout man, gazing over the parapet, pointed to his right. 'See – Saint Michael's Rock – shaven bare – stranded in the midst of the sea! Where has the forest gone from round about it?' he ended in an awed tone.

'Cast your eyes over the waters before you,' Vivian answered in a grim voice, trying to hold it steady, 'to the sea that has risen in height over the sands to splash and thrust against the cliff. See how a vast amount of wreckage floats there, intermixed with whole trees, some uprooted and some with their trunks riven!'

He closed his eyes as if to shut out the dreadful truth. 'Oh, Lyonesse! Oh, my lost land, my poor people and my dear friends!' he cried, kneeling to pray, as did the others. 'God have mercy on them – and upon us in our sorrow!'

They remained thus for some little while, each person making a personal plea for the souls of those they feared taken, amongst the smothered sobs and louder outbursts of weeping from the women and children. At last Vivian rose to his feet, his body bent over with sadness and, in sympathy, gently pressed the shoulders of the men with him on the walkway, all turned aside to wipe away their tears, but as he moved along to descend the steps a full-throated shout brought him to a halt.

'M'Lord! Stay! Can it be possible? Look – down there – climbing the hill from that thicket at the top of the cliff – a man comes – leading a white horse!'

# 15

---

*Reunion*

The sun was quickly dispersing the vaporous mist to herald a fresh, clear day, and picked out the lonely figure wearily trudging up the hill, being more supported by the horse than leading it. Those on the walkway were asking: 'Who comes? How can this be?' but the bedraggled figure, head down, gave no clue as to its identity.

There was one maiden, however, who had no doubt at all, and another who could only guess, but more than half believed her instinctive feeling. Lowenna, having had Martin constantly in her thoughts, fervently hoped it would be him and heedlessly made to rush out, eager for his arms about her, but the maiden who had no doubt was before her. Meralda had raised herself on shaking legs, benumbed as they were, and stumbled through the gate left open by the guards gone to replace the bridging structures, her bare feet running over a bridge and down the gently sloping hill towards the sea, the white gown and pale gold hair flowing out behind her, her eager face alight.

'My love! My love!' she was calling. 'I have been so lost without you – but I knew you would come for me at last!' When she came close enough to recognise the man she abruptly stopped, as if she had run into an invisible barrier that both impeded her progress and turned her into stone. The horse, indeed, was Mordon, but she was clearly shocked, and at first disbelieving, to find the man to be her father.

Richard was offering his loving greeting and forgiveness by the hand held out to her. In the first instance, seeing her clothed as she was, he had almost been beguiled into thinking he had died in that terrible irruption, and that she was his long-lost bride, Ysella. Sadly dismissing that fancy, he had then persuaded himself that Meralda's hurried and excited progress had been occasioned by her anxiety and love for him, her past disobedience and indiscretion forgiven and forgotten in his joy at being reunited with her, his fairest swan. When, though, she suddenly ceased her headlong advance, and he saw no sign of welcome on her stricken face, he would have counted upon a surge of anger and resentment to rise up within him. Instead, he felt a deep, compassionate sorrow, but whether for himself or her he had no time to probe.

Lowenna and the others, eager to see who was approaching, ran past Meralda to reach him, Lowenna embracing him with a degree of heartiness that all but robbed him of what little breath he had left. She had to beg his pardon for her vigour, causing them both to laugh and cry at the same time.

'Oh, Father!' she gasped. 'I was so sure you were Martin 'til I saw you were not clad in a habit, but now 'tis of no concern to me. I find it a matter for wonderment that you have both been saved from death and have arrived hereabouts, for I have been teased by the certainty that he is very near to me.' Her eyes darted here and there, searching for him. 'But why does he remain hid…?'

By now they were encircled by the rest of the company, Tressa and Hicca hugging their father, while Vivian clasped his hand as if he would never release it, and all amid a babble of voices saluting his return and asking for news of their kin. When his silence had lasted longer than it would take to clear his throat, a hush fell upon them, like a vast, smothering fur pelt, while they waited, suspended in the moment, conscious only of the sea birds screaming in the sky above as if echoing their own, as yet unreleased, inner pain.

Richard slowly walked to a flat-topped boulder and sat down heavily, as if his legs were no longer able to support him, the enormity of what he had to impart draining away what little strength he retained. He knew he had to find the words that would rob family, friends, all of them, of any hope they might still have, and his courage failed him. As he sadly regarded the pleading faces, his gaze alighted on a small figure clad in saffron yellow and was held again by those large, green-flecked grey eyes he had last encountered on Lyonesse. He held out an open palm to her, mutely asking for support to harden his resolve to reveal the bitter, unpalatable truth. She at once went to him, putting her hand in his, and thus sustained to bear what he had so far been unable to admit, even to himself, he stood tall so that all might see.

'I have to confess I have no way of bringing comfort to any who await the sight of their kin, all those who remained on Lyonesse in order to follow and do service with me. The events that overtook us when we failed to remove the evil before the new moon, although forewarned of the consequences, yet caught us unawares with the speed and ferocity of God's judgment on the land. I cannot say with surety that I am the only survivor, but...' he shook his head with resignation.

'Then Martin and Old Jowan...?' Lowenna's voice faltered. 'I had a certainty that Martin...'

'I'truth, neither of them would be turned from staying, and I doubt there could be the smallest chance of them having escaped the havoc. 'Twas as if they knew they could not evade their destiny.'

Richard resumed his seat sorrowfully, scrutinising the familiar faces. 'I give thanks that the ferry brought to safety the others dear to my heart,' he said, and turned to the small maiden standing beside him, her hand still held in his. 'I cannot put tongue to a name for you.' He spoke gently, seeking an answer.

'My name is Ruth.' Her voice was clear and matter of fact. When she saw Lowenna's start of surprise she addressed the explanation mainly to her.

'All who entered into the priory took the name of a saint. I was earlier baptised Ruth and, now the link with the Sisters has been severed, that I shall remain.' She returned her attention to Richard, noticing him wince as he pressed her fingers and saw that his hands had been torn and grazed by some mischance.

The crowd had broken up into smaller groups, individuals consoling one another. Lowenna went to Gweniver and the children, who were crying bitterly and clinging to her. She wiped their tearful cheeks and then her own.

Vivian decided he must talk with Richard, hoping to divert him from what he knew must be the agony of his inner thoughts, and also eager for an account as to how he had arrived at the hillfort, comparatively unscathed. He approached discreetly, glad to see that his friend was being tended by the fresh-faced damsel with the yellow cloth about her head, knowing that he must make an effort to rid his mind of her erstwhile name, Adwen, that yet sprang readily to his lips.

'Richard, my dear brother,' he began, sitting beside him. 'I ache with you for the pain you have to bear, but trust you might find it offset, in a small measure, when I say we must show gratitude that the charges you left in my care have survived. I will leave Ad...Ruth to acquaint you with the tale of how we four might have drowned when the ferry was wrecked, but were thankfully delivered up, though at this precise moment I have an urgent need to know by what miracle *you* escaped death. We saw you on the horse as you were carried on the wave, and it seemed there could be no avoidance of you being hurled to pieces against the cliff.'

'A miracle, ay, and I am yet mazed by it.' Richard mused upon his hurried departure from the now vanished island. ''Twas as we reached the furthest point of land and were going out towards the water, a great sea came from behind and lifted us. There we were, riding high and, can it be believed?' his expression showed wonderment, 'the horse seemed to skim the top of the wave and remain there! The next thing I recall, we were heading for a cliff that came nearer with each flash of light, and at such a speed that I began to say my prayers – having the certain notion that I would be leaving this mortal coil with no further ado.'

'That would be when our eyes fell upon you...' Vivian began, but Richard, tense with reliving the fearsome event, continued over the interruption.

'I tried to blind myself to the sight of the final moment when I should perish, so closed my eyes, to find on the instant myself unseated and engulfed in water whilst being swept upwards. I was unable to breathe and near drowned when I became aware of a hardness and roughness under my body, along with a feeling of being forcibly drawn back down again. I dug my feet and hands into what felt like earth amidst rock and held on, I know not how, and managed to wedge myself between larger rocks as the waters receded downwards with a frightful, sucking noise. 'Twas then I found I was lying aslope, head higher than feet, and to my joy there was good, clean air and I was able to breathe – once I had rid myself of the water inside me.'

'But how? and where? had you been set?' Vivian was puzzled.

Richard returned his thoughts to attend to his friend's enquiry. 'That, Vivian, I only discovered at first light this day, as before, like you, I had no answer – being merely thankful that I was not yet made a corpse!'

He bent his head to regard Ruth at his side. 'You soothe my hands by your touch,' he said with a fleeting smile. 'You cannot know that 'twas you who inspired me in my struggle to survive, giving me cause to stay in this life.' She shyly glanced away with lowered lids as her colour heightened.

'I am coming to the end of my discourse.' Richard raised his voice to those who had gathered about him, following his story. 'As I was saying, my friends, I lay gulping the air in great discomfort, eager to know my whereabouts, when I heard a whinny from close by and saw, by another flash, a hole just above me, and outlined on the edge of it stood the stallion I had thought doomed. I managed to clamber up and out onto the grass and then, exhausted, lay as one dead 'til I awoke to the peace of the dawn and found myself brought alive to this place.'

Lowenna was among those clustered round him, intent on his tale. 'Father, as I am not blessed with an ease of imagining, I beg you to give meaning as to how you came to be lying aslope with a hole above you from riding on the wave?'

Richard nodded. 'Have patience, Daughter, 'twill be made plain. When I roused myself and looked about me I saw I was laying in the midst of that thicket yonder, on the cliff's edge. It conceals the hole that, I believe, must have been the roof of a cave that fell in long ago, forming a sloping shaft to its open mouth lying high up on the cliff face. 'Twas into that we had been forced, the sea pushing us up as in a funnel – then trying with all its might to suck me down again,' he ended, smiling.

After a pause he continued. 'I think that splendid horse was guided to that singular point of entry by Saint Perran himself, desirous to protect one of his tinners. Only a saint – or God – or one who protects horses – could have wrought this miracle of deliverance for us!'

His admiring eyes sought Mordon, to find the horse had moved to where Meralda had remained frozen into immobility, only the breeze giving movement to her hair and the fine material of her gown. Pity for her evident suffering filled her father's heart and he made his way back to where she stood, solitary and aloof, positioning himself near but not touching her, exercising caution.

'My very dear and, of late, ill-used daughter,' he said, attempting to convey an understanding of her unhappiness. 'Let your sorrow flow from you.' He hesitated. 'I am a harbinger of further sadness, should you not have heard. I fear our beloved Martin has been lost to us with the rest.'

As she failed to respond he went on, flinching at her apparent lack of concern for her brother. 'Weep – weep with us for those who have been taken from our sight, but wrest comfort from knowing that you, my daughter, possess our heartfelt love.'

Only then did Meralda acknowledge his presence. 'Weep? Why should I weep?' she asked defiantly, 'when I have the love of the only one who loves me truly! If you had really loved me, Father, you would not have made me suffer so.'

He did not try to defend the accusation. 'You must believe me that you are in error.' Richard's voice was kind. 'You have my word on't that the love you crave is truly lost to you forever. I saw him die, brought to his end in Kellimargh, and is now held in what remains of Lyonesse at the bottom of the sea.'

Meralda tossed her head angrily, dismissing his words. 'You lie!' She spoke as if to a stranger. ''Tis not lost! I am minded of some words from the Scriptures that Martin would read to us – I recall them because they pleasured me…"Many waters cannot quench love, neither can the floods drown it"…so I know what you say is untrue – my lover will never forsake me. I say it again to you – you lie!'

Richard had begun to feel his old impatience and anger rising at what he considered a gratuitous impertinence, never before having encountered such a flat statement of disbelief from any of his children, and could not let it pass. He managed to hold back the torrent of charges he longed to hurl at her, only stilling his tongue because he knew she would not heed him and, having been reminded of Atlan's death and the conflict at the foot of Carrag Uthek, he remembered the pouch at his belt. As his searching hand encountered it, he was relieved to find it had not been torn away by the force of the sea. He pulled it open, withdrawing the huge pearl in its protective cage and wrathfully thrust it in front of Meralda's eyes, swinging it to and fro.

'See – the Vivian Jewel – taken from the infamous throat of that miscalled high priest – and not yet cleansed of his blood despite the efforts of the waters to wash it away! Regard it! Your pagan died soon after I whipped the head off the neck that held this, though neither were slain by mine own hand – as I shall forever have cause to regret!'

Meralda shrank back with a small cry, a look of horror stirring her pale features, compelled to believe him despite her reluctance. Richard turned away, already reproaching himself for his pitiless action, to find Vivian at his elbow. He held out the pearl to him.

'This belongs to you, m'Lord,' he declared shortly, his tone sounding thick with stifled rage and remorse. ''Twas never properly bestowed upon my daughter.'

Vivian accepted the gory jewel with distaste. 'It has been defiled and robbed of any beauty it once held for me. I'truth, I feel curiously impelled to give it back to the sea which gave it birth and from whose unknown depths it was plundered.'

Without further thought he moved nearer to the cliff's edge, and holding it aloft by the chain, whirled the jewel several times around his head before releasing it. The sun glinted on the gold as it was flung far out over the waves, to fall in a clear patch of water free of the debris floating on the surface, trees jostling with splintered timbers. To those watching the spot where it fell it seemed as if the sea began to

261

bubble and froth, but the moment was brief, and by the time they had blinked again there was no sign of disturbance.

Vivian then realised that Lowenna was beside him and was taken aback by his hasty action. 'My dear...I did not think to ask...'twas ere bestowed upon each Lady of Lyonesse at her espousal, as you must have heard, but now I reflect on't, it appeared to occasion every one of them nought but sadness in their lives – even my mother died early of a melancholy – and hers before her. Did you covet it? If so, I stand abashed.'

He showed his relief as she shook her head. 'Pearls are said to be ill-fated, bringing tears and grief – and we are already overburdened with those.' Lowenna's voice was tender with her love for him. 'Mayhap we will be free of both now you have rid yourself of it, and since our island is no more, there can never be another Lady of Lyonesse to wear it. Meralda would have been the last had she stood in church yester-morn.'

She glanced across at her sister as she spoke, to see her stroking Mordon's gleaming white coat, fresh from its immersion in the sea, hiding her face in his mane and caressing him with one hand, while with the other she had pulled Atlan's talisman from the neck of her bodice and was pressing it to her heart.

Ruth had come to stand with Richard, seeking to quieten his anger with Meralda and console him. 'There is nought you can do to pacify her,' she said. 'She is no longer able to bethink with any clarity, so lost is she in her consuming love. I am blessed with greater awareness for her because I felt so close to Saint Adwen, the saint of lovers, while I bore her name. We can but offer our sympathy, when we consider the dreadful dearth of happiness she must feel the future holds for her.'

He put an arm about her shoulders and they began to walk down to join Vivian and Lowenna. 'You speak truth. I will endeavour to bring her aid in the only way that comes into my mind,' he agreed, and raised his voice. 'Lord Vivian, family and friends – all – hear my plea. Though you are in the midst of your own sorrow I beg you to join with me to pray to our merciful God to bring my dear daughter, Meralda, back to Him and to us.'

Murmuring assent they prepared to kneel, but just as they did so a strong wind blew in off the sea, disconcerting everyone, whipping up skirts and loose garments. It carried with it what some were certain they heard, a voice calling insistently, soft and persuasive yet penetrating and evocative. Others, equally sure, heard nothing more than a solitary gull wheeling and crying above their heads, but Mordon had pricked up his ears, alert, and Meralda was suddenly vividly alive, transformed, radiant.

'I hear you, my love! You be Poseidon and I will be Cleito…!' Her joyful voice rang out, loud and triumphant, subduing all other sounds as she stepped on to a rocky prominence beside her. In an instant she was on Mordon's back, hands firmly twisted in his mane, and they were away, galloping headlong down the hill towards the edge of the cliff. Men ran out to try to halt their impetuous charge, but Mordon evaded them, speeding onward in wild abandon, nostrils flaring, hooves pounding the grassy slope, kicking up the turf – going too fast either to be stopped or stayed. The crowd watched, horrified, as they came to the very edge and the horse, without hesitation, leapt, soaring, appearing to be borne up on a cushion of air, his long tail flowing out behind him. Meralda sat serenely on his back, her pale, gold hair and the abundantly delicate material of the white wedding gown floating on the wind around them, the long, full sleeves streaming out on either side, fluttering buoyantly, giving the impression of great, white wings…

Then, it seemed to those staring aghast, that the very next instant they had vanished from view, leaving nothing but the plaintive sighing of the wind as it began to die down…The cry went up: 'Where are they?' Those who dared ran to look over the cliff's edge into the cluttered, watery depths below, but nobody claimed to have had a sight of them and their bodies were never found washed up on the shore – as were so many others.

It had all happened too quickly for anyone to receive more than a fleeting impression of that tempestuous escape from the confines of this world, so there were conflicting reports of what people thought they had seen. Some, like Gweniver, who were the most anxious to believe it, said an angel had taken Meralda up to heaven. Others were certain that Mordon had sprouted wings – like Pegasus, the winged horse they had learned about from stories handed down – to depart in a manner as mysterious as his arrival on Lyonesse had been, to fly away triumphantly with the willing, exultant rider on his back. Or did they, perhaps, dive down into the waiting embrace of Atlan in the deep, mysterious ocean…?

Her father, however, had seen Meralda, his beloved swan, the morning sun shining brightly upon her outline, her beating, outstretched, feathered wings framed against the blue of the sky, flying away from him for ever.

And he wept…

He remained near the edge of the cliff standing alone, head lowered, his pain apparent for all to see. No one approached him, deeming it wiser to leave him to fight his way through the confusion of his troubled anguish. After a time, he raised his head and gazed for some time out over the sea to the empty horizon beyond, before lifting his face to address, aggressively, what he felt to be the equally empty sky.

'Can You still be up there, safe in heaven, God? And if that be possible, have You now ceased playing with us like a cat with helpless mice?'

The shouted words were delivered passionately and with emphasis, as if he were determined there should be no doubt but that they were heard from above. After a long pause, he made a supreme effort to speak with more restraint, though his voice sounded achingly hoarse when he failed to control his tears.

'God...? Are You content at last with all You have taken from us? The prophecy has been fulfilled – yet I am left confounded. Is this how You requite me for my probity? You had my trust whilst I believed my son would be saved from Your wrath, but now I find him gone – and a daughter, too! 'Twas never promised I would have to bear such a dreadful loss – I could have borne aught else – earnestly hoping for something other that would not wrench the heart from my body! 'Twas merely said I would lose one to right and one to wrong, and now, in the event, which cleaves to which? Or is it but the same to You? How do I choose 'twixt my son who killed and my daughter – who loved?' He paused, searching for a logical argument. 'Is it not writ that You are the Creator of all things in this world? Well then, that must include right and wrong, good and evil. Can there be white without black? Day without night? Love without hate? Life without...death? You spread out your hand to freely bestow Your gifts, only to snatch them away again. I know I am neither able nor meant to see with clarity Your ultimate plan for us – You merely bid me have faith – blind, unreasoning faith! You know I have never once swerved from that faith, but this time, Heavenly Father, this time You have tried me beyond endurance!'

He began to stride up and down, shaking his head from side to side, striking his hip with his fist until he suddenly stopped, passing a hand across his brow as if just reminded of something that had slipped his memory. A mantle of calm appeared to envelop him, as he sank to his knees and lifted his face to the sky.

'Your just reproach has descended on my head, O God, and I humbly ask forgiveness for this ungrateful creature, undeserving of Your mercy, for my folly in querying what You have seen fit to impose on us. You have brought clearly to my understanding that 'twas You, indeed, who created Man – but 'tis Man himself who created evil – prompted by the Devil. Those people of Lyonesse who turned their faces from You deserved to suffer Your anger – and will continue to do so for all eternity – unless any truly repented before the end. In a like way, I deserve the pain I must endure, for I let pleasure divert me from Your bidding. I failed, too, in my care of Meralda,' he bowed his head, 'but happily recall the many blessings You bestowed on us that do remain, and for which I thank You with all my being. I make You a solemn vow to spend the rest of my earthly life proclaiming Your Word amongst the peoples of this new land, unknown to me as yet.'

He arose and turned to face the assembled company, increasing the power of his voice. 'Let all you men and women hear me well! Lyonesse may lie drowned, but this I know. As long as men keep her name on their lips and in their hearts, they will remember God's promise of eternal life for whomsoever believes in His Holy Son and repent of their sins, and all those faithful souls that are gone – and Lyonesse – *will live forever!*'

# 16

## Aftermath

The following days were employed with the burial of those bodies found washed up amongst the wreckage, an attempt being made to return to a semblance of regular, everyday life as the chill of winter began to make itself felt. A subdued air and feeling of unreality hung over the fort, and Vivian had immediately been faced with the unenviable task of riding back to Trevivian with the news that the men who had fought on Lyonesse were no more of this earth, and offer condolences to their families.

The Cornish fisher folk, who eventually ventured out over the watery expanse covering what had once been a proud and flourishing land, reported that the very top of Carrag Uthek remained visible above the water, so the evil rock would continue to provide an altar for sacrifice on the surface of the sea, ready to wreck any unwary vessel. They also reported that the tops of the seven hills of Breonseyth, which had surrounded the Town of Lyons, could yet be seen on the approach to Scilly. The water level around that land-mass had risen, forming a number of small isles, Saint Elid's Carn being one of them, and although searches had taken place for survivors from Lyonesse, none had been found.

When he returned to the fort, Vivian was gladdened to hear that Richard was so gratified by the prospect of his betrothal to Lowenna that it had banished his constant melancholy, but it sadly returned, as he seemed unable to entirely rid himself of it, despite all efforts to divert him.

It was not long before Vivian again left the fort to choose a site some distance from the fire-damaged Trevivian, suitable for building another residence in which to install his future wife. He intended it to be constructed as soon as possible, insisting that, since the building destroyed by fire had to be replaced in any event, it would be as well to move away from that locality, inferring that he was doing it for Lowenna's sake to keep her from being reminded of Kweras and the child he had sired. Lowenna had protested that she felt no ill toward them, but agreed, with no further demur, when Vivian confessed that it was he who wished to put his memories behind him even though he had made his peace with Kweras. He also had to arrange for the pledged chapel in Sennen Cove to be built; it was to be of small dimensions because of the restricted area in the cove available, hence its given name, Chapel Idne – the 'narrow chapel'. When he visited the proposed site, he gave bounty to the fishers living there and also sought out the ferrymen, now stranded on the Cornish mainland, to offer them a living amongst his retainers.

The days passed more slowly for Richard, who continued to suffer a reaction to the violent events that had taken place the night the new moon was born. He displayed but a shadow of his former assured self, seemingly robbed of any purpose or initiative to try to establish a permanent home for his dependents, while aware the hillfort could only be a temporary stopping place. His workers in tin had been entrusted to another master, but those concerned with the milling of grain had become restless, and there persisted the mourning and dejection of the families of the men who had perished to haunt him. Some days he would ride out to hunt, roaming the countryside whitened by frost, but never showing any decisive intention for his family's future.

The one with whom he spent the most time was Ruth, teaching her to ride, amongst other things. She had cast off her head covering to reveal a fine, sprouting growth of curly, bright red hair that enhanced those often merry, ever-wise green-flecked grey eyes and glowing, fresh complexion. She it was who managed to persuade him to loose his tongue, hoping it would encourage him to disclose what was troubling his mind, but he remained reticent.

It was on Christ's Mass Day, the day on which Lowenna celebrated her birth, that Richard came to a decision, when the entire community of the fort were gathered together in celebration on their return from the nearby church. Vivian was enjoying Richard's hospitality during the festival, everyone supping food and drink and managing to enjoy themselves despite the austere, cramped surroundings. During a lull in the simple games being played, Richard drew his family and Vivian, Ruth and Gweniver aside into a sheltered alcove, saying he had matters to discuss. When they were comfortably seated he looked about him, regarding each one with love and affection.

''Tis for your ears alone I unburden my soul,' he began. 'The time has come for me to address myself to you who are nearest my heart, who have shown such patience with my lack of vigour and purpose these last weeks that I am beholden to each and every one. I'faith, I have given a deal of pondering as to how I shall spend the rest of my days, and how 'twill bear upon you. Whenever my thoughts drift, they always return to my inescapable belief that I cannot continue to live amongst you with the spectres of those who were lost ceaselessly parading before me. They torment me with the guilt of their loss – for 'tis mine – and I must atone for it. So, I deem it meet and proper to take the only course left open to me...' He momentarily closed his eyes and took a deep breath before completing the sentence: '...which is for me to seek elsewhere for how to live out my destiny and discharge my vow to God.'

269

No one moved or spoke as he ended his statement, neither believing nor wanting to understand what he had said. It was Vivian who first broke the uneasy silence. 'Old friend...' but he could find no further speech.

Richard grimaced. 'You speak truth, Vivian, and indeed, I feel my years hanging heavily upon me, 'twas ever a jest to us. Remember how we used to make merry about it in our youth? That I was older than you and therefore the wiser, more aware of my actions, and thus carry more blame and reproach for misdoing. Sadly enow, and to my shame, it has proved to be true.'

Tressa and Hicca had thrown themselves on his knees, excited, arms about him. 'Where do we journey to, Father? When do we depart?'

Richard gently disengaged himself but still held them close. 'My beloved children, I must go alone. The road I shall travel will lead I know not where. Believe me when I say I have only your welfare at heart – 'twould be too great a hardship for you to have to endure certain discomfort and possible discontent, when you have Gweniver and, I trust, Lowenna and her lord to look to for your future care. I also have the pious hope that m'Lord will be able and well-disposed to enlarge his new household in order to lift the burden of responsibility from my shoulders and take into it all who have been outcast from Trevelyan.'

Vivian, although dismayed, was quick to show agreement, readily conscious of Richard's need, nodding in willing assent. Then Lowenna pleaded with him, shocked and bewildered with the surprise of his resolve, reluctant for him to be leaving them.

'I understand that you must have time to recover from the adversity that has beset you, Father, but I would beg you to delay and remain with us 'til after we are wed, when winter is done and we all move to the new house. Nay, hear me out,' she said, as Richard shook his head forcefully, already dismissing her plea. 'Then be content to stay 'til it offers more clement weather for journeying – since I see you will refuse to be stayed from your intention.'

'In the hope I will be turned from that intention by the passage of time, you shrewd maid!' Richard smiled at Vivian. 'You are fortunate to have found a love so suited to you that it can but heighten the lifelong happiness of you both. I shall go from here greatly cheered in the knowledge that you will continue to care for each other and our kin – and all my people here!' He gave a sweep of his hand.

'When will you leave us?' The quiet voice came from Ruth sitting huddled at his feet, resting her chin upon bent arms supported by her knees, like a child.

'On the morrow – at sunup.' Richard's reply was short, sharp with regret. 'Whate'er betides, I cannot remain longer in idleness and infirmity of purpose.'

Lowenna took his hand as if to hold him there by force. 'But what is your plan? When shall we see you again?'

'I have no plan, and will go as God guides me to spread His Word as I promised Him. When, and if, He is satisfied with what I have done, I shall live in the hope of being allowed to return here. Now, 'tis time for prayers and rest in readiness for the day.'

And so, some slept and some did not…

\*

The dawn had begun to spread its rosy fingers to touch the surrounding frost-covered countryside, the hillfort and the sea. Richard was already examining the horses that had been led out from their stabling for him to make his choice, white vapour bursting from their nostrils as they snorted and pawed the cold ground. He indicated the one he would lead on a rein – the one to carry the pack containing his necessities, and the grooms set about making it ready. His

271

family and friends stood nearby, waiting to bid him farewell as, wrapped up in furs, he chose a sturdy roan for his mount, stamping his feet impatiently until it was saddled, anxious now to be gone.

Vivian ventured to remark on its appearance. ''Tis a fine creature, but bears no likeness to the white stallion that brought you here.'

'The one that carried away my daughter, d'ye mean?' Richard's tone revealed his deep, underlying rancour.

'The very same that saved your own life, my friend, and to which I, for one, shall be beholden for as long as I draw breath. I intend to keep one such saddled always in my stables awaiting your return, and will make a white horse the emblem of my house – although it should be of your own house, Richard of Trevelyan – if you would but stay!'

Richard regarded him sadly. 'It grieves me that I cannot be persuaded, but I must go where I cannot set my eyes upon the sea to trouble me, as it constantly does, without pity. I am told that if I follow the road to the east I shall be far removed from it, unable even to breathe in its smell to bring my memories crowding in upon me. Ay, and forgive me for admonishing you, Vivian, but I am no longer Richard of Trevelyan, for where is my mill house now? So, since I must be known by some title, let it simply be Richard Trevelyan.'

He hugged Lowenna and the children, lingering over it. 'Dry your tears. Talk to God and say your prayers every day and think joyfully of me, as I shall think of you 'til I hold you once again. And Hicca, since your name is but a childish rewording of mine own, I charge you to bear it with honour.'

He next embraced Vivian. They clasped each other silently before Richard broke away and went to the waiting horses. He searched the tearful faces watching him for the singular pert one he had become accustomed to find always somewhere within his vision, an expressive face that rarely stayed solemn for long, now topped by a neat cap of red curls. He felt saddened to find her absent, but accepted that she might find the parting painful and was hiding her reddened eyes from him.

When he had mounted and taken the rein of the packhorse, he leaned down to place a final kiss on Lowenna's brow. 'I bid you take the greatest care of Ruth for me,' he said quietly.

'Nay, Father, that I will not to do – not I!' she answered, her lips emphasising her refusal while her countenance showed her smiling love for him. 'I charge you to do that for yourself – and Godspeed you both on your way!'

Surprised, he made to turn his horse to find another beside him, Ruth sitting on it comfortably while tying to the saddle a bundle of warm clothing and commodities given her by the women. As he caught her quiet gaze with his own, he decided to waste no time in what he knew would be useless argument, fully aware of his inner delight that he was being blessed by having her companionship.

With no further tarrying or looking back at what they were leaving behind them, they straightway rode out together to follow the shining path on the frosty ground made by the early-morning sun, leading them…

Who knew where…?